AN AMIABLE FOE

Castles & Courtship
Series

JENNIE GOUTET

Development edit by Jolene Perry at Waypoint Authors

Proof edit by Theresa Schultz at Marginalia Editing

Cover Design by Shaela Odd at Blue Water Books

Dedicated to my talented son William, who came up with the idea for the ending.

CHAPTER ONE

March, 1810 - Kent

It was the first true day of spring, and Marianne Edgewood stood, at present, the sole occupant of the rose garden on the southern lawn of Brindale Castle. Her late uncle had employed—through the expedience of a new land steward who had the courtesy to take orders from her—a gardener and an outdoor servant who acted as groom. She'd sent both of them to scythe the eastern lawn. This left her in perfect peace to skim her fingers over the rosebushes' thick, thorny stems and pluck the browning leaves that must give way for the budding green ones. Her mother had loved these roses, and spending time in their company was one of the few ways remaining to Marianne to spend time with her mother, a loss now going on ten years.

She glanced at the garden fork beside her and left off her pruning to tackle the more robust task of airing out the earth around the base of each plant. As she worked, her blood pumped and a smile came naturally to her face. Loosening the earth and pulling the fledging weeds before they could fully take root brought the satisfaction of instilling order to an estate that otherwise refused to be tamed.

The wind picked up, cooling her cheeks and sending a chill along her back where a trickle of perspiration collected. The gust of air whistled through the branches of the dogwood trees, carrying with it the unexpected sound of hoofbeats. This was not unheard of, as the Brindale property was bordered on the west by a public road. The distraction was, however, noteworthy—and most unusual when the sound of those hoofbeats grew louder until a rider emerged through the western gate of the castle grounds and entered the estate. The sun had peaked three hours earlier and was now on its downward path, and Marianne squinted at the uninvited guest until he drew near and she could discern more than a dim outline.

"You." The gentleman sitting astride a stallion of an impressive size pulled up along the path—*her* path—that intercepted the row of Lancaster and York roses on one side and yew hedges on the other. A few rogue curls sprang out from underneath his top hat, and the muscled thighs encased in calfskin breeches, along with the tight-fitting coat visible under his folded cape, proclaimed him a man of no paltry size and breadth.

"Run and fetch your mistress and inform her that Mr. Peregrine Osborne, nephew and heir to the baron Lord Steere, has come and requests an audience with her."

Marianne thrust her garden fork into the pliable soil and lifted her head to better appraise the man, her heart beginning to beat a fearful rhythm. The news of her uncle's death six months prior brought with it the information that she had not inherited the castle, as he had all but promised. Instead, an unknown baron, Lord Steere—the thought of whose visit she had trembled over in the months following her uncle's death

—was given possession of the deed to Brindale Castle. And now, it appeared she must welcome his nephew—a man who had not seen fit to give notice of his visit. Her hour of reckoning had come.

With her forearm, she brushed a lock of hair out of her face in time to catch the look of surprise that flitted across his expression, followed by hesitation. She had taken her time to answer, and her attitude showed nothing of the submissive servant he must have expected, although she could hardly blame him for assuming it of her. She was garbed in her oldest dress and wore the grass-stained work apron that even a lady's maid would have disdained. Her soft bonnet was hidden on the bench behind the boxwood shrub.

In an effort to delay the inevitable, and perhaps seized by an uncharacteristic flash of devilry, she dipped into a brief curtsy and responded in the unrefined speech of a servant.

"Ye'll find the stables on the north end of the castle, jest beyond the pond, milord. I'll inform the mistress."

Leaving her gardening tools in place, Marianne turned without another word and went at an unhurried pace to the closest entrance to the castle. This happened to be the kitchen, tucked on the near edge of the southern tower. There was an absence of movement behind her—what seemed like a puzzled silence, as if the gentleman wondered whether he should take her to task for having dismissed him—before she heard the sounds of the horse turning and walking in the direction she had indicated.

She stepped inside the kitchen and went past the stillroom, her eyes adjusting to the sudden decrease in light. Mrs. Malford set down a bundle of apricots in the sink and wiped her hands on her apron as she came over.

"Oh, no, please don't trouble yourself, Mrs. Malford. I am not in need of anything."

Marianne pulled her own apron over her head and draped it across her arm as she rounded the wooden table in the direction of the door that led to the narrow corridor. She pinched her lips together, flustered. "Although, perhaps I will require refreshments to be sent to the drawing room. We have an unexpected visitor, and I suppose I shall have to offer tea or brandy or some such thing. Do we even stock brandy?"

"Brandy? 'Haps there's a bottle or two in the cellar. A visitor, ye say? A gentleman?" Mrs. Malford's voice held a note of curiosity, and Marianne indulged her.

"The heir has sent an envoy at last, after all these months of my dreading it. It is not Lord Steere, who we might have expected since the property is his, but rather his nephew. And Mr. Osborne has not left me with a favorable impression, I must own, with his imperious command that I summon my mistress."

"Summon yer mistress?" Mrs. Malford had followed her to where the kitchen met the servants' corridor, her brows raised in confusion and very likely outrage. She was as protective of Marianne as her own mother had been.

Marianne gave a weak smile. "I did not look the part of a gently bred lady, and he did not see one in me. I merely... encouraged his prejudice by not revealing anything to the contrary."

"Miss Marianne—" Mrs. Malford shook her head, but a smile tugged at the corners of her mouth. She turned to the kitchen maid who had stopped to stare. "Annabel, don't jes' stand there. Put a kettle on to boil."

Mrs. Malford had held the position of cook since Marianne was born and knew her better than anyone alive. She merited more than the meager salary the castle provided her, but she had made it clear her devotion to Marianne kept her from searching for another position. In truth, Mrs. Malford was better suited to the role of confidant and advice-giver than Marianne's actual companion could ever hope to be, although such was not her official title. The aged Miss Fife was one of the banes of Marianne's existence—along with the loss of her parents, the death of her uncle, and now the arrival of the handsome and most unwelcome Mr. Osborne, come to snatch Brindale from her and hand it over to his uncle.

Marianne sighed. That was a lot of banes.

"Ye must let Miss Fife know of his arrival, so she might sit in the room with ye," Mrs. Malford insisted.

Marianne shook her head wearily. Miss Fife would somehow find a way to make things worse. "I believe the less Mr. Osborne sees of Miss Fife, the better it will be for me. I would rather speak of my having a companion than let him meet her, for he might think as unguarded as I am that I'm a chicken for plucking."

She stepped into the hall, and Mrs. Malford followed her out. "Yer not unguarded, Miss Marianne. We're all looking out for ye. I'll have the tea made ready and ask Charlie to see about the brandy."

"Very good. But don't bring it to me until I ring for it. As Mr. Osborne has not had the courtesy to write and inform me of his visit, I will not attempt to make his welcome more salutary than I must. I wonder how long he plans to stay. I saw a traveling portmanteau, which does not bode well for me."

Marianne continued along the corridor, following the rounded edges of the castle walls until she reached the circular staircase leading up to where her bedroom was located. Only the southern wing had been fully refurbished, holding some element of protection against the chill of spring air, or the icier drafts of winter. She mulled over in her mind, should Mr. Osborne expect to be put up for the night, whether she should consign him to the worst-kept wing where he would not be inclined to remain or whether she should have an ounce of humanity and place him in the wing adjacent to hers that had at least been partially restored.

She opened the door to her room and went to her tall wooden armoire. There was no need to summon a maid to dress her, as there were only two on the estate and she was accustomed to dressing herself. Annabel was preparing the tea, and Sarah had been set to beating the smaller rugs. Marianne wondered how much of this activity Mr. Osborne had seen and what he would make of this partly rundown castle his uncle now owned—a dwelling to which he had no more connection or attachment than any other set of stones in all of England. That was not the case for her.

She selected her finest day dress, although it was faded and several years old—the one she wore only to attend church. Made of thin white muslin, it had corded lace trimming in a darker blue that perfectly matched Marianne's eyes. Her hair needed styling, but she had plaited her hair more neatly and pinned it up, and it would have to do. In this encounter, she would look every inch the lady, despite the fact that she shook like a girl.

Standing outside of the door to the drawing room, Marianne smoothed her dress in front and glanced at the mirror in the broad hall. From the echoing stairwell, she had heard the knock at the front entrance and the sounds of Charlie ushering Mr. Osborne into the drawing room, where he now awaited her, likely with impatience at having been left to cool his heels.

She took a breath and stepped into the room.

Mr. Osborne was in the process of examining her father's collection of nacre snuffboxes on the mantelpiece, his back to her. He turned at the sound of her entrance, and the measure of his surprise was betrayed only by the lift of one of his eyebrows. He held her gaze as he strode across the room, then bowed.

"Sir." Marianne dipped into a curtsy, her heart racing anew at this long-dreaded envoy from the new heir, propelled by the whisper of fear over what awaited her should he announce that Lord Steere had decided to take up residence in the castle. One thing was clear. If Lord Steere took immediate possession of Brindale, there would be no place for her in it.

"Miss Edgewood, I presume. How lovely to make your acquaintance." The initial impression Mr. Osborne had given led her to expect him to do no more than pass a cursory glance over her, but he held her gaze quite steadily. And what did she read in it? Was it accusation for her lapse of gentility in working outdoors like a servant would? Condemnation? But what, then, was that quirk of the lips that was gone as soon as it had appeared?

So he would not refer to their first meeting. Marianne's breath quickened as an unexpected urge to laugh came over her. His behavior showed either a delightful and well-hidden vein of humor or a pompous refusal to acknowledge anything but the most correct behavior between a gentleman and a lady. She hoped for the former and suspected the latter, but only time would tell.

"Will you have a seat, sir?" Marianne peeled her gaze from his firm jaw and the gray eyes that seemed to read her too intimately. He would not find her so easy a conquest of his charm, if that was his objective. She moved into the middle of the room where there was a green quilted sofa flanked by two wooden chairs with embroidered cushions and armrests. In the middle was a table set to hold refreshments, though the castle had not welcomed a formal visitor in ten years.

Mr. Osborne followed and sat where she indicated, waiting until she was seated. After a moment's silence, which Marianne refused to fill, he crossed one leg over the other, rubbing his chin, then resting it in his hand as he continued his regard in a disconcerting way that raised her hackles.

"I am to understand from my uncle's man of business that you have resided at Brindale since your parents' untimely death."

"I have resided at Brindale my entire life, sir." Ten years was enough time that the mention of her parents' death and the subsequent uncertainty as to her future should not have caused any sudden surge of emotion, but her voice hitched at the end of her sentence. This was her home, yet he'd hinted that she merely stayed here as though she were some passing visitor.

"And who is the trustee looking after your affairs?" he enquired. "My uncle did not mention one, although I must own, he gave me little information of things pertaining to the estate before I set off."

Although Mr. Osborne's voice was perfectly civil, his manner of tossing questions at Marianne left her wishing she could toss something at him in return. Instead, she commanded the corners of her mouth to turn up in a polite smile.

"Mr. Mercy, Brindale's steward, has continued to oversee all matters concerning the property even after my uncle's death, and he consults with me on what must be done at Brindale."

Mr. Osborne's manner of drawing back before snapping his brows together showed that he found this both curious and appalling. "You make decisions for a property you do not own?"

Marianne was, in general, a rather timid thing. But if there was one area where courage seemed to spring up from nowhere, it was that which concerned her castle. "Would you have me allow it to go to rack and ruin because the new owner is not in place to approve a steward's decision to trim the hedges or repair the gates?"

"Why should you have any say in the matter at all?" Mr. Osborne stopped short as though catching himself and continued in a milder tone. "The land steward should have corresponded with my uncle about these details."

"And what should the steward do if he has sent no less than four letters, not one of which received a reply that gave indication of Lord Steere's wishes?"

The baron had answered two of the letters, but one was only to say that he was still reflecting on what he wished to do with the castle that had been unexpectedly bequeathed to him, and the other was to say that Mr. Mercy would shortly be hearing from the attorney attached to the estate.

Mr. Osborne turned his gaze to the window, where a thick iron framework held tiny panes of glass that allowed little light to come in. The drawing room was situated in the northern part of the castle, close to a grove of towering trees, and it therefore received little light. The wall near the rounded tower held the portraits of her parents, which gave the room a welcoming air, although the modern paintings had been set in oppressive black frames. The drawing room was also the first place Marianne's father had looked for her when they played hide-and-seek.

"He has left it completely up to me, then." Mr. Osborne spoke the words more to himself, though it brought her back to the present. He allowed a silence to fall that Marianne did not break.

His words had confirmed her worst fear. He had come to prepare for his uncle to take immediate possession of Brindale. Until now, she'd had one ambition in life, no matter how impossible such a thing was to achieve: to remain at Brindale

Castle, the place which held her only ties to this earth. Mr. Osborne's sudden appearance made her see how foolish a hope it was.

At last, Mr. Osborne seemed to come out of his reflections. He looked around him, his brows lowered. "This is a singularly ugly room."

His words hurt and showed how little worthy he was to even visit her castle. Marianne folded her hands on her lap and sat up straight as she brought her eyes to his. "To what do I owe the pleasure of your visit, sir?"

The lift of the eyebrow was back and his reply was given in a smooth voice she could easily grow to detest. "I should think the answer would be obvious to you, Miss Edgewood. I came to look over the property."

Marianne could bear it no more. She stood, causing Mr. Osborne to hasten to his feet. "Have you? Perhaps you will explain what right you have to do so. I have been awaiting Lord Steere's pleasure to come examine his bequeathment, and instead I must receive a strange gentleman whose name I have never before heard and who did not see fit to inform me of his visit. If someone is to come and look over the property, should it not be Lord Steere himself?"

Mr. Osborne froze in surprise at her outburst, before his features relaxed and understanding dawned. "But Miss Edgewood," he replied in a voice that was maddeningly complacent, "Lord Steere is not in possession of the deed to this castle —I am."

CHAPTER TWO

Peregrine Osborne—Oz to the gentlemen at the clubs and Perry to his intimates—had worked hard to arrive at his current level of standing. He had overcome the stigma of possessing a wastrel gentleman of a father and a mother who had not been given the upbringing of a lady. He had endured the scorn at Oxford of having been educated by the local clergyman and having no knowledge of the sporting disciplines. This led him to study all manner of the Corinthian arts as much as he did his classes at university and put every penny he had into turning himself out in proper rig. But it was not until the unexpected acknowledgement of his uncle, who had lost his only son and heir, that he had been received at the clubs in London. With Brindale as the first piece of property rightfully in his own name, Perry would live up to every expectation he had set for himself.

He now observed the young woman standing before him. Even without the servant's attire, she could not be described as fashionable, and her hair was much too heavy for her slight face. She was an odd mix of timid and defiant. However, he supposed the fair Miss Edgewood had a right to be irritated—a sentiment that brought out her flashing blue eyes, one could not help but notice.

But what could he have done? No sooner had he left the meeting with his uncle, where he'd been handed the deed to the castle with instructions to make something of it, than he set out to look over his new property, stopping first in London to boast of his inheritance in the clubs. His uncle had mentioned something about the daughter, or niece, or some such thing of the last heir being still in residence, but he'd promptly put it out of his mind.

It was only now that he saw with perfect clarity that of course she could not have known about his uncle's gift. His name would have meant nothing to her in relation to the castle.

"You...you are Brindale's new owner? How did this come about? We received no word of it."

He could see that she was troubled by the news; she seemed smaller somehow. "My uncle did not find it convenient to have another estate to oversee and one which was far from his other holdings. Since I will be inheriting anyway, he wished for me to take over the estate at once." *To test me*, Perry thought. *And I must pass.*

"I see." Miss Edgewood blinked, her eyes staring straight through him. "Then as owner, you have no need of me. You will know how to direct your servants to accommodate all of your wishes. If you will excuse me." She turned to leave.

"Miss Edgewood," Perry called out from behind. If she left, he might be stuck here waiting idly until the sun set. "I will trouble you to tug the bell pull that I might meet with the housekeeper."

She stopped short, and without turning to look at him gave

two sharp tugs on the pull, then swept from the room in a manner worthy of a member of London's ton.

Perry resumed his seat, waiting for the housekeeper to arrive, and went through the conversation that had gone less smoothly than he might have wished as he remembered Miss Edgewood's mouth pulling down in a frown. There was the surprise of his inheritance, of course. But then, he supposed his disparaging remarks about the drawing room had not helped. He had not intended to insult, although she had possibly taken it that way. Perhaps her mother had designed the drawing room with particular care, unaware of the latest London fashions, and Miss Edgewood saw a barb in his words.

From what he had been able to assess from his glimpses of the castle's exterior and the hall leading to the drawing room, Brindale would have to be turned inside out if he had any hopes of making the place comfortable. The bones of the castle might be solid, but the interior was positively Gothic and would not charm any but the most lugubrious. He would need to see what could be done about bringing more light inside. Or perhaps there was a room better situated on a different side of the castle that could serve as the drawing room, and he could assign this one to perdition.

Indeed, there was a great deal of work to be done, and his uncle had not increased his quarterly allowance to help him to do it. Oh, it was most definitely a test.

The door opened, and a servant that he now doubted from her lack of formal attire was the housekeeper curtsied as soon as she entered. She looked around the room, her gaze searching and her brows raised as though in surprise to find him sitting there alone. Perhaps she had expected to see Miss Edgewood. He remained seated and put on his warmest smile. He would need an ally in Brindale's head servant.

"Mrs....?"

"I'm Mrs. Malford, Brindale's cook, sir. How might I assist ye?" Her appearance was crisp and neat, at least. Diligence in appearance meant diligence in household matters. With her hair neatly tucked into a cap and a face that held only the beginning signs of age, she stood, hands clasped and awaiting his orders.

Peregrine glanced at the table in front of him, suddenly struck by how hungry he was. "I would be glad of some tea to start with. I will also require a room to be made up for me, and"—he sent his most self-effacing smile—"if you can possibly have a hot supper on short notice, no matter how humble, I will partake of it in the dining room. Tomorrow, I suppose I must meet with the other servants and the steward and look over the castle. I assume Brindale has no housekeeper or butler?"

He paused, struck by doubt. Whom should he appeal to if there was no housekeeper? "Perhaps you might give me a tour of the interior?" he added. With the way Miss Edgewood had run off, he would not propose that she be the one to give it to him.

"As ye wish, sir," Mrs. Malford replied after a slight hesitation, and he was left to wonder if she'd felt Miss Edgewood should perform the duty of giving Brindale's tour. But Miss Edgewood was not mistress of the castle, nor was it its employee.

The door opened again, and another neat—but much younger—servant entered, cutting short his musings. Mrs. Malford presented her. "This be Sarah, the upper maid, and she'll help ye on matters pertaining to Brindale."

"Sir." Sarah curtsied and listened while he explained his need to have a room readied for him. She had an air of competence and nodded when he finished speaking. "The master bedroom, and the best to be found in Brindale. 'Tis the room that belonged to Mr. and Mrs. Edgewood when they were still alive."

"That will do very well for me." Perry rose to his feet, prepared to end the discussion.

"Except the master bedroom is near to Miss Edgewood's room," Mrs. Malford added. She had remained at Sarah's side, and Perry was brought up short by the firm expression on Mrs. Malford's face. He had no serious designs on the young lady but even if he had, he was not such a simpleton as to miss the protective mien the cook had adopted. Miss Edgewood appeared to have the loyalty of her servants, which spoke highly of her.

"Well then, take me to the best room that is not in the same wing as Miss Edgewood's." Fatigue overset Perry, and he allowed his gaze to drift aimlessly over to the tiny glass panes that distorted the scenery beyond it. They were in need of cleaning.

Neither Mrs. Malford nor Sarah moved to get the tea, and it was the maid who spoke. "'Tis the eastern wing near to Miss Edgewood's, and it's not got the same comfort, I'm afraid, sir. There'm some chinks in the wall as needs be looked to, and 'tis said the bed hasn't been slept in for a century. But it 'ull be a sight better nor the other wings that have leaks in the roof."

He snapped his gaze back to the maid. Panic at the monumental task ahead of him set in, lending a sharp tone to his voice. "It is a pity the Edgewoods did not invest more in the upkeep of the castle. Maintaining the roof leak-free is the most fundamental of necessities." He shook his head as a desultory laugh escaped him. "And a centuries-old bed? Did the castle never receive guests?"

His question was rhetorical, but Mrs. Malford answered it. "When Miss Edgewood's fader was alive, he did all he could to improve Brindale, but there 'us not time enow before he died.

His broder Mr. Joseph Edgewood was busy with the East India Company overseas to worrit 'bout his English estate. I fear the bed ye 'ull sleep in tonight 'ull not be what yer used to."

"Bring the bed from the Edgewoods' room to mine and that will do," Perry said, ready for the conversation to be over and for the tea to be brought. He would think about the remaining problems once he had something in his stomach.

Sarah nodded her acquiescence but did not turn to get the tea, merely exchanging a glance with the cook. Despite her meek comportment, she was showing herself to have strong opinions. This might work in his favor if she was diligent, and he could rely on her to see that things were properly done. But a maid who did not easily give way in most matters would be more of a headache than a help.

"I'm afeared 'tis not so easy a task, sir. The bed in the old master bedroom is a mizmaze—made up of thick beams of oak that'm nailed to the floor. Charlie can have the bed unmounted, but not against nightfall. Mrs. Malford 'ull have a hot meal for you, and I'll see to the fire in yer room and that a set of Brindale's finest sheets is on your bed, such as it is."

Perry let out a quiet exhale. There was little point in complaining about what could not be changed. "That will suit me very well."

When the servants left the room, its silence fell upon Peregrine in a way that felt almost accusatory. With the drooping curtains and low gilded frames, the room seemed to frown at him, as though he were trying to take away someone else's home, although the thought was ludicrous. Everyone knew that rooms could not frown, and inheritances were not personal. They were the natural order of things.

And this castle did belong to him now. Even if Miss Edgewood, who had shown herself a chameleon, appearing one minute in servant's clothing and the next in the outmoded raiment of a young lady, had looked every inch Brindale's natural owner. He would not think of that just now. Although the question of what steps she had taken to acquire a new lodging would need to be explored, Perry was not here to displace her. He was here to prove to Lord Steere that he was worthy to inherit the barony.

His gloomy musings improved after the tea tray was brought with such sustenance as warm bread and slabs of ham, along with the lightest Bath cakes he had ever eaten. After three cups of fragrant tea mixed with cream and sugar, Perry felt ready to continue his quest to tame his new surroundings. He decided to escape the oppressive nature of the castle and go check on his stallion before night fell. This was a Percheron from France with the unoriginal, though apt, name of Beau that he had bought from an ex-soldier, and he was partial to him.

He opened the front door and nearly ran into a gentleman who had been on the point of knocking. The man's features were unremarkable, his stature short, and his countenance friendly—a country gentleman from the look of it. His amicable expression fell into one of surprise, then distrust, when he saw Perry.

"Who the devil are you?"

Not even in his worst periods of school tyranny had anyone ever spoken to Perry like that, and his surprise at the address almost outweighed his irritation at the nature of it. Almost.

"Mr. Peregrine Osborne at your service." He delivered the words coldly and with a slight bow. The stranger continued to stare at him, and although Perry should not have said more, he added, "Heir to the baron, Lord Steere."

Only then did recognition dawn on the man's features. It was clear he was on intimate enough terms to know who Perry's uncle was and what had likely brought him here.

"Forgive me my presumption, sir." The gentleman returned the bow and more deeply. It seemed to express his chagrin at a greeting that could only be called rude. "We had been expecting the baron. Related to Lord Steere, are you? Nephew? Where is she?"

The barrage of questions bewildered Perry as he tried to grapple with the man's knowledge of Brindale's successors and his uncivil approach at gaining more information. He folded his arms across his chest.

"Excuse me, sir. And you are?" He would not give this man the upper hand, even if he did know quite a bit more about the castle, its inhabitants, and Perry's ties to Brindale than one might expect in a stranger.

"Ah, of course. My name's Robert Vernon." He put his hand on his chest as if swearing an oath. "My father's squire and owns Grinnell, a property not far from here. I've known Marianne my whole life."

Understanding of the man's peculiar behavior now dawned at this admission. Vernon had likely been stirred by the embers of jealousy when he'd confronted Perry like that on his betrothed's doorstep. Theirs was likely a match arranged from childhood, or a love that had blossomed as they spent time in each other's company. He was not a bad-looking fellow, and she was probably habituated to his coarse manners, not having other men to judge him by. Perry hoped he was not a frequent visitor.

Then again, Miss Edgewood proving already engaged would provide a simple solution to the matter that had become more of the moment than sprucing up the castle. He would not have to worry about finding a new place for her to live. These thoughts turned around in his mind, leading him to speak with uncharacteristic forthrightness.

"A pleasure, Mr. Vernon. If I may be so bold as to ask,

considering that I am here with the object to see to Brindale's future...might I inquire if you have an understanding with Miss Edgewood?"

"You mean marriage?" Vernon laughed, flushing a deep red. "I should say not. At any rate, we have no understanding at present. But I am the closest thing she has to family."

He struck a belligerent tone, and Perry simply nodded. He would not get in the way of this one, who seemed to be suffering from the throes of love, or at least of possessiveness.

Vernon looked around, then folded his arms across his chest. "I must tell you that Marianne has dreaded your visit since she received word of her uncle's death. Or I should say, she dreaded Lord Steere's visit. She was certain he would arrive unannounced and turn her out of a home that is of great sentimental value."

He stopped and looked at Perry shrewdly. "And here you are, unannounced. It may be none of my business, but given the unusual frankness of our speech upon meeting, will you tell me if your uncle is planning on selling the castle? You have every right to tell me to go to the devil, of course."

Vernon laughed again, and the sound grated on Perry like the braying of a donkey. That was precisely where he would have liked to send him. The man was not altogether unrefined, although he certainly seemed it compared to the gentlemen Perry was accustomed to frequenting. And he did have some right as Miss Edgewood's friend to ask such a question, but Perry was not about to reveal anything to a perfect stranger other than a truth that would soon be widely known.

"I am the owner of Brindale Castle, as a matter of fact." When Vernon's jaw dropped, Perry hurried on rather than allow him to respond. "As for the castle's future, I'm afraid I cannot disclose my plans at present. I will need time to look over the estate and judge what is best to be done." The air had grown colder with the loss of sunlight, and he wondered if he should go in search of his cloak.

Vernon narrowed his eyes. "So you are here on an extended stay."

"I am," he replied. The two of them stood, feet planted and arms folded, facing off as though in a pugilist match, in what Perry thought was the most ridiculous manner. Vernon had nothing he wanted, and Perry owned something that was none of Vernon's business. They should have nothing further to say to one another.

Vernon dropped his arms first. "Where's Marianne, then? I came to tell her about my new foal. She'll want to visit her." He looked beyond Perry into the house, where the door was still cracked open, then brought his gaze back to him.

"I'm afraid I cannot be of any help. I have only just arrived here myself. But I will inform Miss Edgewood that you came to call when I next see her." He stood, effectively barring the door in case Vernon should have any thoughts of darting past him. It was *his* castle, after all.

Vernon did not attempt it. "Ah, very well. I suppose the foal will have to wait. She's a beauty, though. Got a star on her nose and the longest legs you've ever seen. Tell Marianne about her. That will have her wanting to come around as soon as she may." He looked over at the sun, which was about to set between the trees on the western end of the castle wall. "Good evening, then." He lifted his hat and turned to walk toward the stables.

Drat. Vernon must have driven to Brindale. The stables had been Perry's destination, but he had no wish to continue the conversation with a country gentleman who, despite having a basic grasp of proper decorum, acted as though he had been raised by the stable hands rather than by a gentleman's tutor.

Vernon took only a few steps more before turning back,

flicking his eyes to Perry at last. "Marianne is not without protectors, I'll have you know. In case you had any less than noble thoughts in that direction, I'd advise you against it."

The implication in his words was as surprising as it was insulting. "You've fallen far from the mark. I do not need such a reminder." Perry clenched his fists and spoke through gritted teeth. "I ought to call you out for suggesting I do. A gentleman does not seduce innocent maidens."

"Not in a perfect world," Vernon said, taking a step backwards. He put his hand on his chest and bowed, a gesture which, following his words, seemed like a mockery. "Forgive me if my protectiveness for her led me to speak rashly. No insult was meant."

After a moment, Perry nodded, his heartbeat steadying. He could not like the man, but it would not do to make enemies of his neighbors. And it might further be to his advantage to keep a close eye on him. "None taken, then."

CHAPTER THREE

Marianne's flash of bravado completely deserted her by the time she'd made it to her room. What courage did she have, truly? None. She might imagine herself a lion, but she was really just a mouse.

She had been bent upon teaching Mr. Osborne a lesson by showing him that *he* was trespassing in *her* home, no matter what relation he was to the baron. And then to learn this modish gentleman from London was the owner in truth? That unexpected piece of knowledge had stolen her breath, and she needed to sit in silence to come to grips with it. After a time, she did, although the realization only increased her despair because he was yet another person who stood between her and her home.

I should think the answer would be obvious to you, Miss Edgewood. I came to look over the property. And this spoken in a faintly ironic, condescending, *infuriating* manner.

Well, best of luck to him in learning the workings of a crotchety, beloved castle, whose personality took a lifetime to know intimately. She had never allowed herself to imagine this day coming. Against reason, she had hoped the baron would leave her alone—that he would forget all about this castle that did not have much to recommend it in the way of income or comfort.

Marianne stood and walked to the window, placing her hands on the cool gray stone ledge where the window was set back in the wall. She absently picked up the candle holder that sat there, the candle now a mere stump, and then set it down again before pacing away.

Mr. Osborne may have rightfully come to take charge of what was his, but it didn't make it fair. How could her uncle have left her castle to a stranger? Had not his letters over the years promised she would be well taken care of? True, she did not know her uncle well—had no recollection of his visit when she was a small girl. But they had corresponded for the ten years after her parents' death, and he knew how important Brindale was to her. For him to disregard what mattered without a word of explanation was a betrayal of the highest order. This was why she preferred her home to people. A solid, centuries-old stone structure could not betray her. Stones did not change.

It didn't signify that her uncle had carved out a tiny parcel from the estate and bequeathed it to her, along with the cottage that sat on it. Nor did it signify that her mother's dowry had also been kept aside for her and she possessed a modest amount of coin to live upon—Marianne had never had the least desire to move. Now, the decision had forced itself upon her as one she could no longer avoid. It was nearly impossible to imagine taking a house within eye's view of the castle that had someone else living in it, a home which she would always feel in her heart was hers. Of course, if she did not wish to live in the cottage, there was always the possibility of residing with the Vernons, who looked upon her quite like family.

But living with the Vernons would provide her with little relief. She would still have to cross paths with Mr. Osborne in the village—a thought that left her cold—unless he were simply looking over the property with a mind to sell. That would be just like a man such as him. What need had a stranger of an out-of-the-way castle in Kent? The attorney had never hinted at whether Lord Steere was pleased to have received the deed to the castle or not. He must not have been if he could so easily hand it over to his nephew.

Marianne continued to pace until she nearly tripped on the woven cloth rug. Its position must have shifted when Sarah last cleaned her room. She lifted the nearly empty wooden chest that was set against the wall and tucked the corner of the rug underneath to secure it.

Perhaps the nephew was just as loath to acquire a castle that could not bring him much satisfaction. It wasn't a particularly harmonious structure, and one loved it the way one loved a mongrel. There was no denying that the castle needed an influx of money for restoration. She had done what she could with her uncle's sparse instructions from India, sent with small allotments of money, and she had even used some of her own small income. But as the steward Mr. Mercy had reminded her, that had only fixed the minor issues. The roof still leaked in places.

Marianne gave up pacing and went over to peer at herself in the glass, studying her set chin and glowering eyes. Her initial thought had been to take dinner in her room, but she now saw how impossible it was to remain closeted up here while Mr. Osborne roamed her castle at will. She needed to walk its halls and breathe in the scent of the ages, to trail her fingers over the cold stones and give them warmth, to place her hands on the quilted tapestries that had been put in place to keep the chill out. Her mother had begun restoring some and creating others with considerable talent, but Marianne had never learned. Therefore, the tapestries remained unfinished needlepoint landscapes, reminiscent of happier times.

She grabbed a warm shawl and left her room to seek solace in the lower-level apartment that always had a small fire burning. The apartment in question held a sitting room she was fond of, with bedrooms adjoining it that were not quite fit for use, as they were in a passageway and gave little privacy. She had long learned to view the bedrooms as places of storage, unfit for the public eye. Not that anyone visited her, except Robert and his mother.

The sitting room there was papered in yellow with faint silver scrolls, and there was a waist-high dark wooden sideboard that ran along the edge of the room. Above it hung soothing pastels with touching scenes of the countryside in gilded frames, warm and unlike anything else in the castle. Once inside the sitting room, Marianne set down her candle and went to stand in its center, hugging her arms to her chest. She turned slowly, taking the room in, checking that everything was in place as her mother had left it, although not a single servant would think to displace the items here. Despite the sacred nature of the room, Marianne had not allowed it to become a museum, untouched and dusty. It was a life-giving space that held clues to how her mother had been able to live so joyfully, if only Marianne could decipher them. It was a room that brought peace to her still, ten years after her mother's last embrace.

The close of day meant there was no longer any sun to stream into the room, but the diamond-shaped window panes gleamed in the flickering light of her candle. The book on the table was set exactly where her mother had always left hers, but it was a different book, replaced regularly with the one Marianne was currently reading. This one, published anonymously and entitled *Marriage*, was a gripping tale of a woman who had married for love and repented of it heartily when she discovered she was not suited to live as the wife of a penniless man. Once Lady Juliana came to this belated realization and took steps to alter her destiny, it could not be denied that the ill-fated heroine's life grew increasingly sinful and foolish.

Foolish. Marianne tore her eyes from the book that had, until now, brought her diversion. That was precisely what she was. To have believed that she might live out her days in this castle—after the death of her parents, perhaps, but even after the death of her uncle? It was nothing but the unobtainable dream of a foolish girl. She was paying for her naïveté now.

It was not long before Marianne let out a long sigh and turned to leave her haven of peace and tranquility. This was not the time to gather wisdom from her gentle and unassuming mother, who would probably have advised Marianne to give up a battle she could not win and set her sights elsewhere. No, now was the time to see what might be done about the dilemma of Brindale's new heir and then set about doing it. She could not lose her home—such a thing was impossible to contemplate, even if it meant living with Mrs. Malford in the servants' quarters. *No, Mama, of course I could not do such a thing, but it is a sore temptation, let me tell you.*

She crossed over to the wooden door, fitted into the thick stone wall that peaked at the arch, and lifted the metal latch. It was time to seek wisdom from her father, and that was found in a different part of the castle.

Marianne would have to proceed cautiously in the event that Mr. Osborne had already begun his appropriation of Brindale Castle and was wandering liberally about its halls. The drawing room must be free of the unwelcome presence of the heir if she were to ask her father what to do. Of course, her father was not bodily in the drawing room. There were no specters to be found, and the castle was not haunted—although the thought struck Marianne as funny. Would it scare away Mr. Osborne if he thought the castle haunted? Could she conjure up such a farce and have it be believable? Probably not. Even if he did believe it, he would be more likely to attempt to frighten the ghosts into submission with that dour face of his than run away quaking himself. There were no phantoms, though. It was just that her father's presence was there all the same if one knew what to feel.

She traversed the adjoining corridor from her mother's apartment into the bedroom and antechamber beyond, where they stored household linens and various trifles under lock and key. There was also a tall stack of books that she had read and cast off that needed to be returned to the library, but which remained another unfinished task the castle's few servants had no time for. She crossed the antechamber and put her ear to the door to listen if Mr. Osborne was in the drawing room, but was instead greeted from behind.

"Marianne, there you are. I've not seen you since breakfast."

It was the feeble, petulant voice of Miss Fife, who had never earned the more familiar appellate of her Christian name. In fact, so scant was the affection between them, Marianne had planned to search for a new companion as soon as she reached her majority in three months' time. Over the years, her appeals to her uncle to find someone new had met with deaf ears, so the task must fall to her. If only she had an idea of where to begin.

Miss Fife's gray curls escaped from her cap at odd angles, and she was wearing the same faded spencer she always wore over a nondescript dress, a shawl of a most unfortunate green draped across her shoulders. At all times, Miss Fife's presence was something to be borne rather than sought. But right now, with such emotions swirling through Marianne, it was nothing short of a bother. For one thing, she still had no wish for Miss Fife to meet Mr. Osborne, although such an event must be inevitable. Once he'd met her companion, he might decide that it was a simple matter to take advantage of her, or he might push her to quit the castle without delay. For another, she was too tense to deal with Miss Fife's irritated nerves or flights of fancy. She could barely deal with her own.

"I have been here all along," Marianne replied, retracing her steps toward her companion, wondering where she could stash Miss Fife before the woman fell under Mr. Osborne's keen eyes. "Of course, I did spend some time in the rose garden, as I told you I would do at breakfast."

"Did you tell me so?" Miss Fife reached up and adjusted her cap, sending it positively crooked. "I cannot recall you saying such a thing. But, Marianne, you should not wander about the rose garden at this time of year. You will catch your death of cold."

This was word for word what Miss Fife had said this morning when Marianne told her of her plans. It was also coming from a woman who never left off her shawls, even at noon on a hot summer day.

"The fresh air does me good," Marianne repeated for the hundredth time, attempting a cheerful tone as she turned back toward her mother's sitting room. "I think I would go out of my mind if I had to stay inside the castle walls all day."

It struck Marianne that perhaps Miss Fife was losing her wits early for that very reason. She spent all of her time within doors.

"Nevertheless," Miss Fife said, attempting to scold as Marianne took her by the arm. "Were you going into the drawing room? It's so cold in there. You should have tea laid out in the yellow room."

It was perverse, perhaps, but as little as Marianne wished for Mr. Osborne to meet Miss Fife did she also wish for her companion to catch wind of Mr. Osborne's arrival. If a stranger inserted himself upon Miss Fife's notice, the shock might change her into the model companion, attempting to admonish and curtail all Marianne's activities as she had done in fits and starts in the past. Miss Fife was wholly unpredictable, at times demonstrating an alarming lack of reason, and at others, showing behavior that was so petty as to be almost spiteful. And at the most inopportune moments she became acuity itself—or guile. It was impossible to tell. Her meeting Mr. Osborne would likely snatch what little peace Marianne had managed to carve out for herself.

"I think tea is a wonderful idea." In the yellow sitting room, Marianne drew Miss Fife to a comfortable chair she knew the spinster loved. "Why don't you settle here with a book? Here is the one on wildflowers that I've seen you looking at before. I will call for tea."

"That is good of you, dear."

Miss Fife looked up at her with a smile while patting her arm, and Marianne almost felt guilty for her perfidy. She would get tea sent to the woman as a diversion, hoping and expecting that her companion would forget all about her once she had some tea and cake in her and there was a book she could read —or pretend to read. Marianne was not sure if any of the words remained in her companion's head. She had rarely seen her turn a page.

Marianne cut through the library on her way to the kitchen, deciding to approach the drawing room from the front entrance rather than the back after she had called for tea. Now feeling like a fugitive in her own home in her attempts to avoid the uninvited guest, she held on to the wood newel of the staircase that led to the upstairs and peered around it into the main hall. No sounds could be heard, so she crept forward in a furtive fashion to the kitchen, unable to entirely mute the clip of her boots against stone. She reached the kitchen, out of breath from the unaccustomed stealth, where Mrs. Malford looked up at her in surprise, her hands deep inside a capon.

"Ye might've rung, Miss Marianne, if ye be needing something, even if we're preparing Mr. Osborne's dinner. Annabel, ye'd best be getting started on those potatoes." Turning back to Marianne, she asked, "Will ye be taking dinner with him?"

Marianne hesitated still. Was it indeed what she wanted? Continuing with her latest resolution that Mr. Osborne should not have full run of the castle before he could see her as the true owner of it, she came to her decision.

"Yes, I will be joining him for dinner. In the meantime, Annabel, please see that tea is brought to the yellow room for Miss Fife." Still hoping she might avoid Miss Fife's presence at dinner, she added, "Along with something substantial in case she is hungry."

"Yes, miss." Annabel left the potatoes and paring knife, bustling over to stoke the fire and put the kettle on.

Sarah entered the kitchen. "Miss Marianne, I'm glad to find ye. Charlie put Mr. Osborne's belongings in the blue-papered room off the eastern tower."

Marianne could not stifle the laugh surprised out of her. "You placed him in the blue room? But the bed is the worst we have in the castle. Are you hoping, as I am, that he will not be induced to stay?"

Sarah was too earnest a maid to respond lightly to such a comment, even made in jest. "Ye must see, miss, that the blue room was the only one we could put him in. The chimney does smoke a bit, but there'm not so many cracks in the wall that he 'ull freeze to death at night. Ye can all-a-most see your breath in the rooms on the west wing. Mr. Osborne asked to have the bed from yer parents' room brought to 'im as soon as it might be arranged."

Marianne sobered at the thought of her beloved parents' bed being used by this heartless interloper. It was only the memory of her mother's kindness that made her choke down the response she would like to have given.

"I suppose it is only right. I hope he may not find it too uncomfortable until his room can be made up properly. I should not wish his death from smoke or cold, although I little wish his presence."

On those words, Marianne escaped from the kitchen before she could do something silly like burst into tears—or into a bout of mad laughter from an excess of emotion. All the servants were looking at her with such sympathetic eyes which made it worse.

No sounds came from within the formal drawing room, and she dared to open it and slip inside. The room was empty, lit only by the dying fire, two candles in the sconces, and the one she held in her hand. She walked over to the corner of the room, next to the rounded wall of the northern tower that held her favorite spot, and sat on the stone ledge that formed a perfect, natural seat for her. Years ago, she had placed cushions on each side, and somehow the spot felt like a hug from her father. Her feet did not quite touch the floor, and she swung her legs back and forth. The only sounds in the room were the slow ticking of a standing clock, and the crackle of logs in the fire. Mr. Osborne had found the room ugly, but he surely could not think it so once he had seen it like this. The soothing atmosphere was all she needed to pour out her heart.

"Papa, what would you have me do? Mama would tell me to give up. That it is time to take the cottage as Uncle intended.

But it's not what I want. I have done everything I could to honor your memory and to run Brindale as well as if I had been your son. Robert always warned me that I should be prepared to abandon it the day my uncle died without an heir, but I was sure Uncle would make *me* his heir. The truth is—" Her voice failed, causing her to stop for a moment, but she had to get all the words out. "The truth is, if I leave this castle, I will be leaving you. And then I will truly be orphaned."

The fire snapped loudly then, just as the clock began to ring the hour with deep gongs. The second gong had not yet sounded when a terrific crash came from the antechamber outside of the drawing room. The noise could only be from her stack of books, which had fallen. And that could mean only one thing—that someone had been standing there, listening to her.

CHAPTER FOUR

Perry froze at the resounding crash he had just made. In the seconds that followed, no sound reached him from inside the room, but he didn't stay to find out whether Miss Edgewood would come to inspect its source. *Who leaves piles of books in a darkened corner, anyway?*

Earlier that afternoon, after the encounter with Vernon had thwarted his mission to inspect the stables, Perry made a half-hearted attempt to locate his bedroom but found it impossible without a candle to light the way. He had instead returned to the drawing room with the goal of finding a servant or a candle, but once he reached its depressing familiarity, he was loath to leave it again.

He had to admit that his initial impression of the castle had not excited his curiosity. He dreaded beginning the exploration of his new property for fear he would find little to rejoice in. The drawing room, taken in with fresh eyes, showed itself to be as sad a room as his first glimpse had impressed upon him. He wandered around it, looking over its frayed curtains, the dark burgundy walls so blackened with age they had nearly lost all traces of color, the large oppressive furniture that littered the walls and occupied some of the center of the vast space, and the stone ledge along the far wall that forced upon one's senses the medieval origins of the castle. There were two doors on adjacent walls of the drawing room. One led to the main hall and the other...

Suffering from the oppression of his surroundings, he grabbed a candle set in a holder on the side table and decided to enter the other door. Perhaps he could explore the castle before the dinner hour.

The door led to a passageway that appeared to follow the inside perimeter of the castle. Its corridor continued on to the outer edge of the rounded stone wall and, after a few feet, led to another room. He crossed the living space, which held an armoire and a four-poster bed that might do for visitors, if he could rig up a system for privacy. What possessed the former owners to decide a passageway was the ideal space to put a bedroom?

The following room was the library, which was modest, despite the vast space. He didn't linger. Curious as to the workings of the castle, he continued on, crossing two more rooms containing beds and old furniture. But as with the first bedroom, they were in passageways, and it seemed the placement of furniture was more for the purpose of filling the room than it was to offer a weary soul a place to sleep. The rooms he went through appeared to be squarish in nature rather than shaped like the slice of a pie. He knew the center held the main hall and central staircase, but what about in the basement? Was there an oubliette at its center? Skeletons chained to the wall with rusted irons? Such a thing was beginning to seem less fanciful.

After he traversed a few more cold, dark rooms, the

corridor broadened, and he came to a wide wooden door set in the stone arch, which opened when he lifted the iron latch. This one led to a spacious room with more of a lived-in look than the rooms he had thus seen, and it had the benefits of candlelight and a small fire burning in the grate. Elsewhere, the original trappings of the castle were in evidence, dusty medieval armor in one place, frames blackened with soot in another, and cracked vases that could just as easily be a hidden treasure from the Ming dynasty as a cheap replica. As a whole, not one room he visited inspired him with satisfaction over his new acquisition. Rather, it was hard to keep the pulse of panic at bay, because there was no hope of readying the castle for guests in such a short time.

Throughout his inspection, only this room had given him the first hint of promise that some parts of the castle could be turned into something lovely. Its many feminine touches led him to guess that it had once belonged to Miss Edgewood's mother. The papered yellow walls retained their brightness, showing evidence of cleaning. The sitting room had also been given a modern touch with its short bookcases, sofa table, comfortable chairs, and wide fireplace. In fact, it was so tastefully done he was not sure he would need to make any alterations.

A series of miniatures caught Perry's eye on the sideboard, and he started toward them before stopping short at the unexpected sight of an older woman sleeping in a chair. He had not realized the room was occupied. A tray of tea was in front of her, although the plate contained nothing but crumbs. She did not dress with an eye to fashion, yet neither was she wearing the clothes of a servant. It could only be Miss Edgewood's companion. It was a relief to find out that she had one, in truth. He had begun to wonder.

Not wishing to wake the woman, he had continued silently

across the room to study the miniatures that were set in three frames. He had no trouble recognizing that of Miss Edgewood as a girl of no more than ten years of age. Her eyes held a softness she appeared to have lost when she became a woman, and her smile was mischievous. Darling, actually, if he were being honest, with a pronounced dimple on either side. The other two miniatures could only be of her parents, painted by the same hand. Her mother had been pretty, but it was the father whose portrait caught Perry's eye. His expression retained the same sort of playfulness that could be found in Miss Edgewood's miniature. Mr. Edgewood's eyes seemed to communicate something from the grave. It was compelling enough that Perry took a step backward. What could have caused their deaths, both of them, at such a young age?

The woman behind him stirred, and Perry quickly moved out of her line of sight in case she chose that moment to open her eyes. He had no wish to strike up a conversation with her. Pretty young women, he had learned to charm. Old companions held no intrigue, and in his experience were more likely to trap him into conversation for a lengthier stretch of time than he could possibly desire.

With noiseless steps, he slipped through the door left cracked open, entering the corridor on the far end of the room, now curious as to what lay on the other side of it. He had been walking for some time in his exploration before he'd come to this room and surely must have reached the full perimeter of the castle. This stretch of the corridor, like the others, was dark without any sun coming through the window, and he had set his candle down in the yellow room and forgotten to retrieve it on his way out. However, there was a sliver of light from the room ahead, and he heard a young woman speaking through the open door. It could only be Miss Edgewood addressing a servant. He inched forward.

She seemed to be carrying on a conversation, and he peered into the room from the doorway that was cracked open, quickly stepping back again to avoid being seen. He was now enlightened as to his whereabouts. He had come full circle, as the saying went, for here he was back in the drawing room, but on the opposite side from where he'd left.

His quick glimpse had revealed Miss Edgewood, seated on the stone ledge on the far end of the room almost facing him, her legs swinging as though she were a child. Now, hidden in the dark of the corridor, her bright image remained lit in his mind as though he could still see her. If he had not heard her voice continuing to speak from where he stood, he would have been sure she must have seen him. But it appeared she had not.

Her speech was conversational but muffled, and Perry strained to listen. A silence stretched before the distinct words could be discerned.

"The truth is, Papa, if I leave this castle, I will be leaving you." The rest came out in a quieter, resigned voice, but he could not miss them. "And then I will truly be orphaned."

Perry had steeled himself against having any emotion for so long, the unfamiliar sensation struck him like a small blow upon the heart. Miss Edgewood sounded particularly forlorn. The last thing he wanted to do was burst in upon such a scene, as he could hardly have words of comfort to give to a young woman who was being displaced because of him. He turned to go, which was when he knocked over the large pile of books that had escaped his notice, thereby giving away his presence in a most unmistakable way. Dismayed at the disaster he had created, he quickly stepped over them in the urgency of his escape, stumbling as his foot caught the edge of one of the covers.

Surely the sleeping companion had now awakened. He would be well and truly trapped, since she blocked his access to the front hall. Nonetheless, Perry took his chances and retraced his steps as quickly as his need for stealth would allow. To his infinite relief, the woman slept still. It was time to stop his exploration of the castle and begin dressing for dinner.

Miss Edgewood's words haunted him as he reached the main hall, still empty, and found the staircase leading to the bedrooms above. Just as he reached the bottom step, a maid entered from a door on his left and, after exclaiming in surprise at the sight of him, offered him her candle. He thanked her and continued his journey upward. Word must have reached the other servants that he was here. He wondered how many there were of them.

Miss Edgewood had been talking to her dead father. She seemed to truly grieve for her parents, even after so many years, and he began to wonder what her life had been like at the castle after their death. That she had at least one friend in the local squire's son let him know she was not completely isolated. And she had a companion. But the resolve grew to find out more about her; he could not otherwise advise her on a good situation. And she most certainly could not remain here, now that he had come to take possession of her home.

Perry found his room upstairs only by incorrectly entering the southern wing, which he recognized from its refurbished state. From there, he was able to figure out which direction he should go to find the eastern wing. Then, he passed through a succession of rooms in his search, one after the other, each one appearing more neglected than the one he'd just quit.

At last, he stumbled on the room that contained his effects —the room that had been assigned to him. His perusal of it did not make him want to linger. The meager fire let out unencouraging puffs of smoke, although he was relieved to see that a fire was burning in the hearth. He went over to call for some hot water, only to realize that the bell was broken. Letting out a groan of exasperation, he went to face his worst fears and tested the bed.

He had slept on patches of ground more comfortable than this. It seemed there were boulders of straw lumped in various places most designed to torment his bones. However, the sheets were crisp and clean, so he would not have to fear soiled linens. He changed his clothes, grateful that his valet would arrive in a couple of days. He was not a vain man, but he would not be able to bear such conditions for very long. Matley would set everything to rights.

Having an idea that the dinner hour had been reached—or if it had not, that he might enjoy a glass of sherry while he waited—he made his way down a nearby circular staircase, set in what must be one of the towers. This led to a square hall on the first floor, with several doors that were all closed. He opened one and found the billiard room. At least the castle had that, although it appeared the green baize, propped on its side on the floor, had been nibbled on by rodents. He returned to the hall and was about to open another door when the footman who had first admitted him into the castle came upon him. He had introduced himself as Charlie.

"If yer wanting the dining room, Mr. Osborne, ye 'ull find it right through this door."

Charlie led him back through the billiard room and opened a door on the opposite end, then stood back to allow Perry to enter a small sitting room. It was adjacent to the dining room that was visible on his right, confirming what a labyrinth Brindale was. Here was another room that could potentially be used to entertain guests. The sitting room had been designed with an emphasis on gothic elements but it did not appear in need of repairs. He turned slowly to examine all four walls, and only then did he discover Miss Edgewood seated on the row of chairs behind the door where he'd entered. He gave a start. Were women forever popping up from unexpected places in this castle?

After their unusual beginning, he'd had a difficult time imagining that Miss Edgewood would make an appearance for dinner, but here she was. He went over to her and bowed. "Miss Edgewood."

She stood and dipped into a light curtsy. "Mr. Osborne." Gone was the forlorn sound of her voice from her private monologue. Back was that nagging feeling that she belonged to this castle more than he did.

Charlie went ahead into the dining room as Sarah stepped out and curtsied. "Dinner is ready, if ye'll care to take yer places." The maid waited until they had both entered before following them in.

The footman helped Miss Edgewood into her seat before addressing Perry. "If ye care for it, sir, I've brought up one of the bottles of Burgundy from the wine cellar. The late Mr. Edgewood—Miss Edgewood's uncle, 'tis to say—bought a case in India, and he had 'em shipped here."

With England's war with France, true Burgundy was a rarity, and Perry began to look more cheerfully upon his inheritance. At last, Brindale had given him something to rejoice over that would undoubtedly impress his friends. He remained standing until Miss Edgewood had taken her seat.

"Water for me, Charlie." She smiled at the footman, and he returned it with a deferential nod. It seemed there was both affection and respect from the servants toward their mistress.

When the wine had been poured and Sarah handed them their napkins, she opened the door for Annabel to bring in the first course. Perry had to own that—pressing need for repairs aside—the castle ran smoothly, despite having a young woman at its current head and engaging, it appeared, only one indoor male servant. It was a shame the Edgewoods had not tackled the larger domestic projects of restoring the castle's elegance and making it fit for visitors. Perhaps her uncle had been tight-fisted in handing over the money needed for castle repairs.

When the food had been served, the maid moved to stand behind them near the wall, and Perry supposed it was to protect Miss Edgewood. He was grateful for that since the companion was nowhere in sight. This was a most unusual situation, and he did not wish to be forced to marry Miss Edgewood for lack of chaperonage. Although he had no idea if she even had a protector who would force the point.

Ah, yes. She has one—Vernon.

As though in rebellion against the neighbor's threats and innuendos, Perry's mind began to wander on its own path, and a rogue vision of kissing Miss Edgewood senseless with no one the wiser seized him. His neck began to heat, and he reached up to loosen his cravat with a discreet gesture. Despite not having the most spotless reputation, he was not the sort to kiss an unprotected, genteel woman, and he would do better to banish such thoughts. Where was her companion, anyway? One look at *her* ought to remove any temptation.

Miss Edgewood picked up her spoon and took a quiet sip of the soup and he did the same. He searched his mind for something agreeable to say, but it was not needed. Miss Edgewood spoke first.

"Mr. Osborne, there are not a great number of servants at Brindale Castle. You will, perhaps, wish to rectify that fact and hire some more. There is, at present, our cook, one footman, a gardener, and a groom who helps with outdoor work, and only two maids."

"Is that so?" he asked politely.

"It is. Therefore, if you have the misfortune to knock over a pile of books again, you may find it expedient to pick them up, for you will be hard-pressed to find someone else to do it."

CHAPTER FIVE

arianne peeked at Mr. Osborne from under her lashes and took wicked pleasure in the flush that crept over his cheeks at her words. It afforded her some satisfaction to let him know she had outed him for snooping, and it had taken only a discreet inquiry of the servants to be sure it was not one of them. She had so few weapons in her arsenal. After all, he was the official proprietor of Brindale Castle. He had upset her peace by arriving on the doorstep without a word in advance and had taken her entirely by surprise by revealing that he was the new owner. Now, in her own small way, she had the upper hand.

Mr. Osborne regarded her for a moment and reached for his glass. "I see now that I should have contacted the steward before coming. I might have learned of the castle's needs ahead of time and been better able to meet them." He had sidestepped her comment neatly.

So, he would not admit to eavesdropping. Marianne took another sip of the cream soup, contemplating how best she should answer and whether she might put him in his place. Nothing came as she lifted her eyes to him. "Why did you not?"

"When my uncle informed me that he'd had the deed to Brindale put in my name, he expressed his expectation that I should waste no time in seeing to castle renovations. I am afraid I took his instructions to heart and came without delay, not thinking through the implications—that the castle might not be ready for me."

Marianne's little experience with men had led her to believe they were all of them rather self-absorbed, and Mr. Osborne only reinforced that belief. It had not occurred to him that perhaps *she* might not be ready for his unannounced arrival either. Sarah and Charlie stood behind her, and their presence lent her courage. She was not the interloper. He was. She risked the question that had been burning inside of her ever since he'd arrived. "Now that you own Brindale, what do you plan to do with it?"

"Ah." Mr. Osborne pulled apart his bread and brought a piece of it to his mouth. He glanced at her as he chewed, then drank more of his wine. Charlie stepped forward to refill his glass while Marianne waited in breathless anticipation.

"My immediate plan is to begin whatever repairs are necessary at Brindale. Lord Steere suggested I consider readying the castle so that I might eventually lease it out to a gentleman who wishes to have easy access to Ramsgate, since we are situated so nearby. Perhaps a military family of some sort. It is indeed the most logical step, as my own home is in London. But renting it out won't be for some time yet, as there is much to be done first."

The little Marianne had eaten turned sour in her stomach. "You wish to rent Brindale out? I hope you will reconsider the idea. This castle is meant to be lived in by someone who cares for it. It is not meant to provide convenient lodging for a carousel of random people who wish to live in proximity to Ramsgate."

Mr. Osborne had finished his soup, and she would not be eating any more of hers. Charlie walked forward to retrieve the soup plates and handed them to Sarah, who set them on the sideboard. He brought fresh plates as the maid placed dishes of hot food on the table. Mr. Osborne pushed the fish toward Marianne, and she served herself for something to do with her hands. Something meant to look natural, although she was too agitated to eat.

When the servants had stepped back, Mr. Osborne caught her gaze and smiled at her in what she could only view as condescension.

"May I remind you that leasing is not an option I can consider at present, so you need not fret. I must have time to assess how much restoration is necessary, and that will, of course, take time. However, in the long term, no other choice presents itself to me than the one I have just proposed. The castle must be restored with the aim of it becoming inhabitable. Profitable. I hope you can understand that, Miss Edgewood."

Marianne set down her fork and hid her trembling hands under the table. "I don't understand it. I care not about profitability. I care about Brindale—its stones, its land, every windowpane and door latch, even the tapestries whose patterns I could trace with my eyes closed. This is my home."

Mr. Osborne did not seem moved by her spirited outburst. He simply looked at her with his cool gray eyes that made her think he was used to getting what he wanted, and he would have his way in this.

"Your passion for Brindale is admirable, but surely you understand that I must handle the estate in the way I see fit. There are mercenary considerations that you can know nothing about. Perhaps we should instead turn our attention to what you plan to do next."

He looked around suddenly. "Where is your companion? I believe I stumbled upon her sleeping in a sitting room when I was exploring the castle."

"She's likely still there," Marianne said, crossly.

She fixed her eyes past Mr. Osborne, attempting to keep her temper under control. It would do her no good to lose it. And as ridiculous as it was to voice what her hopes for her future were, she felt she would be lacking in courage if she did not at least try.

"As for what is to come next, my goal is to continue to live in the castle, where I've spent my entire life. I will not hide that from you, sir."

Mr. Osborne glanced behind him in the direction of the servants, then gave Marianne a wry smile. "Your loyalty to the place does you credit, but it is hardly reasonable. You will find *me* reasonable, however. I will allow you to stay here in the time it takes for you to find a suitable place to live. But I must insist that your companion begin to join us at mealtimes. Ours is otherwise a most unusual plight, and I must have a thought for your good name."

He had heard nothing of what she had expressed, and Marianne felt something crumple inside of her. It would be folly to resist against such determined opposition.

"Very well. I will request that Miss Fife join me at mealtimes." She helped herself to the peas that sat beside her untouched fish. "As for where I plan to go next, my uncle left the cottage on the edge of the property to me. So I suppose I will go there. But you will either have to move Buttercup to the cottage or allow me access to the pighouse behind the stables."

Her statement, slipped into the conversation in such a casual way had all the effect of surprise she could have wished if such a thing mattered to her. Mr. Osborne lifted his eyebrows.

"Buttercup? I am sorry, but you have lost me. Are you speaking of a pig?"

"Brindale's pig." Marianne nodded. "She lives with two other sows, but she tends towards aggression. She doesn't like men."

"I see." Mr. Osborne seemed to digest the information, then settled on another question. "You mentioned a cottage. You already have a place to live? This is news to me. My uncle did not mention a dependence on the estate property. Where is this cottage situated, and what is it like?"

"It's only two hundred years old, but it used to be occupied by Brindale's land steward when the estate was large and went beyond the castle walls."

Marianne sighed, pushing the peas with her fork and watching them roll to the edge of her plate. "It's a stone house with a clay tile roof similar to Brindale, and it has six bedrooms. It's on the southeast edge of the property—before the lines were redrawn—so you would not have seen it when you rode in. Not unless you went out to explore the land."

"I was about to, but I ran into a friend of yours. At least he said he was. A Robert Vernon?"

"Robert was here?" Marianne met his gaze, soothed by hearing a familiar name. She had been forced so out of her element since Mr. Osborne's arrival that she quite thought she could throw her arms around Robert if he walked into the room at that moment. "Why did you not inform me that he had come?"

"I would not have known where to find you," Mr. Osborne said prosaically. "Mr. Vernon said something about a female foal being born that you would want to see."

Marianne nodded. Robert had been waiting for this event,

and she was glad for his sake that the foaling had been successful.

"I will visit him tomorrow." It might bring her relief to pour her heart out to Robert or Mrs. Vernon, and seeing the foal could not help but bring her pleasure. She fell silent, and even managed to eat a few bites.

"If you would accept my company, I would like to go with you."

Marianne looked at Mr. Osborne in surprise, and he gave a little shrug, before adding by way of explanation, "You might show me around the castle grounds on the way, and I am hoping you will introduce me to our neighbors. Mr. Vernon led me to understand that his father is squire, so it would be useful to make his acquaintance, along with any other family in the neighborhood. Besides, you and I might further our acquaintance. In the future, it is likely our paths will frequently cross, and I am hoping you will look upon me as something of an ally."

"Mr. Osborne, since you are taking away my castle, I am more inclined to regard you as a foe." When he refrained from responding to her outburst, she almost regretted her pique. It caused her to add in a milder tone, "However, you are welcome to accompany me, so that I might make the introductions."

She could hardly refuse.

That night, as Marianne tossed once again to her side, she wondered at herself, that she could have agreed to go calling with the man who was all but her mortal enemy. She didn't even like him enough to keep him company. But she had given her word, so there was nothing to do but go through with it.

She and Mr. Osborne did not cross paths at breakfast the next day, but at their designated hour, Mr. Osborne met her in the main hall, a puzzled look on his face.

"I've just been to the stables and have noticed that there is no carriage. Does Brindale not have one? What do you generally do when you wish to go somewhere?"

Marianne tugged on her glove as she moved forward. "Sometimes I ride, but as we have nothing but a nag, it's not much fun. We do have an old gig, but the axle is broken, and the blacksmith is repairing it. Come to think of it, the carriage should be ready, and the smithy is located on the way to the Vernons'. We can stop in there on our way out."

"Do you hitch your nag to the shafts? Or is there another horse secreted away somewhere that does the job?" Mr. Osborne's playful tone surprised a laugh out of Marianne. She would not have expected her foe to have an amiable side.

"We could always use yours," she suggested in the same vein, and was pleased to see mock indignation light his face. That was one thing missing from her relationship with Robert. He was much too serious and did not know how to tease.

"Mine?" He shook his head. "Beau would never condescend to such a thing." They had entered the stables and Marianne reached for the traces from the peg as Mr. Osborne leapt forward to help her, quite towering over her. He was indeed a tall man, and broad—even when not sitting on top of his impressive horse—but oddly enough, he did not make her feel uncomfortable.

"You're handy at harnessing your horse," he observed. "You're nearly as quick as my own groom."

She shrugged. "Marcus is not often needed in the stables, so he helps Neville tend the gardens. It's easier to do it myself at times rather than fetching him." They finished harnessing Sweet Nips and Marianne led her to the doors of the stable while Mr. Osborne went over to greet his stallion, promising him some treats when he returned.

Soon, they were on their way in the direction of Cliff's End, with her leading the horse and Mr. Osborne walking at her other side. It was a journey of twenty minutes' walk to the smithy, and she filled the time by pointing out features of the local landscape. His questions about the castle and the area were intelligent, and he responded without any of the haughtiness from the previous day. They were at the smithy before she saw the time fly.

Joe Dobson was the assistant to a more established blacksmith, who rarely deigned to come to his workplace. Marianne had become touched by Joe's plight because, although he was a hard worker, he did not earn enough to set up his own establishment. As a widower with a young family, he had little flexibility to move and was forced to work the smithy of a man who left all in his charge yet paid him very little. Marianne wished she knew how she could help him.

Upon their arrival, Joe came outside in his leatherwork apron, leaving her with a glimpse of the forge's orange heat through the opening. He smiled and lifted his hand in greeting.

She handed the reins to Mr. Osborne and stepped forward, holding her hand out for him to clasp. Mr. Osborne might think it unusual, but she did not care about that. Joe was like a friend. "Good day to you. Have you finished with my gig? We are in need of it."

He gestured to the carriage sitting outside of the wooden storage. "I was to send Ant'ony over this morning to let ye know 'twas ready, but I've had a rush of orders and had need of him. I see ye've brought Sweet Nips." He glanced at Mr. Osborne.

"I was that confident. Mr. Osborne, may I present Joe Dobson? Joe, this is Mr. Osborne, who has inherited Brindale

Castle." The words left a bitter taste in her mouth, and she had difficulty in refraining from a grimace when she spoke them.

Marianne looked around in search of the children. Anthony rounded the smithy at that moment, trailed by his little sister Beth. Marianne waved when they spotted her, and they came running over, Anthony in front. "Miss Marianne. I was to come to ye today."

"I know." Marianne bent and pointed to the wooden toy he was holding. "Your father has told me. What is that you have in your hand?"

"Ant'ony fixthed my dollth carriage. The wheel'th broke." Beth's strong lisp made it difficult for some to understand her, but it only endeared her more to Marianne.

She leaned down and hugged the girl, who was always covered with soot. Beth needed a mother to care for her, and Marianne wondered at the fact that Joe had not yet remarried.

"Did he now? Your brother is such a clever boy. Anthony, you must still come for your treat. I'm sure Mrs. Malford will send you off with two biscuits, one for each of you."

"Yes, miss! If Papa lets me, I'll come roun'." Anthony was a mature six-year-old who could do anything he set his mind to, Marianne thought, but who would probably become a black-smith like his father.

In the time she had been speaking to the children, Joe hitched her horse to the gig. It was quite an old conveyance, but it ran smoothly enough. He led the horse forward and waited until she had finished.

Marianne stood. "I am most obliged, Joe. As I was telling Anthony, he can come to Brindale as soon as he's free, and Charlie will see to it that Mr. Reacher is paid. I don't suppose the payment for this job could be given directly to you?" She smiled as she said it, wishing she could help.

"It's kind of ye, miss. But ye know I can't do that." Joe

tugged his cap off and bowed, giving his son a swat with his cap to do the same. "Good day, miss. Sir," he added, bowing to Mr. Osborne.

"Good day, Joe. Goodbye, Anthony, Goodbye, Beth." Marianne raised her hand and gave a gentle swish of the reins and a cluck of her tongue to the plodding horse, then drove the gig out of the yard.

With Mr. Osborne at her side, she steered in the direction of the Vernons' estate, finding herself in an unexpectedly benign mood for someone who was about to lose her home. Perhaps it would not be so terrible to have someone like Mr. Osborne living nearby. At the very least, he was easy to talk to. And from the number of questions he'd asked her on their walk to the smithy, and the way he seemed to consider her answers, she began to hope he would allow her to have some hand in Brindale's future.

"You seem on awfully intimate terms with the blacksmith and his family," Mr. Osborne observed. "Where is his wife?"

She looked at him, surprised, and the burgeoning feelings of conviviality suffered a check. Not only his words but his tone showed disapproval, and she allowed indignation to color her own.

"I've known Joe much of my life. He lost his wife when she was brought to bed with little Beth. Now he must raise two children on his own." She kept her eyes trained ahead. "His grief caused his business to suffer so that he lost his smithy and is now dependent on another blacksmith, but he is a good man. Why should I not care for him?"

"It's just that he appears to take liberties." Mr. Osborne's stiff voice showed his disapproval. "He speaks with great familiarity to a young lady who is unrelated to him and above him in station. He should not do so."

Any vestige of good opinion she'd had concerning him

vanished. "There are no liberties taken, I assure you. None that I have not freely given." They rode on in uncomfortable silence, and she pointed ahead to a sandy gravel path that cut between two rows of trees. "This road leads to the Vernons'. We are likely to find them all at home, as it is early yet."

They continued on without speaking until they reached the stables. Robert came out as soon as he spotted them. "You came, Mary. Morning, Osborne. I hope you have slept comfortably." Mr. Osborne nodded but did not respond. Marianne suspected that he had not slept comfortably at all.

She looked around the stables. "Where is she? And what have you called her?" She then spotted the mare in the birthing pen with the foal at her side.

"I was hoping you would help me choose a name." Robert led them over to the small caramel-colored hackney that had a large star on her forehead. She was nursing from her mother but was solid on her feet.

"Oh, she is a darling. You must have a name with the word star in it, of course," Marianne said to the foal, refraining from caressing her while she nursed. "Stardust? Starlight?"

"Whatever you wish. I told Father I would let you choose." Robert stood close by her, and although Marianne was glad to see him again, especially after a length of time spent in a stranger's company, his proximity caused her to shift away.

"Why not Cassiopeia?" Mr. Osborne suggested, surprising her enough to meet his eyes directly. "The constellation named for a queen famed for her beauty."

"And who was punished by Poseidon? I think not," Marianne responded, laughing. After a moment's reflection, she added, "But Cassie is a pretty name. I like it."

"It's a good name," Robert said with a brief glance at Mr. Osborne before turning to her. "Cassie it is, if you like. Come inside, both of you. Marianne, my mother will want to see you.

And, of course, I must introduce you as well," he added, nodding in Mr. Osborne's direction.

He led them to his half-timber, half-brick house, dominating the conversation in his usual way with the birthing of the foal, the great catch he'd had at the pond on their property, and the puppy that would be added to their kennel and trained for the hunt. Mr. Osborne responded when called upon but had resorted to being standoffish. He did not show quite to advantage the way he had when it was just the two of them. Well, except for that unfortunate remark about Joe Dobson. Mr. Osborne must learn that he would not do well in the village if he were to be high in the instep.

As Robert led the party indoors with a great commotion, Mrs. Vernon came toward them with her arms out. "Marianne, you've come at last to visit us! I was thinking it must be about time. The last visit was after church two Sundays ago, and that is just too long."

Their voices resounded in the entrance, and the squire came out of his study into the main hall, where introductions were made. Mrs. Vernon invited them to sit down to tea, and the squire engaged Mr. Osborne in conversation, asking him questions about the castle. Full of curiosity as to his responses, Marianne attempted to listen, but Robert was in rare form and entertained her with a steady stream of words while his mother looked on fondly. When there was a pause in the conversation, Mrs. Vernon lifted her hands with an exclamation about having something for Marianne. She stood and went to the escritoire.

"I had almost forgotten. The Belfords are to serve as hosts for a public ball in the oast house in two weeks' time. Those who are not on the subscription list may attend with a voucher." Mrs. Vernon turned to her with a determined air. "Now, Marianne, you have managed to evade every social opportunity held in the area, and this time I really think you must come. You are not getting any younger and must see to your future."

"Oh, yes, you must come this time," Robert interjected. "I won't take no for an answer."

"I will see that you receive a voucher, my dear," Mrs. Vernon added, before turning to Mr. Osborne. "And that you do, as well, sir."

Marianne turned her gaze to him, curious how he might react. As for herself, she could not accept this invitation any more than she could have each of the previous times Mrs. Vernon had tried to invite her. She had not been raised knowing how to go about in society and would only make a fool out of herself. But Mr. Osborne... Whether he decided to accept would say a lot about him and how well he would fit into local society. He must show them he did not consider them beneath his notice.

He set down his teacup. "I would be much obliged to you if you might procure for me not one, but four vouchers. Three of my friends from London are expected to arrive within the week."

"Within the week? This week?" At the shock of his pronouncement, Marianne could not have held back her words if she tried. "You are entertaining at Brindale?"

CHAPTER SIX

Perry glanced at Miss Edgewood, surprised by her outburst. She was clearly displeased at learning the news that his friends were coming, but he couldn't figure out why it should concern her. After all, he was the one who had to worry about housing them in less-than-ideal conditions. And she had already made plans to remove to the cottage. It had been a boon to discover she actually had somewhere to live. He had not hoped for such luck.

He answered in vague terms, allowing Mrs. Vernon to come to his rescue and direct the conversation to easier subjects. Eventually, he and Miss Edgewood spoke their farewells to the Vernons and climbed back into the gig to return to Brindale. Perry was not sure why he had proposed to join her on the visit, except that he thought it important to be on good terms with the squire, even if that meant consorting with the squire's son. It had been the right decision. The father seemed to be a reasonable man, and his son was like any other gentleman Perry might find in London. The main difference was when it concerned Miss Edgewood. *It's jealousy. That was what made him behave like a boor*, Perry thought.

Miss Edgewood had left the path through the row of trees on the Vernon estate and turned the gig toward home. He couldn't help but wonder what it would be like to tool her around in *his* phaeton with two of his horses setting a spanking pace, as opposed to riding in this creaking carriage pulled by a nag that could barely put one foot in front of the other. If they had been in London, he would have offered to take her riding in Hyde Park. That was a fanciful notion, however, as she had likely never been to London and probably never would. Perry decided to broach the subject of his friends visiting. No sooner had he opened his mouth to speak than she beat him to it.

"When were you planning to tell me of your visitors, sir?" Her lips were pinched tight, giving her a prim look that he found oddly adorable.

"To be perfectly frank with you, Miss Edgewood, the news of my London friends visiting did not strike me as the most pressing bit of information to share with you. After all, may not a gentleman invite whom he pleases to his own house without having to beg permission?"

As soon as the words were out, Perry could have slapped his hand over his mouth. That biting piece of truth was a most unfortunate thing to have left his lips, and quite unlike him. He may not have the greatest social address of all his friends, but he had learned a thing or two in his years as a gentleman.

Miss Edgewood's face blanched except for two distinct spots of color on her cheeks. "No, why should you think to inform me of anything at all, when up until yesterday, Brindale Castle has been exclusively *my* home? After all, if you did not think to warn me of your own arrival, why should the inclusion of three extra guests disrupt my comfort in any way?"

Perry owed her an apology. "I beg your pardon, Miss Edgewood. That was most unhandsome of me. Of course you have every right to know—" He broke off suddenly. "Dash it! My uncle should have been clearer about your presence in the castle when he handed me the deed. He was vague concerning the details, and I'm sure it was to test how I would handle it. It's his way."

Miss Edgewood seemed to soften at his words, and she glanced at him sideways as the nag moved steadily forward. "Is your uncle so fearsome?"

In another lifetime, Perry would have wanted to grab the reins and get the gig moving at a faster pace than the deathly amble the nag was executing. However, there was something enjoyable about riding at Miss Edgewood's side. She had borne much in the two days in his company, but was not given to some of the excess emotions or shrill tones he had experienced in the company of other women. And one had to admit she was excessively fine to look upon, despite not owning a single item that had been sewn in the last several seasons.

"Yes, I suppose my uncle does strike a bit of fear in my heart. He is not an easy man to please." Perry lifted his eyes to the green needles of the Scots pine tree above, breathing in the fresh air that held hints of salt from the ocean not far away, although the water was not visible from where they rode. A subject that had once caused him pain was easier to talk about in such a peaceful setting, and so he continued.

"Lord Steere never paid me any attention until his own son was taken from him. I had never even met my cousin in the fifteen years John was alive. Then, and only because I was his heir and he was forced to notice me, did my uncle invite me to visit. I suppose that makes me anxious not to misstep in his presence."

"And your own parents?" Marianne prompted, her eyes trained ahead and the reins held loosely in her hands.

"My father was a spendthrift and a gambler, according to my mother. I have few memories of him. I suppose he was charming, and he must have been to win a woman like my mother. She would not have been won over by his claims as a gentleman. If he were alive today, I doubt he would be someone I could admire. My mother is a very good woman. She is still alive and living in Essex."

Perry had spoken about himself in unusual detail. He could not remember the last time he had done such a thing. A sudden curiosity to know more about Miss Edgewood prompted him to turn for a glimpse of her face, just visible under her short poke bonnet.

"If it is not excessively painful to speak of, how did you lose your parents?"

Miss Edgewood took a silent breath and exhaled. "It is painful. It cannot be otherwise. But I have had ten years to grow accustomed to the idea. My parents went to bed one night and did not wake up the next morning."

Perry frowned. "Did not wake up? Had they been poisoned?"

She turned the gig onto the public road that he had taken yesterday which led to the estate. *Had it been only yesterday?*

"No, the doctor ruled out poison—at least from a food substance, for we had all eaten the same thing. He thought it must be related to the fire in their room somehow, which was nearly out by the next morning and was smoking excessively. He said that when there is an abundance of smoke or sulfurous air, it can be poisonous to the lungs. As they had both been in perfect health when they went to bed and no other symptom was found to give indication to their death, he is most likely right."

"I am sorry to hear it." Perry allowed himself to imagine how difficult it must have been to be so young and deprived of both parents in one go. She did not appear to have had much guidance at the castle. It had been hard enough for him when he was just sixteen and attending Oxford on his own for his first year. He had not been well-liked then, for reasons he could not understand. But at least he'd had his mother's letters to remind him he was cared for by someone.

After a respectful beat of silence, he prodded further. "If I followed my uncle's brief explanation correctly, your parents were then succeeded by your uncle. Were you close to him?"

Miss Edgewood gave a wan smile. "To my understanding, I have met him but once in my life, and that was before I was old enough to remember it. He succeeded my father as Brindale's owner in the ten years before his own death, and although he made plans to come see me within that first year, the visit never came to fruition. I believe it was business concerns that made him put the visit off, and I eventually stopped expecting it."

The tops of the castle towers could be seen from the distance, and she drove off the public road, directing the gig toward the western gate.

"My uncle and I corresponded the best we could with such distance as we had between us. He was the one who engaged my companion for me, and I was too young to know that it should have been a governess. He was a bachelor, you see, and had spent his entire adult life in India. I think he was rather ignorant of the social niceties or needs of a young girl."

She fell into silence as she drove on to the estate, headed in the opposite direction of the stables. He did not question where she was going. After all, he had asked her to show him the castle grounds, and it seemed she was taking it to heart. The lawns had been kept up beautifully considering the small team of servants that she had numbered, and the castle itself had little outside appearance of decay.

The four towers and crenelated walls gave the structure an appearance of a fortress. Its walls were rounded in between the towers, and they extended up to where a gabled roof was covered with clay peg tiles. This gave the only outward sign of disrepair, as some of the tiles were discolored and in evident need of being replaced. He had already decided that the roof would receive the first of his attention.

They drove by a series of decrepit wooden boxes that must have once been an apiary. "Stop here, would you?" As Miss Edgewood pulled the gig to a stop, Perry asked, "Are these no longer in use?"

Miss Edgewood looked around and almost smiled in nostalgia. "My father loved honeybees, and had the gardener plant all the flowers that might attract them. Comfrey, heather, Michaelmas daisies.... It's all here." She sighed as she brought her gaze to his, her blue eyes reminding him of all those flowers she had just named. He would not allow himself to be distracted by a pretty set of eyes.

She broke his gaze and turned to look at the empty hives. "The hives at Brindale produced a fine honey that was well-known, and it fetched a very good price all the way in London. And our bee liquor was famous locally and sold excessively well."

"Bee liquor?" That had caught his attention.

"It's a mead you get from cleaning the combs. I remember my father boasting of it but I was too young to try it."

They had left the remnants of the bee colonies behind and were now climbing a slight hill that masked the view beyond it. "I was just a girl when my father died and was unable to upkeep the colonies. The beehives lost their queens. All of them are dead now, and the hives are no longer in use."

"I will have to do something about that," he mused as they crested the small incline and a lawn stretched in front of him that might be broad enough for a few sheep. He would eliminate nothing in his search for methods to make the estate profitable. It was not a large estate—there were no tenant farmers to bring in crops, but perhaps something like the apiary could be brought to good account.

"*Hm.*" Her smile seemed hopeful. "I would like to see that."

"Miss Edgewood," he said, prompted by some stirring in his heart he could not quite identify, despite his desire to maintain a formal distance. "I can see that life has not dealt you an overly generous hand. But it's just possible that some of the changes I bring about will be things you approve of."

"Perhaps." She refused to look at him, but her expression relaxed, giving him hope that they might come to a better understanding.

If he were to achieve the formal distance he aimed for, however, it would be best if they did not live together. "If you are indeed ready to move to the cottage, perhaps you might allow me to assist you with the move."

"And take away precious time from readying the castle for your friends?" she asked, an ironic lift to her brow.

She was perfectly right. He hadn't considered that. The thought of all there was to do in preparation sent panic running through his veins. "I will do my best," he answered valiantly.

"I would be much obliged. As a matter of fact, I was bringing you to see the cottage. You can see the side of it there, just ahead."

Perry looked to where she had pointed and saw that the cottage, partly hidden by trees, was situated on the corner of the property, along the wall, as she had indicated. It was a friendly-looking stone house with even windows and matching gabled roofs. This one appeared to be in better shape than the castle.

"When was the last time you came here?" he asked, staring at the small lawn in front of it which was overgrown with weeds.

"I visited it only once when I learned that this would be my fate, and that my uncle had not bequeathed the castle to me, as he had all but promised he would." Miss Edgewood's expression had closed up again.

"Perhaps he feared you did not have the means to restore it," Perry suggested, treading cautiously.

Miss Edgewood pulled the gig up in front of the cottage, dropped the reins, and climbed down before he could do the same.

"My uncle left me alone to raise myself for all intents and purposes. I would have figured out a way to make the estate profitable again. And if I did not, I would have managed just fine, living as I have been for the past ten years. It was the cruelest thing he could have done, and that without sending a word of explanation."

She marched forward, and Perry was saved from having to respond. He would not have known what to say if he were forced to it. Miss Edgewood had had the foresight to bring the keys with her and now pulled a large iron skeleton key from her reticule and went to the front door, where she turned the key in the lock. Perry followed close behind and entered the hall, finding it dark and damp from having all the windows permanently shuttered.

"My new home," she said, her words echoing, melancholy in the empty space.

"It's nice," he offered, but his words sounded feeble even to his own ears. It was barren and damp, the dingy walls giving more the appearance of a prison than a fortress. This would take more than just restoration. It would take hope.

The next day, Miss Edgewood announced at breakfast that she would be moving her things into the cottage that same day. Perry lifted his eyebrows but did not argue her sudden determination when it accorded so well with his own view. It would be much better for her to be gone by the time his friends arrived. It was hardly appropriate for him to be residing in the castle with her, but he could claim he had no inappropriate designs on her. As much as he admired his friends, he could not say the same for all of them.

He had just short of one week until his friends arrived, and with Miss Edgewood moved out, he would make his own room where her parents had stayed. Adam Raifer must have the largest room where Perry had been staying until now, once the bell pull was repaired and the chimney had been cleaned. The bed would not need to be moved, although it was imperative the mattresses be changed in all the rooms. He could give Laurence Wilmot the bedroom where Miss Edgewood had been staying, and Harold Banks—nicknamed "Neck"—whom he judged to be least particular would have to have one of the corridor bedrooms downstairs.

When the servants carried out Miss Edgewood's trunk and he had a glimpse of her room, all he could think about was how Lorry would turn his nose up at the dismal green silk wallpaper there. He didn't expect much of a fuss from Neck, but even he would have a reason to complain when he saw that his bedroom had no privacy. And Raife would just protest mildly in that ironic way of his that Perry must not think of him. After all, *his* butler would have ensured the rooms were inhabitable, but one could not expect such a level of comfort everywhere. Perry feared Raife's reaction most of all.

The day proved to be a busy one with Miss Edgewood supervising the packing up of items throughout the house that held sentimental or practical value, including some of the furniture. Perry was glad to see the gloomy paintings from the drawing room taken from their spots and understood her desire for them when she explained they were portraits of her parents. He was less delighted to see the light patches left behind on the wall that would have to be filled with some other artwork, and the more charming aspects of the yellow apartment disappear that she had said were her mother's. This was the one room in which he'd thought he might tolerably entertain his guests.

However, Miss Edgewood proved to be more generous than she had any right to be by promising to secure him some green baize that could repair the billiard table, and sure enough, a servant came from the Vernon residence with the same that very day.

Perry was faithful to his offer to help with the move and took one end of a rolled-up rug that he had thought he despised from the drawing room, but regretted the sentiment when he saw how cold and barren the floor was without it. He helped the gardener carry it to the cart. His efforts left an unfortunate patch of dust on his pale pantaloons, and as he leaned down to attempt to brush off the stain, the familiar sound of his carriage rolling into the property brought his head up.

"John," he exclaimed in relief when he saw both his groom and valet pull up in his curricle. Marcus had not been able to care for Beau in the way John could, although the man had done his best. And it appeared that Perry could not care for himself. "Matley, how glad I am to see you."

"I arrived as soon as I could, sir." His short valet looked down his nose at the streak of dirt on the pantaloons. "And not a moment too soon, I see."

Miss Edgewood walked by at that moment with a large sewing basket under her arm and directed Sarah to where she wished to have the tea set placed on the cart. She nestled her sewing basket beside it.

"Miss Edgewood," he called out. "My valet has arrived. Sarah, this is Matley. Would you see to the accommodations we spoke of yesterday? John, Marcus will show you where you'll be staying above the stables."

The maid nodded and indicated for Matley to follow. Charlie and Neville moved from the castle to the cart with brisk efficiency, and Perry asked Marcus to assist John in removing the trunk from his curricle so that they might bring the carriage to the coach house and have his horses stabled and brushed down. By the time the carriage was empty, and John had Marcus up on the curricle beside him to go to the stables, Sarah returned with Miss Edgewood, who climbed up onto the cart before he could assist her.

He rested his hand on the side of the cart lest she nudge the horse forward. "I believe the servants have things well in hand at the castle. I will join you at the cottage and assist in whatever way I can if you'll accept my help."

"I would be much obliged. Sarah, would you climb in the back and allow Mr. Osborne to take your place, please?"

There was a flat surface for sitting on one of the trunks, and the maid climbed nimbly over the carriage seat and allowed Mr. Osborne to take her place. Miss Edgewood snapped the reins and the nag started off at a slow pace, covering the short distance in her own rhythm.

As soon as they reached the cottage, Perry swung off the cart and went to the back, where he picked up the heaviest of the trunks, regretting that he had not thought to command one of the male servants to come and assist. The estate was in desperate need of more help, and Matley and John had been hired for specific purposes, not as multi-function servants. They would not take too kindly to being asked to perform the services of a footman. What he needed urgently—and before his friends arrived—was at least one more footman and a maid. However, the task of hiring more servants was daunting, especially in a village he did not know well. He didn't know where to begin.

Miss Edgewood picked up a loose portmanteau and held it along with her sewing basket as she accompanied him into the house.

"I shall have to go back and fetch Miss Fife, who cannot move at anything faster than a snail's pace. I know the servants have been hired by the castle's steward; however, I should be much obliged if you would leave Sarah here with me, for otherwise I shall have no one."

Perry's anxiety only increased at the request. He turned sideways to carry the trunk into the stone house, grunting as he bumped against the door jamb which sent a bolt of pain to his thigh. He grumbled his reply.

"I am afraid that is out of the question, Miss Edgewood. I will not be able to spare a single servant. I do not have enough of them as it is."

She stopped in her tracks behind him, and he heard her utter, "How very generous," under her breath before she followed him over the threshold.

He suffered a blow to his conscience, but really, he could not go back on his decision. She must know how to hire servants more easily than he. And he simply could not do without the help of each one the castle currently had on hand.

CHAPTER SEVEN

At the end of a long day spent moving, Marianne settled by the fire next to Miss Fife in the sitting room of Brindale's cottage with a teapot and two cups of tea. The holland covers had been removed from the chairs in the room, and some bread and other goods Mrs. Malford had thought to pack for her were spread before them on the low table. She was more exhausted than she'd ever been in her life.

Mr. Osborne had not backtracked on his selfish and astonishing refusal to send Marianne her most valuable asset—a maid—and Sarah left her with regret. However, he did spare Charlie, plus Marcus and Neville to bring the rest of the furniture in cart loads. In what revealed her extreme naïveté about how easy it would be to set up house for herself, she had not even given any thought to the sleeping arrangements. The beds and furniture were in place, but the existing tick mattresses were not designed for comfort.

After his earlier miserly display, Mr. Osborne had surprised her by sending Miss Fife's and her own mattresses, and a variety of other useful things such as candles and tablecloths that could be spared. Marianne had thought only of the items which reminded her of her parents, and which she held dear.

"I don't see how we shall get along with no maid," Miss Fife grumbled again for the fourth time. "Never in my life did I think to be brought to such low circumstances."

Marianne sipped her tea and offered no response. From the little she had been able to understand from her uncle's brief mentions of her companion's background and the few words she could get from the woman herself, Miss Fife was a distant and impoverished member of the family. She had never displayed any gratitude at being given a situation, and such an undemanding one at that.

How easily Miss Fife might have won Marianne's affection at that tender age when she had lost everyone she held dear. Instead, she focused on correction and what she termed her "duty," of which she neglected the most important part, which was to train Marianne in how to go on in society. But Miss Fife insisted only that she show no unwomanly display of temper —or even personality. If it had not been for Marianne's memory of her gentle mother and playful father, Miss Fife might have succeeded in crushing her completely.

Hiding her personal anxiety about how well they would do without Sarah, Marianne replied, "Nonsense. Have I not been running the castle single-handedly? I have assisted Mrs. Malford plenty of times in the kitchen and will have no problem reproducing those efforts here. I dress myself with regularity, as do you. I'm sure I shall learn how to wash our clothes just as easily as I have learned these other things until I can hire someone reliable."

Marianne bit into her buttered bread and ignored the fluttering in her breast that reminded her she had not overly paid attention when Mrs. Malford was preparing sweets. She had mainly been occupied with eating them. And she had never assisted her in preparing a more substantial dish. She had gone for the cook's company.

"It has been a long day, and I'm going to bed. I am sure everything will look more promising tomorrow."

Marianne stood and went over to the tall windows, unfolding the wooden shutters and clasping them shut. The noise resounded through the nearly empty room. She would learn to love this place. At the very least, it was hers.

She could only suppose her uncle's illness had been too quick for him to be able to send her any explanation of why he chose this path for her. Why he hadn't given her the castle itself, when he knew how much it mattered to her—why he'd given it to a stranger instead. She would never have those answers, but she was young and could manage what life had handed her.

With the possible exception of much more time spent in Miss Fife's company.

Her companion stood as well and took one of the candles, leaving Marianne to finish the task of closing up. It seemed she would have absolutely no assistance from Miss Fife, despite there being an absence of hired help. It was a daunting task to envision the next couple of days doing everything alone, but she would hire a maid as soon as she could. She would also, upon reaching her twenty-first birthday and gaining her independence, seek out a new companion who would be more agreeable than the one whose presence she had endured for the last ten years.

The next morning, Marianne woke up aching in places she had not even been aware of, but the sun streaming into the room did make her feel more cheerful. It would be impossible to hang her parents' portraits without help, but she set about making the cottage comfortable and trying her hand in the kitchen before the day was well underway.

She had just finished pulling her burned first attempt at almond cakes out of the brick oven tucked on one side of the kitchen fireplace when there was a knock on the door. The blackened lumps on the pan were puffy on one side and flat on the other, and she stared at them in dismay, wondering how the addition of five minutes could have wreaked such havoc on her culinary efforts.

The knock came again, but she didn't bother to move. Either Miss Fife would answer the door, or the person would go away. In any event, it was most likely Mr. Osborne, and she had no desire to see him. She began spooning dough for a second batch of cakes, and as soon as the pan was full, placed those in the enclosed brick oven. This time she would watch the pan carefully and would not allow them to burn.

A knock at the window of the kitchen brought her attention from her discouraging first attempt at baking. "Marianne. It's me. Open up." She could see the top of Robert's head from where he stood, and she opened the window.

"Go around to the front door, and I will let you in."

Cheered at the thought of seeing a familiar face, she hurried over to the front door, crossing the drawing room where Miss Fife slept. She had woken up with the complaint that the bed was not what she was used to, despite the fact that it was her same mattress. Marianne opened the door, and Robert grinned at her, stepping inside.

"So you have your own place now. Thought I'd come and take a look. I had thought to come yesterday, but I didn't want to get in the way."

"Far from being in the way, your presence yesterday would have helped," she said frankly. "I only had the servants' help for the move, and not even all of them. Mr. Osborne has refused to let me keep Sarah."

She regretted the words as soon as they left her lips. She

did not like to spread bad reports of somebody behind his back. It was not good practice, and it was not *her* practice.

Robert reacted much as she could have expected. "Refused! I shall have a word with him. You must have a maid, at the very least."

Marianne was shaking her head. "I beg you to leave it be. I may not agree with Mr. Osborne, who was only thinking of his own needs, but Brindale must have servants, too. If you really want to be of use, find me another maid who might serve the purpose."

"What is that awful smell?" Robert pointed at the evidence of her poor attempt at baking and laughed. "Oh, my word, Mary. Is this how you plan to feed yourself? It looks like nothing short of a disaster."

Marianne pulled herself upright and lifted her chin. Besides his insult, he knew she didn't like that nickname. "I may not have a great deal of knowledge of baking or cooking— or anything domestic for that matter—but I will learn. Now, what about finding me a maid?"

"You must not count on me for that." He poked at one of the burnt cakes, which crumbled at his touch. "What do I know about getting a maid? That's a woman's domain. Or it might be the steward's job. Have you asked him?"

She hated to admit it, but Mr. Mercy had not attempted to discuss matters with her pertaining to the castle ever since Mr. Osborne had arrived. He'd requested an immediate audience with the new owner, probably assuming—and rightly so— that the man who would be paying his salary was the one he should be applying to.

Marianne sat at the well-worn table. She picked a remaining bit of uncooked dough from the bowl and put it in her mouth. It was not terrible. She would just have to learn how to use the oven properly.

The oven! She jumped up and went to peek into the brick oven to see if the cakes were done yet. No, they were not yet baked but it would be only another minute. She would have to try to understand the workings of the oven in the time it would take her to hire a servant.

"What did you come for if it was not to help?" she asked, turning to him. He was an easy target for her irritation, considering how long she had known him—and how irritating he could be.

"I came to see how you were getting on. And I brought you a gift." Robert snapped his fingers and left the kitchen, returning to the front door. She heard him open it, and moments later, he reentered the kitchen carrying a basket. "My mother thought you might need this."

He set it on the table, and Marianne pulled the cloth aside, discovering it was loaded with things to eat: cheese, a crock of butter, and another one of jam. There was some tea, a small cloth carrying eggs, one of which had broken, and smoked ham. Mrs. Vernon had also thoughtfully placed some of the fruit grown in the hothouse located on the Grinnell property.

"Oh, lovely. How generous of her! It would have taken me an age to purchase all of this, and to learn how and where to find it. This will give me a couple of days' respite as I learn my way around."

"You'd better use that time to find a new maid," Robert advised helpfully.

Later, when he had left and Marianne was placing the uncharred, but still lumpy, cakes onto a plate, which she covered with a cloth, there was another knock at the door. This time, she went to open it. It was Mr. Osborne.

"I came to see how you fared." He had what she thought was a sheepish look on his face, and she wondered if it was for the spiteful way he had denied her the one thing she needed most. He should be feeling sheepish.

She swallowed a retort, deciding she would be dignified. "I am getting along very well, I thank you."

Mr. Osborne stood just inside the vestibule, and he looked around her at Miss Fife, who had gotten to her feet. "Mr. Osborne, how do you do?"

Marianne was surprised that she even knew Mr. Osborne's name. He responded with a slight bow. "I am well. Might I come in?" These latter words he addressed to Marianne.

"Please do," she said, although she was still provoked enough to want to deny him access. But he was the possessor of her beloved castle, and she couldn't bear it if she were never to see the inside of it again. They must remain on good terms.

"Have a seat," she said, gesturing to the nearest chair. As she was about to take her own seat, she hesitated. "Would you like some tea?"

"If you have some, I would be glad of it." He remained standing as well, until she left the room.

Marianne went to the kitchen, and as she put the kettle of water to boil and the canister of tea leaves on the tray, she looked over at her plate of almond cakes. They were pitiful, but she had nothing else to offer him that seemed appropriate for a light tea tray. It didn't seem right to put out a slab of ham so close to dinner.

After a moment's hesitation, she arranged the cakes on the tray as well, and when the water was hot, brought the tray out. If he wouldn't give her a maid, he could very well eat the cakes she'd made with her own hands.

She steeped the tea as Miss Fife spoke, loquacious as she expounded on the inconveniences to be found in the cottage. Marianne handed him a cup of tea and a small plate with an almond cake on it, then sat back to watch.

He listened politely to Miss Fife as she informed him that the dining room could not be used to entertain more than eight. As she continued, he drank all of his tea and ate the cake. He made no comment about it whether it was good or not, but he finished it.

At last he was given enough pause from Miss Fife's soliloquy to turn to her. "Did you have a good night's sleep? Were you able to have everything you needed?" He seemed anxious, and she refrained from snapping at him that she would have been much better off if she'd had some hired help.

"I am perfectly capable of taking care of myself," she replied.

"I have no doubt." Mr. Osborne reached over and took a second cake and began to eat it. He'd liked the cake well enough to take another! The small gesture brought her more pleasure than she could have imagined.

"My friends are coming in five days," he said in between bites. "And they are quite particular. I had Charlie go buy proper bedding for them as the most urgent task. And I'm making up a room with more privacy for Neck downstairs in your mother's apartment."

That touched her as well, that he'd called the yellow sitting room her mother's, the way she thought of it. When his words registered, she drew her brows together.

"Your friend Nick will be staying in the bedroom attached to the yellow sitting room? Yes, I suppose of all the downstairs bedrooms, that is the one with the most privacy."

"Neck," he clarified. "Short for 'neck-or-nothing.' And Lorry will stay upstairs in the southern wing—" He stopped short suddenly, and she grasped that this friend would probably be staying in her room. "But I think the hardest task before me will be to repair the roof. I won't have it done by the time they come, yet I must get started."

"Will you be able to do so?" she asked. "It has been many years that the need for repair has been pressing, but my uncle was never a nabob and could not send the funds."

"I will have enough to do just the roof repairs," he replied. "But I won't be able to see to repairing the walls that have been damaged by mold and damp right away. At least I can repair the source of damp so no further damage is done." He took a third almond cake and Marianne was beginning to feel quite charitable toward him.

"It was kind of you to come to see how I was doing."

"I wish for us to be on good terms," he replied. He turned and caught her gaze. She dropped her eyes to his strong chin and lifted them to his mass of tousled curls, suddenly aware of his attractiveness—a thing she most certainly should not allow herself to dwell upon.

Miss Fife, who had finished her tea, then took the conversation hostage in an unexpected spurt of volubility. Marianne was not able to get another word in edgewise. Before long, Mr. Osborne took his leave, and she surprised herself by finding that she could almost forgive him for keeping Sarah after his visit. He had eaten her cakes.

She spent the rest of the day scrubbing what corners she could reach while Miss Fife pointed out some of the spots she had missed. When her stomach began to growl, and the light started to fade, Marianne went into the kitchen and stared at the dwindling fire there, nearly extinguished after her midday efforts.

She leaned back against the wood table and put her hands on it at her side, unable to muster the zeal to attempt to cook something new. How would she do this every day? Her first task tomorrow must be to hire someone local, but no one could replace Sarah in her affection. The sweet maid was only a couple of years older than she, and Marianne had known her since she was ten.

Another knock came—the third visitor for the day. Perhaps life here would not be quite so lonely as she'd feared. This time it was on the door to the kitchen that led to the outside. She could have shown Robert into the kitchen this way earlier, but she had forgotten it was there. She went over and turned the stiff key, already set in the lock, then tugged on the door until she was able to open it.

Standing on the other side was Sarah, her crisp white cap over her blonde hair and her neat apron covering her dress. She dipped into a curtsy, her lips turning up in a cheerful smile.

"'Tis me, miss. Mr. Osborne said he no longer had need of me and that I should come to ye. Said my wages 'ud still come from Brindale Castle for the present, and that I should apply to him for 'em."

Marianne's mouth fell open in surprise as she opened the door wider and stepped back. As she welcomed Sarah into the cottage, she couldn't help but wonder what had come over Mr. Osborne. To have a change of heart like that, to go back on his decision and do something so selfless as to give her back her maid when he so obviously needed every servant at Brindale, showed there was more to him than she had first thought.

It was too soon, however, to apply noble attributes to his character with broad brushstrokes. He might have done so on a whim.

CHAPTER EIGHT

Once Perry had visited Miss Edgewood and seen the state of affairs at the cottage, he had not been able to live comfortably with his conscience. It had been an act of pure selfishness that prompted him to deny her the one thing that was absolutely essential—a maid. The decision was prompted by the wave of panic stemming from not having enough servants for his own estate. The thought of losing one was untenable at this juncture.

However, it had taken only one glance around the room to see that the little touches of comfort from a well-run establishment were missing and that Miss Edgewood deserved better. Then, there was Miss Fife's unpleasant conversation peppered with querulous undertones, showing her to be of absolutely no help to her mistress. Even a glimpse at the lumpy cakes Miss Edgewood had been obliged to make herself—which were surprisingly tasty, he must own—made him ready to repent of his selfish refusal and send her Sarah straight away.

Mr. Mercy's unexpected visit that afternoon only solidified his decision when the steward promised to arrange for more hired help. When asked about the lack of servants at the castle, Mr. Mercy informed him that Mr. Edgewood had not had the funds necessary to run Brindale as needed. But with the new servants in place, Perry would be able to meet his friends with his head held high.

The next couple of days were spent in a frenzy of readying the castle. He had one of the hired hands put lime plaster in the chinks of Raife's room, and he'd had all of the mattresses restuffed with fresh straw, including his own. He was still missing the extra footman, butler, and maids that his friends were accustomed to from their own establishments, but the cook was skilled, and he would do all he could to see they were well entertained.

He certainly hoped to impress them—and hoped he could find enough to do to keep them occupied. These were the first friends he had made in London after having made few at Oxford, none of which proved lasting. The fact that he had only made these connections after being named heir to a barony reminded him of just how difficult it was to form friendships. He couldn't lose the ones he had.

Perry decided to examine all aspects of the castle and grounds. He would not again be caught by surprise at the mention of a pighouse, or a cottage that had been carved out of his bequeathment, or the sight of an unused apiary. He would know every inch of the castle grounds, used or unused, in perfect order or in need of repair.

The walls damaged by damp in the northern wing led Perry to inspect the roof more closely where he discovered the timbers to be rotted beyond repair, and the tiles above it decayed with age. Mr. Mercy was looking into what they might accomplish in the short term with a limited budget. Repairing the roof was a matter of utmost urgency, and although he had spent the majority of his father's small inheritance most foolishly, he should have enough for these most pressing issues.

He stopped by the stables and visited Beau, then went around to see the pighouse with the famous Buttercup that Miss Edgewood had spoken of. He didn't know much about swine, but surely the sow couldn't be as aggressive as Miss Edgewood had indicated.

Perry approached the wooden gate that enclosed the covered pighouse and leaned against it, looking down. A large white pig turned in his direction and charged against the wooden beams, ramming against them and shaking the wood. Although he was well-protected by the gate, the aggression caused Perry to take a step back.

Very well. The pig had won this round.

Continuing on the path behind the stables, he came upon another covered wooden structure, whose center was open and whose roof attached to a decently sized dependence. The door and shutters on the house were falling apart, showing it to be unused. But it was the brick structure near the far end of the sheltered area that caught his eye, along with the iron rings and bars that were meant to hold tools. Perry examined the forge and determined it to be in working order, before turning to see if he could access the building next to it without a key. He could not, but this was still a very good find. He supposed no medieval castle was complete without a resident blacksmith.

His return to the castle was filled with thoughts about what might be done to put the smithy to good use and the recollection that the steward must also look into purchasing a few bee colonies to set up the apiary.

The second of April arrived at last—the day his friends were to come. Matley and John remained nearby to direct the gentlemen's servants when they arrived. The grooms would have lodging above the stables, but he feared the valets would have cause for complaint. And thus it was with both trepidation and excitement that he lifted his hand in greeting as the three of them pulled into the castle at last. Lorry was the first one down from his traveling carriage.

"So this is it, eh? Not quite Steere's estate, I imagine, but it should do for you in the meantime. A bit out of the way, is it not?" He signaled to his valet who was sitting beside the groom at the front of the carriage.

"He said he would be renting it out," Neck reminded him. Unlike Lorry, he'd not brought his valet, which meant that Matley would be serving more than one of them. "Keep that in mind should you wish for a repairing lease."

Lorry looked up at the castle. "A repairing lease? This? I should hope my need for a repairing lease would lead me to something slightly more congenial should I need one."

He spoke in jest, but Perry couldn't help but look at the castle with fresh eyes. It was true that Brindale didn't look precisely hospitable.

"You're always on the brink of needing a repairing lease," Raife said as he stepped to the ground. He had come in a closed carriage and let his groom do the driving with his valet seated beside him. He handed his gloves to the valet and went over to shake Perry's hand, the only one to do so.

Perry was gratified at this attention from the most distinguished member of their circle. Raife was not of the peerage, but he came from a family that could trace their lineage back to the Norman invasion. He was also the wealthiest.

Perry waved them forward. "Gentlemen, allow me to show you Brindale after you've had some refreshments."

"Tell me you have something better than lukewarm tea," Lorry said, removing the offense when he slapped his hand on Perry's back.

"I will have you know the tea here is of the best quality. But perhaps you would prefer a bottle of real French Burgundy?" Perry hadn't intended to reveal his find so early in their stay, but his mouth seemed to speak the words without his consent.

Lorry whistled. "The real thing! Astonished you were able to get some. I see we have come to the right place after all. What do we have in the way of female entertainment?" he asked as Perry led the way indoors.

"There's an elderly spinster residing in the cottage on the estate," he said cheerfully, excluding all references to Miss Edgewood. He might not be able to prevent them from meeting her, but he would do his best to keep her out of their view. "Miss Fife is quite skilled at conversation and has an excessive amount of it."

Raife gave a visible shudder at Perry's side, then turned to his valet, who was following them. "Grant, I trust you will alert me to the presence of prosy spinsters lurking about. Have these brought up to the room I've been assigned. I am sure you will see to my every comfort."

"Ah, quite so," Perry added, bothered that his inexperience in hosting should be so obvious. "Matley, show the valets where their gentlemen will be staying. And see to it that Neck's belongings are brought to his room."

"Very good," his valet said in a wooden voice as he bowed.

He had already protested to deaf ears that he would not be able to show his face to Neck's valet, when he brought him to the downstairs room. Perry could only agree with him and counted himself fortunate that, in the end, there was no valet to turn his nose up at Neck's accommodations.

Moments later, when the men were seated in the yellow

sitting room, Perry sent Charlie for a bottle of the Burgundy, already worrying about what he would do when the stock ran out. There were fifteen bottles, and he wasn't sure how long his friends were staying. But surely they would understand he didn't have an unlimited supply of it. Nobody in England did. The fact that he had any French wine at all was already a thing of amazement considering the English had been at war with the French for nearly a decade.

Neck and Lorry began comparing notes about their trip. They had convened last night at the coaching house Perry recommended for the last leg of their journey, which was how they arrived all at once. As the two of them argued about how close Neck had come to overturning a mail coach, Raife looked on idly.

Perry had not even heard the knock at the front door, but Charlie came in to announce a visitor. "Mr. Vernon here to see you, sir."

Perry got to his feet, less than pleased to see Vernon at Brindale. He could not think his friends would form a more favorable impression of the man than he had himself. However, civility forced him to perform the introductions as soon as his neighbor entered the room. He went through them all, then indicated for Vernon to sit and join them.

"Will you have a glass?" he asked, holding the treasured bottle up. "There are a few left in the wine cellar."

"What's this? Not Burgundy, surely. Had I known these bottles were lying around, I would've convinced Marianne to give them all up to me." Vernon stopped short, likely realizing that sounded an awful lot like theft, and forced a laugh. "Not that she would have, of course. These were always meant for whomever owned Brindale."

"Marianne?" Lorry inquired, his voice perking up with interest. "And who is she?"

Perry could not delay the inevitable, although he privately thought Vernon a dunderhead for bringing up her name amongst a set of London bachelors. "Miss Edgewood is a former resident of the castle." He hoped to leave it at that, but Lorry, who most appreciated female company, would not let it lie.

"And where is the lovely Miss Marianne now?"

Perry glanced up, and his gaze crossed that of Raife's. He needed to dampen the idea quickly. "She inherited the cottage on the property in her uncle's will, and that is where she currently resides. Of course, she is a gently bred lady and will not be joining us at our suppers. In fact, I should be astonished if you meet her at all during your stay."

"Friend of yours, is she?" Lorry asked, turning to Vernon and ignoring Perry completely.

Vernon had his glass raised to his lips, and he stared at Lorry over its rim. "I've known her all my life. I would say we are more than friends."

Neck stood, stretched, and walked over to the small desk and fiddled with the feminine objects that Miss Edgewood had not removed.

"Well, I hope you will join us for our suppers. It's always good to have an extra hand at cards." Neck was an excellent card player, and although he would generally not stoop so far as to ruin a man, he was known to declare that if a chicken asked to be plucked, he was not one to refuse the feathers.

"As it happens, I have my evenings free," Vernon replied after a beat, without looking at Perry to see if the welcome had been extended to him. Not that Perry could have done anything differently, but it would make things complicated to have Vernon here on a regular basis. He was not exactly the model of good ton, and Perry somehow feared his friends would associate Vernon's lack of breeding with him.

Even after so many years spent in their company, he was not sure of his place. The continual need to prove his worth was beginning to be exhausting.

When the men had finished their glasses, toured the parts of the castle that could be shown, and politely declared themselves perfectly satisfied—Perry was vastly relieved when none of them voiced an open complaint since there was nothing he could do to improve their situation—they decided that it was fair enough outside to walk about the estate.

The property was not quite two square miles, which meant they could visit much of it on foot. They strolled at an idle pace, and Perry showed them the woods where they could get some hunting in when it was the right season. It was on the northeastern end of his property, and they rounded the pond that bordered the castle, which he surmised was part of what had once been a moat.

He had purposefully steered them in the opposite direction from that Miss Edgewood usually took to go to the cottage in hopes they would not cross paths with her. It was therefore with consternation that he saw Miss Edgewood walking in their direction and without a maid accompanying her—this despite the fact that he had expressly given her one.

She stopped short when she saw Perry and curtsied before turning to his friends. At the sight of her, a broad smile spread over Lorry's face, and he bowed deeply. "Miss Edgewood, I presume."

She lifted inquiring eyes to Perry. There was a hint of surprise there, and he couldn't help it if his explanation sounded more like a defense. "Vernon was over and mentioned you by name, so my friends asked for an explanation."

"To be sure. After all, I was the first to live in Brindale." She looked past him to where the castle could be seen in the distance, and the sight of it seemed to cause her to deflate. "Of course, I have a different home now."

"I hope you will join us for dinner one of these evenings," Lorry said, ignoring both her melancholy tone and Perry's express warnings. He had a sudden fear that she would accept, showing her to be even more artless—or less innocent—than he had first believed.

She shook her head resolutely. "It would not be seemly. I do not, in general, attend societal functions of any nature." She looked behind her as Sarah hurried from the direction of the cottage to meet her.

"I must be off. Good day," she said, dropping a general curtsy in their direction, before turning to walk with her maid toward the western gate that led to the village.

Perry thought he had escaped any further comments about Marianne and was in the process of congratulating himself when Lorry sidled up to him. "I thought the bottles of Burgundy were a find, but it appears Brindale has offered you a treasure of even greater worth."

"Don't think of it," Perry said firmly. She was strictly off-limits, and he could only hope his friend would hear him.

Mrs. Malford had outdone herself with their first dinner that night, and Perry was pleased to see his friends partaking liberally of everything set before them. Vernon had sent a note explaining that they should start the meal without him, as he had a family obligation to attend to first but promised to come for the cards.

They were sitting around a shared bottle of port, his friends already in high revelry, when Vernon eventually arrived. Raife fiddled with the salt cellar that had been left on the table while the others spoke, appearing not to pay heed to any of the conversation, but Perry had come to know that this was just an act. Raife was much more awake than he let on.

When Vernon was seated at their table with his glass of *porto* in front of him, a lull settled over the conversation. Neck folded his arms and sat back. "Are you originally from Kent? Who is your father?"

"Spent my whole life here," Vernon answered with pride. "M'father is squire for the eastern coast of Kent. We live at Grinnell a mile or so from here."

"Where were you schooled?" Lorry asked, and Perry felt for Vernon but didn't know how to stem the inquisition. It seemed as though he were on the opposite end of a firing squad, although only two questions had been asked.

Given the flush that lit Vernon's cheeks, he must have felt the same. "The squire wanted me close by to learn estate business, so he hired tutors."

"Shame you've never had a formal education. It's a great load of fun," Neck said. "Well, except for the studies." Vernon wasn't given a chance to respond, because Lorry picked up the thread.

"And so you're an intimate of Miss Edgewood's. She's a rare piece of beauty, isn't she? I don't suppose your two families tried to set the two of you up?" Lorry gave the appearance of making idle conversation, but Perry did not like the direction in which it was headed.

"Shall we try some fishing tomorrow?" he proposed, but Vernon did not let the matter drop.

"There's some interest there. We shall see what the future holds." He put his glass down and set his hands on his knees. "But I imagine Marianne will soon see the benefits of marriage, now that she no longer has the security of her castle. Her relationship with my family is of long standing, and she would be foolish to turn down such security too quickly."

"You'd better hurry before Lorry makes a stab at it," Neck

said under his breath, his remark nonetheless perfectly audible.

It was not well done of them to discuss Miss Edgewood so openly, even for gentlemen who had a tendency toward the bawdry whenever they were far from the company of women. Raife remained quiet throughout it all, merely lifting an eyebrow as though such matters were beneath him. Perry was as irritated as he could be for the sake of a woman he could hardly claim to know, but Vernon was no longer able to contain himself. He grew quite red and jumped out of his seat.

"I'll not sit here and listen to Marianne's name be sullied. Whatever gentlemen may speak of in their own time, their conversation should not involve the name of an innocent maiden. And not one of you"—he pointed at each of them but kept his gaze longest on Perry—"is worthy of her. So stay away from her." He enunciated each of the last five words, then grabbed his hat and gloves and stormed out of the room.

Raife dropped the spoon in the salt cellar. "As much as it pains me to admit it, he is not wrong."

Perry remained silent as Neck and Lorry made a snide remark at Vernon's expense before turning the conversation to other matters. After a brief reflection, he decided that Raife was not entirely correct in his agreement with Vernon. If Perry was bent on wooing Miss Edgewood, he would make certain he was worthy.

CHAPTER NINE

Having Sarah working beside her brought Marianne immense comfort. In the day and a half she'd spent without a servant, she had learned to value the maid's assistance even more. With just the two of them at the cottage—she would not count Miss Fife—it would not be long before their relationship turned to friendship rather than mistress and servant.

Miss Fife had never been and would never be the companion or friend Marianne needed, and apart from the Vernons, none of the village families had ever paid her any heed. She supposed it started with her being a mere child when her parents died and therefore beneath their notice. Then, when she had grown enough to make friends with other girls her age, there had been no one to sponsor her among the local families. Her parents had been civil but had not worked on developing village relations, content to live at Brindale Castle. It was only because Mr. Vernon had occasionally applied to her father in his duties as magistrate that she had even been permitted to frequent the Vernon family at all.

When she became old enough for invitations to balls or suppers, those invitations never came. Miss Fife was beneath the social status of the other important families in the village, and she did not have a congenial nature or desire to make herself agreeable to society for the sake of her charge. Mrs. Vernon had attempted to bring Marianne to balls and parties when she had come of age, but after years of solitude, the thought terrified Marianne. She grew tongue-tied around people her age and felt more comfortable with ones like Joe, the blacksmith, or Mrs. Malford. What likely did not help matters, despite having a small independence of one hundred guineas a year from her mother, was that she preferred investing money in running the castle rather than purchasing clothes that were modish. After all, if she was not going to go about in society, why would she need the latest fashions?

Now, things were changing. Having Mr. Osborne's friends from London invade the intimacy of her estate made her feel shabby in ways she never had when dipping polite curtsies to familiar faces at church. Being forced from the haven the castle had provided her, she was beginning to see the value of learning to dress correctly and move about in society. It had been foolhardy to think she could avoid it forever. However, dress and manners were not something easily learned, and they would become a problem for another day. She had enough to worry about with turning the cottage into a home.

"I've swept the 'earth clean in the spare bedrooms, miss. However, I fear we 'ull need to have the chimney sweep come in. There's a buildup of soot, and it's that what makes the fire smoke there." Sarah bustled about the drawing room, looking hardly worse for wear despite the task of cleaning the hearths. She always managed to look tidy.

That morning, Marianne had asked Sarah to test the chimneys in each room to see which ones were usable and which were not. This she was forced to do after Miss Fife woke her up in the middle of the night, complaining that there was too much smoke in her room and that the chimney wasn't drawing properly. As much as Marianne's weary bones had screamed to be left alone so she could go back to sleep, she couldn't ignore the danger of a room that was not properly ventilated—not after losing her parents in such a manner. She roused herself and saw that, true to Miss Fife's word, the fire in her chimney was more smoke than flames. Rather than disturb Sarah for something she could not fix, Marianne gave up her room to her companion and slept on the chair in the drawing room.

Now she stared at Sarah, suddenly tired. She sat, brushing the dirt off her work apron—an item that would need to be washed as well, though she had worn it only one day. At least Sarah was here to help with laundry. She dropped her chin in her hands.

"I will see if Joe knows of a chimney sweep. In any case, it must be done."

Sarah cocked her head at Marianne's pinched brow and rested a hand on her forearm. "Don't ye fear, miss. My cousin, Jeremy Brown, is a master chimney sweep, and he has lads as 'ull scurry up that chimney and clean it grandly."

"He doesn't..." Marianne couldn't finish the words. She had heard that chimney sweep boys were often orphans who were taken on young, then treated as slaves. She might not be able to do anything about the institution of chimney sweeps, but she did not want little orphan boys to suffer in her house.

"No, miss. My cousin is a kind master. Ye won't find him whippin' 'em or lightin' fires under their feet to get them to go higher."

Marianne smiled in relief. "You are an angel. I am so relieved that Mr. Osborne let you come to me. I honestly don't know how long I would have lasted without you."

"That he did, miss, and I'm right glad to be here." Sarah glanced at the chimney in the drawing room and went over and rubbed at the marble sides with a cloth. "Mr. Osborne asked if I could pack up my things before the sun set, and he drove me over when I said I could."

Mr. Osborne was a perplexing man. Imperious and looking out for his own interests in one moment, then surprisingly easy to talk to and showing great kindness in the next. But she would do well not to think too kindly of him, for life had taught her that people could not be relied upon. They would either die, or snub you at church, or hand your most prized possession—your home for the last twenty years—over to a perfect stranger without the blink of an eye or a word of explanation. No, she needed to keep her mind and focus on her own life, for she had to make a new one here.

Early in the morning, Sarah had gone to market to buy viands and produce that would keep them for a week, filling the pantry in a satisfying way. She now prepared to scale a fish for their supper while Marianne went outside to look at what might be made of the garden. She would never have her mother's rosebushes, but she might create something of her own here. It had rained that morning, and the grass sparkled with drops of water like crystal, and the budding leaves of the trees had begun to open. The sight lifted her spirits. She was looking at an enchanting fairyland.

The sound of a horse snorting came from her left, and she turned to look. In a moment, Mr. Osborne's friend with the neat, pomaded hair and trim whiskers stepped through the clearing. He was not as tall as Mr. Osborne, and objectively not quite as handsome, but he possessed charm. She did not remember his name.

"What's this?" The gentleman leapt down from his horse and sketched her a bow. "Miss Marianne, I presume."

"Miss Edgewood," she corrected, pulling her basket containing the gardening shears closer.

"Miss Edgewood. Lawrence Wilmot at your service, in case you might not have remembered. My friends call me Lorry. So, you have been ousted from the castle by that poor devil, Osborne."

"I have been ousted by my uncle." Marianne looked more closely at his horse, which was an English Thoroughbred with a shiny black coat, as fine as any she had seen. "Robert would offer you his fortune for this horse if he had a glimpse of him."

She spoke without thinking and then turned red. Perhaps that was not something appropriate to say to a perfect stranger. However, Mr. Wilmot only laughed.

"Yes, I have met your Robert. He joined us last night after supper for a game of cards. However, we did not get to the game in the end."

"Did he? I am very glad he was invited." Marianne did not know where to look after having expressed herself so freely regarding the horse, so she dropped her gaze to her feet.

She could feel Mr. Wilmot's regard, studying her in a way that was both flattering and made her feel somehow exposed. "Vernon had a few things to say in your regard. Apparently, he has proprietary views towards you, given your longstanding relationship."

At that, Marianne darted her head up. "Robert has no hold on me whatsoever."

She didn't like the idea that Robert was going around making it seem as though they had an understanding. And if she examined her thoughts too closely, she feared to find that she also didn't wish for this fine London gentleman to view her as some country miss who had buried herself away and subsequently sold out to the first man who showed an interest. Although it was the perfect truth that she had buried herself away. That was not something she would be changing any time soon.

"Of course," he said soothingly. "Anyone might see that you are much too fine a lady to accept the offer of the first gentleman who makes one."

Honesty pushed her to say, "He has not exactly made me an offer." Then heat crept up her cheeks, for that seemed a pathetic thing to say. How she wished she had been taught to converse with gentlemen. Although it had not been difficult to talk to Mr. Osborne, despite his provoking ways at times.

To her surprise, Mr. Wilmot did not laugh at her. Instead, he said, "Oh, but he will. Mark my words, Vernon will try. And you"—he gave her a cheeky grin—"you must resist."

Marianne bit her lip to keep from smiling. "Of course, I must resist. Though, allow me to assure you, it is not as much of a temptation as you seem to believe."

Mr. Wilmot swung back into the saddle. "Happy to hear it. Well, I must leave you. We will be having a late breakfast at Brindale, and if I don't arrive in time, I might get nothing to eat until dinner. Barbaric place, that castle. Good day, Miss Marianne." He lifted his hat and rode off.

She stood there, awash with an array of feelings. Flattered. Irritated by his jab at Brindale. Curious as to what he meant by her resisting Robert, said in a way she could only call flirting. It was only when the noise of Sarah banging a spoon against the Dutch oven from inside the house reached her that she realized Mr. Wilmot had called her Miss Marianne again, though she had asked him not to. And she had not thought to inquire what brought him riding onto this part of the estate.

Before another hour had passed with her still performing small tasks in the garden, Robert came to visit. He used to come often when she was living at the castle on her own, but not every day as he was doing now that Mr. Osborne was at

Brindale and she resided in the cottage. Her first thought was that she would not want Mr. Wilmot to see Robert ride up and confirm his suspicions, but she dismissed the notion. Here was proof she had a true friend who had known her nearly her whole life, and who was solicitous of her well-being. After exchanging a greeting, Marianne waved him to come inside. Now that she had Sarah, she was able to put something on the tea tray she need not be ashamed of.

"I came to warn you to stay away from the castle," he said in his familiar way before he had scarcely entered the drawing room. Miss Fife was upstairs deciding upon which bedroom might better suit her than the one she was in, so they were alone.

His words left Marianne at a loss. "Why?"

"Osborne has friends from London in town, and I think you can't be too careful in their presence." He threw himself down in one of the chairs.

"But they are gentlemen, as you say. Therefore I think I need not fear. One of them rode by the cottage this morning, and when he stopped to talk, he behaved most properly."

"Came here?" Robert said, his voice rising in astonishment. "Who was he? Which one?"

"He said his name was Mr. Wilmot. And as I said, he was perfectly cordial," Marianne said, neglecting to add that he was also rather informal. After all, was not Robert informal as well? Perhaps it was the way of gentlemen.

"I'm telling you, Marianne, you need to stay clear of them —the lot of them, including Osborne. I hear their conversation when no ladies are about, and you must trust me on this."

Sarah did not appear to have heard Robert's arrival, and the tea tray would not bring itself. Marianne waved for him to follow as she led him into the kitchen where Sarah was kneading dough. "I do not need you to tell me this, Robert. I assure you I am fine."

Sarah took a cue from Robert's intense look and Marianne's belligerent one and wiped her hands on her apron with a murmur about fetching something from the cellar.

"You have to allow me to look out for you. I don't think it's a good idea for you to be living here alone. Where is...?" Robert looked around suddenly as though Miss Fife might suddenly accost him from some shadowy corner.

"I'm not alone—" Marianne started to say, but he cut her off.

"And don't tell me that you have a companion, for both you and I know that she is no companion for you. Thunder an' turf, Mary, it's time you were married. You need a husband who can take care of you."

Marianne wasn't tall, but at those words, she drew herself up. "I should not need to tell you that I am perfectly capable of taking care of myself. I did so when I lived at the castle; and as you can see, I am taking care of myself here. I do not need a husband. I have an independence, and I have a place to live. That is all I need."

"You've always been too naïve. Until now you've been young, sheltered. But it's time you leave childhood fancies behind. It's time to start behaving like a woman and see to your future. I'm not a man of honeyed tongue, but you must know how I feel—"

"Don't—please."

Now Marianne was truly distressed. She needed time to adjust to her new situation. And if only to prove it to herself, she needed to show she could manage it. She did not need an offer of marriage. Robert didn't speak right away, and she turned so she wouldn't have to look at his accusatory eyes.

"As you wish," he said at last, his tone curt.

They both fell silent as Sarah reentered the kitchen. "I will bring tea to the sitting room," she said. "I 'ull soon have some fresh-baked scones and jam. I believe the jam's from your house, Mr. Vernon."

Her practical words helped Marianne to relax, and Robert appeared to do so as well. By the time they had entered the sitting room—Miss Fife was not long in joining them as she seemed to have a knack for appearing when the teapot did— Robert and Marianne had resumed their more usual friendly discourse. Marianne was glad of it, for she needed the comfort of a familiar presence. When he was ready to leave, she walked him to the door.

"I won't press you again, but do think about what I said." Robert put his hat on as he faced her.

"If you please..." Marianne shook her head. She did not want to fight with Robert. He might be one of the few friends she had, but he had to see that she would not give in to him. "I beg you will turn your thoughts in another direction and look upon me as your friend, as you have always done."

Robert's lips straightened into a thin line. "I merely asked you to think about it."

It was a losing battle, it seemed. Marianne looked down. "I will."

That night, as Marianne lay in bed, she thought about Robert's reference to her being alone. She would be twenty-one in a couple of months, and she would take steps to find a new companion at that time. She had put up with Miss Fife's presence long enough. A new, more agreeable companion and her maid Sarah were all she needed. If only Robert could see that Marianne had no wish to be married. She had no need to. Even this transition to her new home had gone much better than she could have imagined, and she was perfectly fine on her own.

Well, she was as fine as she could be with her soul having been ripped out of her when she left Brindale.

That night, Marianne had fallen into a deep sleep when a sharp *thwack* sounded from below, causing her to wake suddenly. She sat up, breathing hard. *What had caused that sound?* There was an absence of moonlight, and she could not see the details of her room, but she listened as hard as she could. Was someone downstairs?

Then another sharp noise broke the stillness—the unmistakable sound of glass shattering. Marianne gasped. Somewhere in her house, someone had broken a window.

CHAPTER TEN

A dull, persistent noise pulled Perry from sleep, and a crack in the curtains around his bed showed the faint light of dawn, which allowed him to gain his bearings. However, he couldn't clear his head of sleep well enough to grasp what could be making such a noise at this ungodly hour of the morning. It had not been until sometime in the middle of the night, or perhaps it was early in the morning, that he had been able to fall into his bed, and his head felt like lead. He had not dipped deep—it was not his nature, as he had developed the habit of keeping his wits about him when surrounded by gentlemen who could just as easily be foes as they were friends. But he could hardly leave his three guests to their drinks and cards while he crept off like a wounded dog to bed.

The pounding came again and matched the pounding that would begin in his head if he didn't get more sleep. However, such a thing was not possible. He was the master of the house, and if someone was going to investigate, the job fell to him. Perry arrived downstairs at the same time that Charlie reached the front door. Matley had gone to sleep in the servants' quarters, even farther from the entrance than Neck's makeshift bedroom, and he likely did not hear a thing. He would not expect Perry to call him to dress for several hours at least.

The footman, although in better form than Perry since he had been given leave to go to bed after midnight, was not quite properly attired as was evidenced by his hair falling out of its queue and his half-buttoned coat. Charlie quickly fastened the last three buttons of his coat before unbolting the door and swinging it open, just as Perry arrived at the front entrance. To his astonishment, three women in varying states of undress huddled together in a group at his doorstep, with Miss Edgewood in the center.

"What in heaven's name has happened?" he asked, pushing past Charlie and exiting into the brisk morning air, all thought of his fatigue dissipating.

Miss Edgewood curtsied to him. "Might we come in?" Charlie did not wait for Perry's answer but swung the door wider to allow them entrance.

"It was the most frightful thing!" Miss Fife's voice shook as she removed the handkerchief she was holding to her mouth and waved it in his direction. Of the three, she looked the most disordered, with her hair bound in rags that were likely used to achieve the curls, such as they were, and an open cloak, revealing her dressing gown.

"We have been attacked! We shall be murdered in our beds if we stay there!"

Now truly alarmed, Perry looked to Miss Edgewood for clarification. She was pale but more composed.

"There is some truth to what Miss Fife says. We were not attacked, precisely, but someone broke a downstairs window of the cottage in the middle of the night, and we fear it was an attempt to break into the house." She looked at her maid, who confirmed this with a nod.

"We didn't stay long enough to be sure," Miss Edgewood went on, "but it doesn't look as though anything was stolen. However, after the sound of breaking glass woke us up, we deemed it imprudent to investigate. We did not dare without a male servant in place, so we—Miss Fife, Sarah, and I—took refuge in my room for the remainder of the night. My room at least had a key."

"I couldn't get a wink of sleep." Miss Fife began to cry. "I am distraught—entirely shattered."

Miss Edgewood put her arm around Miss Fife, and Sarah supported the older woman from the other side.

"We pushed furniture against the door in case someone attempted to enter, and although we waited to see if we might hear some evidence of further damage, we heard nothing else. We didn't dare come to see you until daybreak, however."

Perry didn't like the thought of criminals on his estate, although the cottage was technically no longer part of his estate. He especially didn't like the thought of there being a house full of women with no protection, when these women had been perfectly safe at the castle. He had been too hasty for Miss Edgewood to leave, and he deeply regretted it. It was a miracle she had not been harmed. The thought made him turn cold.

"Charlie, rouse one of the servants and bring the women some tea. Miss Edgewood, if you'll please come into the drawing room?"

Sarah separated herself from Miss Fife's side. "I'll help ye, Charlie. Even if I imagine Mrs. Malford, Annabel, and the new maid are already up." She went with him to the kitchen.

"I knew nothing good would come of us leaving Brindale,"

Miss Fife moaned. "The idea of unprotected females setting up house all alone with no male servant to keep an eye on us!"

"We've done very well without a male servant, and you knew it was only temporary until I could hire someone."

Miss Edgewood allowed irritation to creep into her voice, and Perry could hardly blame her. He was running through the decisions he had made since taking up residence at Brindale, and he felt contrite about encouraging the move without providing them with at least one of the male servants along with Sarah. It had not been his best idea. No—it had been positively selfish.

In the drawing room, Perry waited until the two women were seated. "It was wise of you to stay put until dawn came, rather than trying to set out in the night. Did you get any sleep?"

He turned as the door opened and Raife, of all people, entered the room. He would have bet that Raife would be the last one to leave his bed.

Miss Edgewood gave Raife a tight smile in acknowledgement, then turned to answer. "Miss Fife was able to fall back asleep—I gave her my bed so that she might do so—but neither Sarah nor I were able to let down our guard enough to get any rest."

"I shall have to find you both a room to sleep in here, then. You have had quite a fright, and you will need some time to recover your peace of mind." Perry looked at Raife, who took an empty seat in one of the armchairs and raised an inquiring eyebrow.

"There was a break-in at the cottage," Perry explained. "Miss Fife and Miss Edgewood did not leave until morning for fear of encountering the thief on the grounds."

Glancing at Miss Edgewood, he added, "I am glad we can

provide them refuge but regret they should have to suffer any inconvenience."

"Of course they must stay here," Raife agreed.

The door opened again, and Lorry entered the room with the ends of his neckcloth hanging down on either side of his shirt. It looked as though he hadn't bothered to remove his day clothes—or that he'd had any sleep at all.

"What's all this racket?" He rubbed his head, then looked from Perry and Raife to the women. He straightened. "Miss Edgewood. I fear you catch me in less-than-correct attire. I hope you will forgive my appearance. What has happened?"

Miss Edgewood turned her gaze away, and when she didn't speak, Perry cleared his throat.

"There was a break-in," he explained for the second time, then turned to Miss Edgewood. "I will go investigate to see what I might learn, but first allow me to provide a place for you to sleep. Miss Edgewood, you must take my room. The fire has been built up there, and the room can be made comfortable quickly. Miss Fife, you are welcome to sleep in the maid's room that's adjoined to it."

He afterwards supposed that this had not been delicately done. Miss Fife was no maid, but he had thought that surely she would see she couldn't leave Miss Edgewood to sleep alone in a bachelor's establishment.

"I'm afraid I am unable to take the stairs to sleep up there. I have hurt my foot. I shall need a room down here." Miss Fife had removed her cloak and now wrapped her dressing gown more closely around her. Her voice sounded more peevish than it did injured.

Miss Edgewood appeared to think so too because she turned to look at her sharply. "You did not complain of a sore foot when we walked over. You should have let me know. I might have left you at the cottage and gone to get the carriage to bring you. That way you would not have made it worse."

Miss Fife tucked her thin hands into the folds of the gown on her lap. "Oh no. I could never have stayed in that house all by myself. Besides, my foot was not hurting overmuch when we left. It was the long walk that has aggravated the pain, I fear."

Miss Edgewood tightened her lips and glanced at Perry. "I must own that a room where I could rest and recover, and feel in perfect safety, would be most welcome. Has Miss Fife's own room been given away?"

"I'm sorry to say that it has. Please allow me to think for a moment. I am sure we will be able to find a solution that will please everyone," Perry said. Those present seemed only too willing to comply, more likely from fatigue than any other reason.

In his current distress over what had happened, he was nearly ready to give Miss Edgewood permanent residence at Brindale. He liked the idea of being able to keep her safe. The thought of being made useful in such a way restored some of his energy.

Many of the serviceable rooms had been taken, not only by his friends, but also by their servants, who expected a certain degree of comfort. As he ruminated over how he could arrange things, Charlie entered, followed by Sarah, both carrying the tea things. Miss Edgewood remained silent, weary, as she prepared the tea and stood to hand a cup to everyone, including Raife and Lorry.

"Can the house be shut at night?" Raife asked as he accepted the cup from her hands.

Miss Edgewood returned to her seat and nodded. "I've been latching the shutters and bolting the doors each night, but some of the shutters are old and don't fasten well. When the intruder broke the window, it caused the shutters to burst open from the inside. I looked into the drawing room as we left this morning, and I saw glass on the floor. But we were in a hurry, fearful that someone might still be there, so I did not look too closely."

They fell silent as they finished their tea. Perry set his cup down, still without a ready solution for Miss Fife but determined to see to Miss Edgewood.

"Charlie, I will ask assistance from you and Sarah in finding a solution for Miss Fife to be accommodated on this floor so she will not pain her foot by climbing the stairs. You know this castle and its resources more intimately than I do."

Charlie stood at the back of the room, but Sarah had slipped out, likely to sit on the bench in the hall for some rest. He could not blame her. The footman bowed. "I'll do so, sir."

"Miss Fife, we will find you comfortable accommodations soon enough. In the meantime, Miss Edgewood, will you allow me to assist you to your room?" Perry went to her and held out his hand then helped her to rise.

"Oh, I can do that," Lorry said, leaping to his feet. "It would be no trouble at all to bring Miss Edgewood to your room. That way you may get a head start on inspecting what happened."

Perry did not like the eager look in Lorry's eye. He slipped his arm under Miss Edgewood's elbow to support her, surprised by the natural way it felt. She was quite petite, but the difference in height did not make their touch awkward. And a whiff as she drew near brought the faint scent of roses.

"I assure you, it is no trouble," he told Lorry firmly. Turning to Miss Edgewood, he added, "I hope the room will restore a sense of comfort. After all, it had been your parents' room, and very little was changed since I've taken possession of it."

"Thank you," she murmured. The novel feelings of protectiveness he harbored toward her were strong, and they caused his heart to beat almost painfully. He wondered if she also felt the current that seemed to pass through them as he supported her arm. If she did, she did not pull away.

"I'll walk up with you, then."

Lorry fell into step beside them as Perry accompanied Miss Edgewood to the main hall, then followed them up the stairs. Perry remained silent, allowing Lorry to carry the conversation, which was filled with expressions of concern over Miss Edgewood's ordeal. But when they reached Perry's room, he turned to Lorry.

"You had best go back to sleep. Otherwise you'll be good for nothing later." He smiled politely and turned his back on Lorry, who seemed to accept he had been outmaneuvered.

"That is the truth."

As Lorry went back to his bedroom, Perry opened the door to his and allowed Miss Edgewood to enter it. He would not go in himself—that would be inappropriate. He stood in the doorway watching her, and something in his heart softened at the sight of her turning in a slow circle to examine the room as though she were a stranger. She had dressed and put on her bonnet before she'd left the cottage, but the fatigue and fright of the evening were evident in her pale face and the fine lines that were etched around her eyes.

He caught himself staring. Their gaze held for a moment as she stared back at him, mutely.

"You will be safe here," he said. He took a step inside the room when he said it. He couldn't help himself.

"I know it." She offered a wan smile and looked down. Then she gave an intake of breath and reached into her reticule. "You will need the key to the cottage."

She pulled it out and handed it to him. He took two more steps and accepted it from her, their hands brushing. The jolt at their touch caught him by surprise and created a longing to stay and explore these new feelings. But there was nothing else to say, and he turned to go.

Once downstairs, Perry went to check on how Miss Fife was faring and whether they had found her a room. The drawing room was empty, save for Raife.

"Miss Fife has been taken care of by the indomitable Sarah. She is a gem of a maid." Raife said, yawning.

"She is. I'm glad Miss Edgewood has her. I'm seeing how much she needs her." Perry looked through the windows at the sky that had lightened enough to where only faint lines of pink were visible. "I must go to the cottage to see what happened."

"Since I troubled to put on my boots, I may as well go with you."

Raife stood and tugged his waistcoat into place, and Perry raised his eyebrows. Of all the people who would offer to come, it would be Raife? Lorry would certainly have offered except that Miss Edgewood was here. If Perry had been asked to bet between the three of his friends which one would be most concerned, he would have lost the gamble, being quite certain Raife would have chosen to stay firmly abed. He must not know him as well as he thought he did.

"Let's go then." Perry paused only to consider whether he needed fear for Miss Edgewood staying in a room so close to Lorry. He hoped that Lorry would be too tired after last night's *débauche* to think of doing anything untoward, not to mention the fact that he knew she was under Perry's protection.

And here was Raife offering to come. Perry wouldn't look a gift horse in the mouth. They set out on foot, not bothering to harness the horses, for it was not an overly long walk and they didn't want to make the horses stand about while they investigated.

"What do you make of all this?" Perry asked as they traipsed along the path. "Obviously I don't know the area, but it surprises me that a petty thief would be found on Brindale's estate. And I'm troubled that the cottage was targeted."

"I could not say," Raife replied. The roof of the cottage came into view through a clearing in the trees, and they followed the path toward it. "But my guess would be that it was either a poacher whose shot went wide, or it was petty theft and someone hoped to steal something of value, thinking the house still uninhabited."

They walked on in silence for a beat before Raife added, "Given the fact that we are so close to the coast, we cannot rule out smuggling."

It was the last thing that would have occurred to Perry. "You think the cottage might have been used by smugglers in the past?"

He turned the idea over in his mind, frowning as they approached the stone building. "If they had done, they must leave off now, don't you think? Surely smugglers would not be so bent on their mission as to harm innocent people once they knew the cottage was no longer empty."

"I suppose anything is possible," Raife said as they came to the wooden entrance. Perry pulled out the key and fitted it into the lock, then opened the heavy door. Inside, the rooms were dim and absolutely silent. It was impossible to conceive of anyone still being here.

He led the way through the short corridor to the sitting room on the side of the house, which was the only room with any light to speak of. One set of shutters there were indeed thrown open inwards. Jagged pieces of glass on the floor in front of the window reflected the morning sunlight. And there, in the middle of the pieces, was an object that did not seem to belong to the room.

Raife went over and picked it up, examining it from all angles. It was a metal piece, shaped like a tube and with blue engravings on it. Extending from one end was a jagged piece of wood. It appeared to be the head of a cane that had been separated from the rest. Perry took it from Raife and tossed it from hand to hand. It was heavy for what it was.

"Now, look at this. Who could this have come from?"

The shutters in the cottage were built on the inside of the window frames for privacy rather than protection, and Raife went over and pulled the broken shutter open wider.

"It doesn't seem that this was the work of poachers after all," he said. "Someone was trying to get in."

CHAPTER ELEVEN

Marianne did not wake until the morning was long past and the sun was bright overhead, despite the fact that she had forgotten to close the bed curtains to keep out the light. Her parents' bed was comfortable. That Mr. Osborne had replaced the mattress stuffing was evident from its lush comfort and fresh scent, and she wondered why she hadn't thought of doing that herself years ago. She sat up and tucked the pillows behind her, then leaned against the cold stone wall. Pulling her knees up to her chest, she looked around the room.

It had been many years since Marianne spent any time in this room. At the beginning, right after her parents were discovered lifeless and the household had been turned on its end, Mrs. Malford would come into the room and find her wrapped in one of her mother's dresses. In those days, the cook got down on her knees with some difficulty and sat with Marianne, rather than trying to distract her from her pain. Eventually, the arrival of Miss Fife, who had a specific idea of what the routine for a ten-year-old should be, had forced Marianne to grow up. She stopped visiting her parents' bedroom and did no more than clean the room each spring. Her main connection to her parents was downstairs in the living areas, where their presence seemed to pulse still.

She got up from the bed, stretched, and found that she was indeed well-rested. She could not resist the pull to go over to the wardrobe that had once been her parents' and open it to see what filled it now. When she did, her gaze fell upon the familiar silks and linens that she had forgotten to have brought to the cottage. Her mother's gowns were still lined up, and it comforted her to know that Mr. Osborne had not removed everything right away. He must do so—that much was sure—but that he was making changes at a thoughtful pace led her to think well of him.

The washstand held a small shaving bowl and brush, and she lifted the brush from it. When she sniffed at its horsehair bristles, she found the scent leftover from the cream surprisingly sweet. Next to that was a shaving blade, and she picked it up and opened it. The handle was made of smooth wood and the blade proved sharp when she tested it. She closed the blade and set it down, thinking of Mr. Osborne being shaved in this very room, the blade skimming over his masculine jaw. It was such an intimate thing to imagine. It made her feel odd, and yet strangely at home.

She crossed over to the edge of the bed so she could pull on her half boots, and lifted her gaze to a worn pair of pantaloons that were thrown over a chair next to the wall. This also poked at something dormant within her. She could not put her finger on exactly what. To observe the intimate habits of a gentleman —something she had never known—from the safety and privacy of a familiar room made her wonder whether one day she might share such intimacy with a husband. She could hardly picture such a thing. It had only ever been her against the world. And as long as she'd had her castle, it had been enough.

Marianne laced up her boots. Now, she had no castle. It was not hers anymore, and she was here only as a guest. At least she had Sarah, and a home at the cottage she could make her own. But it wasn't the same.

She stood and went to stare at herself in the short glass propped on the table near the washstand. She turned her head to one side and touched the cord of hair that she had hastily plaited and pinned back. Until now, the fact that she did not know how to make elegant hairstyles or requested that Sarah learn had not bothered her. Lowering her eyes, she examined her gown, knowing its gathered bodice was of a different style than what she saw other ladies wearing at church. Their bodices were more fitted than her chemise dresses. This oddity in her dress made her pause—made her doubt. What did Mr. Osborne and his friends see in her, and was it anything good?

She turned aside in impatience. What did she care about how fashionable she was, or how four gentlemen who were all but perfect strangers viewed her?

Going over to the wardrobe, she rummaged through her mother's things until she found a fichu, which she tucked into her neckline for added warmth, having left her shawl at the cottage. The castle had never been particularly warm, even in the hottest part of August, so she would need to retrieve her shawls from the cottage as soon as she had the chance. It was time to see what the rest of the household was doing.

She lifted the latch and exited into the corridor, turning to look back to where her old room had been just days before. Mr. Wilmot slept there now. She turned and hurried down the stairs.

"Miss, yer up now." Sarah paused at the foot of the stairs, carrying a bundle of linens, presumably to be washed. The maid hadn't blinked at their great fright, or the inconvenience of going from one establishment to another, but just done what was needed. Sarah was of great value, both as a servant and a friend.

"I hope you've slept some, Sarah. You did not get any more rest than I did last night, and you're likely to fall asleep at your task if you do not get some now."

Sarah gave her a weary smile, her apple cheeks pink and her brown curls more mussed than usual, and faced Marianne with the bundle in her arms. "Yer right, miss. But I'm not one as is used to napping. If ye'll permit, I'll sleep early tonight."

Marianne smiled at her, descending the remaining three steps. "I will see to it that your tasks are light this evening. I am not sure what I'm to do now. I suppose I must find Mr. Osborne. Have you seen him?"

Sarah gestured with her chin toward the yellow sitting room. "He's in yer mader's apartment, miss. His friends'm in there with him." When she saw Marianne hesitate, she added, "Miss Fife's resting in her room should ye need her, although I do think she might've truly hurt her ankle. She's a plaster on it."

"Thank you, Sarah. I will go see her afterwards."

Marianne put a foot forward, determined that she would not be put off by a room full of gentlemen in what was once her own home. She opened the door to the sound of laughter, which quieted as soon as she entered the sitting room. All of the gentlemen leapt to their feet.

Mr. Osborne approached her first. "It is good to see you up, Miss Edgewood. Are you well rested?"

She couldn't be sure, but it seemed that his eyes were soft when he looked at her, as though their shared adventure had disposed him more kindly toward her. She sensed a solicitude that was new, and it matched the warmer feelings she had begun to develop toward him.

"I am very well rested. It was kind of you to give me your room. It occurred to me that you have not been able to access it for some hours, and I fear I may have incommoded you." She allowed herself to look at him fully, and although his neckcloth was neatly tied, his coat appeared to be rumpled.

"Do not give it another thought. Anything I might have needed, I have done very well without." Mr. Osborne looked around at the other gentlemen and gestured to the chair beside him. "Will you please sit?"

He indicated the chair closest to her mother's desk, her favorite one in a pale blue embroidered silk that had no match. The gentlemen resumed their seats, and she swiveled to face Mr. Osborne. "Did you go to the cottage?"

"I did." He glanced at the friend who had come into the drawing room first after their arrival that morning. From the little she had observed of him, he spoke the least. It seemed he looked at the world through hooded eyes, but somehow did not intimidate her the way Mr. Osborne's other two friends did.

"I regret to tell you this, but Raife and I discovered evidence that someone indeed attempted to break in. That means it was not an accidental poacher, but rather a purposeful attempt to gain entry. I do not feel it prudent for you to return there this evening."

He studied her face before continuing. "We will need to investigate the situation further and contrive a way to better secure the cottage before you do, so I hope I might persuade you to stay at Brindale. You may continue to use my room, of course. I've had the servants prepare rooms for me to use on this floor."

Marianne's eyes met his, which appeared almost blue

rather than gray with the warmth she saw there. His offer was generous. He would be exchanging his own bedroom upstairs —she had begun to accept his right to the castle, beginning with his appropriation of her parents' room—for a room that would not be as private or as comfortable. The gesture touched her.

"As much as I fear to inconvenience you, I cannot refuse. The thought of returning to the cottage gives me cold shivers. But"—she raised her eyes shyly to his—"surely, I can have one of the other rooms made up. I cannot be quite comfortable at the thought of taking yours."

Mr. Osborne was shaking his head before she had finished her sentence, the handsome crease in his jaw pronounced. "I will not hear of it, so there is no sense in pursuing the idea."

After a beat, Marianne smiled. "Very well, then." She allowed her gaze to roam around her mother's sitting room, happy to be back in such a familiar place. "I will not try to dissuade you."

"Now, our dinners will be much more interesting," Mr. Wilmot said.

His hair was the color of burnt caramel, and it fell over his brow. There was a crease on one side of his mouth when he smiled, and he did so now, pointedly in her direction. She could not help but return it, grateful he made her feel welcome rather than a nuisance—which she must surely be, possessing none of the societal arts.

"'Tis the truth," the gentleman called Neck added. She could not remember his proper name and would have to ask Mr. Osborne. She couldn't call him by such a familiar appellation. "Although I'm sorry for the circumstances that led to your stay here, you will be a welcome addition."

Raife, or Mr. Raife—she wasn't sure of his name either— said nothing.

"What did you find at the cottage?" she asked, turning her attention back to Mr. Osborne.

"This." Mr. Osborne stood and retrieved a metal object and handed it to her. There were blue decorative markings that extended from the metal to bits of broken-off wood. "Do you recognize it?" She shook her head, and he resumed his seat.

"The object was on the floor, near where the broken glass lay, and it appears someone used a gentleman's cane to break the window. It must have been separated from the rest in the process."

Marianne handed it back as she tried to decipher the implications. "A gentleman's cane? Does this mean that the intruder was a gentleman?"

"More likely a cane that had been stolen and used for the purpose," Neck replied.

Marianne's insides had gone icy with horror at what might have happened to them.

"I've never been afraid to live on my own. How dreadful that this would occur on my first attempt to do so. I cannot stay in the castle forever, but I fear I shall not be at ease in the cottage either—at least not until the culprit is caught, or perhaps I've hired a manservant there."

"Do not refine too much upon it," Mr. Wilmot said in a light tone.

Mr. Osborne seemed to understand her fears more thoroughly. "I will do everything in my power to ensure you are safe, Miss Edgewood. And we will not have you move back into the cottage until we have bolstered its security and hired a footman. You must simply trust me on this."

"I do." When their gaze met, her smile came naturally. "Mr. Osborne, I've been thinking. If I cannot move back to the cottage right away, I must go there to retrieve some of my more pressing items. Might we do so today?"

Mr. Wilmot raised a hand in protest. "You must eat first. We can't have you fainting from hunger." He focused his charm on her, and her neck prickled in awareness. "And then I will accompany you myself to the cottage to get your things."

Marianne responded with a slight smile. She did not want Mr. Wilmot to think she was too easily won; and besides, she rather thought she would prefer to go with Mr. Osborne, who was more closely connected with her situation. "Very well. I will see about getting something to eat."

"Allow me to do that for you," Mr. Wilmot said, getting out of his seat.

"No, you must allow me." Mr. Osborne rushed to his feet and went to the door. "I will speak to the cook."

A short while later, he returned and his request was quickly followed by a tray, loaded with simple foods. Marianne tucked into them with relish, realizing as her mouth watered when she lifted the bread and cheese to it how hungry she was. When Annabel came afterwards to remove the tray, Marianne asked her if Miss Fife had received anything to eat and was assured she had. Still, she thought it best to go to see her companion, especially if she was truly immobile.

"I will pay a quick visit to Miss Fife, and then I will be ready to set out to the cottage." Marianne directed her words toward Mr. Wilmot, but Mr. Osborne was back on his feet.

"I will go with you as well."

She stopped to look at Mr. Osborne in surprise. Although the news was welcome, his voice held more of the hard, unfriendly tone from when she had first met him. She hadn't the faintest idea what had caused him to turn cold, and it disappointed her. She supposed it did not matter. It would be faster work with both of the gentlemen—and more proper.

"I thank you," she said and nodded to the gentlemen as she turned to go.

Marianne followed the corridor until she had approached the curtain that closed off Miss Fife's room, steeling herself to be gracious and kind.

"Miss Fife?" she called out and entered as soon as she heard her companion bid her come in. "I came to see how you got on."

"My foot is paining me." Miss Fife sighed and rested her head back against the chair, closing her eyes. "This whole ordeal has been such a trial to me."

Marianne walked over to her and glanced at the foot that was propped up on the stool before her companion. It did appear to be more swollen than the other foot. She had misjudged her companion.

"I am sorry you were hurt. We must bear the challenges of being out of our new home as best we can."

As soon as the words were out, it struck Marianne how much she now sounded like the aged companion and Miss Fife the recalcitrant charge. "I am going to the cottage to gather our things. Is there anything you urgently need from your room there?"

"I will need everything brought. I cannot bear the thought of returning there only to be murdered in my bed one day."

With effort, Marianne refrained from delivering a cutting reply. "I understand, but we do not have the possibility of bringing everything just now. Is there anything you must have that is absolutely essential for the next day or two?"

Miss Fife settled more comfortably into her chair. "I suppose you may bring me a spare dress and my soaps. That is all I need for now. Oh, and my work basket. I will need something to do."

Relieved to hear nothing further from Miss Fife about how inconvenient she found her life to be, Marianne nodded and turned to go. "I'll be sure to do so."

After Marianne left Miss Fife, she went to the front hall where Mr. Wilmot stood. "Oz is waiting outside with the cart. We have Charlie with us as well, but your maid is engaged in washing linens. It will be quick work to have anything you need brought over."

She followed him outside and squinted against the sun when she saw Mr. Osborne sitting in the driver's seat of the old cart. It was nice to have the conveyance waiting for her instead of having to go and request it or hitch the horse up herself.

"I cannot thank you both enough for your assistance."

Mr. Osborne smiled at her and hopped down, circling the cart and offering his hand to help Marianne into the carriage. His grip was firm, and he did not let go until she was seated comfortably. Then he rounded the cart and took the reins again as Charlie climbed in the back.

She did not have long to wonder where Mr. Wilmot would sit; he climbed up on her other side, and she was forced to move closer to Mr. Osborne, who snapped the reins. As he drove down the uneven path, she could think of nothing but the presence of warm male thighs on either side of her. She clamped her legs together so she would not touch them more than she could help, but the jolting of the carriage made such a thing difficult. By degree, she allowed herself to shift into Mr. Osborne.

They drove the short distance to the cottage, and when they arrived, Mr. Osborne pulled to a stop. Mr. Wilmot hopped down and lifted his hand to assist her. It was strange how his hand felt foreign while Mr. Osborne's had become familiar. She hardly knew one better than the other.

"Just tell us what you most need," Mr. Osborne said, when she had pulled her hand out of Mr. Wilmot's.

She went through her mental list, then addressed Charlie, who stood waiting. "I suppose if you can gather the perishables from the kitchen—it makes no sense to waste them—then I will gather the personal effects in each of the three bedrooms and bring them out. I believe I am the only one who ought to perform that task."

"Don't suppose we all came for nothing." Mr. Wilmot was at her side, startling her when he took her elbow to walk her the short distance to the house. "We will provide assistance in whatever way we can."

Marianne smiled at the ground, unused to the attention. "You have my gratitude."

As soon as she could politely extricate her arm from his grasp, she hurried through the cottage, going first into her own room. As she folded gowns and placed them in her trunk, she began to rethink the idea of bringing only a few items. It might be smarter to overpack than underpack so that she need not return with the cart again before the cottage could be inhabited safely.

With more haste than care, she placed her most treasured and necessary things in her trunk, then went to do the same in Miss Fife's room. She took most of the clothes and set out the work basket to be brought, but left some of the less important items, like her letters and books. There were more books in the Brindale library.

In Sarah's room, there was only one other servant's uniform hanging on the peg, and a few other items like a hairbrush and tooth powder, all of which were easy to gather and tie up. She brought Sarah's small bundle to the front door and indicated to Mr. Osborne and Mr. Wilmot where they might retrieve her trunk and the pile of items from Miss Fife.

The gentlemen went over to the staircase just as Charlie emerged from the kitchen carrying the last of their food items. Marianne exited to the outdoors, still holding Sarah's bundle, and when she dropped it in the cart, she looked up and saw

Robert riding toward the cottage. She paused, glad to see him, and waited as he pulled up and swung down from his horse.

"G'day, Marianne." His gaze scrutinized the contents in the cart before returning to her. "What are you doing?"

She leaned an elbow on the side of the cart and brought her eyes up to his. "Oh, Robert, you have no idea. Someone broke into the cottage last night, and we were forced to go to the castle for safety."

"You had an intruder here!" he exclaimed. The shock put color into his cheeks. "You didn't go to the castle in the middle of the night, I should hope? That would've been the height of folly. You might have met with anyone."

She shook her head. "We waited until dawn and then we went. We will be staying in the castle for now. Mr. Osborne does not feel that the cottage is safe, and I agree with him."

Robert glanced at Charlie, who was adjusting the pantry items to make room in the cart, and he lowered his voice. "You agree with him, you say? Surely you must see that it is not proper for you to remain in a house with a set of bachelors. Come to my house, instead."

"It is not ideal," she said slowly, "but I am much more comfortable at Brindale. It has been my home my whole life. And Miss Fife is there to lend me companionship. Sarah is with me also, and Mrs. Malford will see that I am protected."

Robert paced away and put his back to her as Charlie discreetly left the cart and returned to the house. Then Robert turned back.

"With this decision, you've placed yourself in a mighty ugly situation. I urge you to come with me to Grinnell now. I can walk you back to the castle, and we can take your carriage from the stable there. Or, I can ride back and hitch up my whiskey. We need only pack a few things."

She frowned and shook her head, and at that moment Mr.

Osborne and Mr. Wilmot exited, carrying the trunk between them. Mr. Osborne's eyes darted between her and Robert as they brought her trunk to the cart.

Before they came close enough to hear, Robert leaned in. "You should be staying at my house, you know. My mother will wonder at your refusal."

There was much truth in what he said, but Marianne hesitated still—almost recoiled from the idea, although she could scarcely admit that to herself, much less to one of her oldest friends. But Robert's intensity showed her as clear as anything that to him, her taking refuge in his house would move them one step closer to an engagement she did not want. She would have to take her chances with the gentleman at the castle.

She shook her head and said softly, "I pray you will understand. I will stay at Brindale."

CHAPTER TWELVE

In the years Perry had spent in the London clubs, he had adjusted to the less-than-honorable whims of gentlemen of the ton. He was not entirely innocent himself in that regard, but his minor indiscretions paled next to the predatory look on Lorry's face when he proposed to accompany Marianne. His eyes gleamed with a determination Perry knew all too well and hinted at attention that was better directed toward a wife or mistress, not a gently bred young lady. He would have to keep an eye on his friend, for he had seen him in action too often to think that his offer to help was innocent or his voracious look easily subdued.

Miss Edgewood had not seemed frightened or put off in any way, but neither did she seem to understand what Lorry was about. She likely had little notion of what it was to be flirted with, as secluded as she had been with only Vernon for masculine attention. Vernon's idea of flirting would have none of Lorry's finesse.

Speaking of Vernon, here was the man now at the cottage,

talking in low undertones that Perry sensed made Miss Edgewood uncomfortable. He didn't care how long Vernon claimed friendship with her. If he was bothering her...

Perry secured the trunk they had set on the back of the cart then gave it a pat before turning to face the visitor.

"Good afternoon, Vernon. You've heard what happened?" He waited until he had the man's attention, which was not easily pulled away from Miss Edgewood. "Are break-ins a common occurrence in these parts?"

Vernon glanced at the door to the cottage that still stood open, then shrugged. "I would not say it's a normal occurrence, but it's not unheard of either. In my father's twenty-five years as magistrate, he deals with a few cases per year of poaching and petty theft. I can only imagine it must have been that. I ought to go in and see what there is in the way of evidence."

"We will need to make the place secure," Perry mused, turning to stare at the windows and shutters visible from their vantage point. "One of the shutters in the drawing room on the side of the house is broken, and some of the others might be weakened with age."

"Likely. Let me take a look. I'll act on my father's behalf in this." Vernon brought his horse over to the iron ring on the side of the house and looped the reins through, then he disappeared into the house.

"Did you see the way he was imposing himself on her?" Lorry said under his breath. Miss Edgewood had disappeared around the side of the cottage.

Perry refrained from rolling his eyes at the irony. Lorry had never been awake to subtleties.

"Miss Edgewood and Vernon are friends of long acquaintance," he replied, ignoring the fact that he had thought much the same thing as Lorry. But if his friend could be persuaded that her heart was already taken, it would be safer for her.

Perry stared at the front door that had been left open. "Perhaps Vernon will find something we missed."

Miss Edgewood came back into view, carrying what looked like gardening utensils, and when she caught Perry staring, she lifted the basket with a smile. "I nearly forgot these."

Vernon exited the house and declared he found the break-in most peculiar. Upon being pressed for details, he replied that he hadn't found anything new that might shed light on the incident. Perry locked the house and handed the key to Miss Edgewood, who climbed back up on the carriage before he could take her hand again. Lorry took his seat beside her, although he very well could have sat on the trunk, and Charlie sat on the floor of the cart toward the back.

"We must be heading back," Perry called out to Vernon before steering the nag in a slow circle. They took their leave, then rejoined the path to return to the castle.

"How will you secure the cottage?"

Miss Edgewood turned to him enough that her bonnet allowed him a glimpse of her face. He found he wanted her face turned toward him rather than Lorry. She was pretty, he discovered again as though seeing her for the first time, and her direct gaze momentarily stopped everything in his orbit. When the breeze carried her fresh scent to his nostrils, he forgot what her question was.

He broke the gaze and dragged his thoughts back to the present with difficulty. "My most pressing need at the castle is for Mr. Mercy to come to an agreement with the carpenter who is to fix the roof. But I will have him attend to the shutters of the cottage first."

"That is most kind of you," Miss Edgewood said quietly, turning forward again, and the spell was broken as Lorry claimed her attention from the other side.

At Brindale, he had Charlie bring the smaller bundles to

Miss Fife and the maid, while he and Lorry brought Miss Edgewood's trunk up to her room. Matley had already removed all of Perry's personals into the room he'd be using downstairs. Unfortunately, this was not one of the rooms that had either doors or a new mattress. But the inconvenience and lack of privacy would be worth it for Miss Edgewood to know herself in perfect security.

"We shall have to adjust our dinner hour, and make it a little more formal," Perry observed when he and Lorry returned downstairs.

"The food has been choice." A rare compliment from Lorry, who seemed to always find fault despite his seemingly easy ways. "How many more bottles of that Burgundy do you have?"

"Only three," Perry returned with dry emphasis. "And as the war with Bonaparte is not set to end any time soon, I hope we might not finish all three in the next day."

"You can hardly expect us to display self-control at this stage with such a temptation before us." Lorry grinned at his own sally, but Perry did not doubt its truth for a moment.

A knock at the front door resounded through the front hall, and since they were at the foot of the stairs, Perry went to answer it himself. Charlie would be in the kitchen unpacking the foodstuffs that had been brought over, and the newer footman who had been hired was assigned to meet his guests' needs. On the other side of the door, a liveried footman stood in stiff attention and extended a thick cream letter, whose Dutch sealing wax was imprinted with a coat of arms.

When Perry took the letter, the footman bowed. "This has come from the Belford household, sir."

"Thank you." Perry shut the door and turned to break the seal, skimming its contents. "True to Mrs. Vernon's word, we have all been given vouchers to the ball that the Belfords will be hosting at the oast house. Did you bring your dancing slippers?"

He looked up at Lorry with a smile. A ball would be most welcome, particularly a country ball that hopefully had none of the crush or airs of a London ball. He wondered what Miss Edgewood would look like in something other than one of her old gowns.

"I always have my evening attire with me," Lorry replied in all seriousness. "You never know when you might need it. The same cannot be said for Neck. But I suppose Raife can lend him something if he needs it." Perry highly doubted Raife would lend any of his impeccable attire to someone as heedless as Neck.

They entered the library where Neck and Raife sat over a game of chess. "We've been invited to a ball," Lorry announced, coming over. Neck grunted and Raife raised his eyes to them.

"When?"

"Thursday next," Perry said, walking over to the window and lifting the vouchers up to read them in better light. "Shall we respond yes?"

"Yes," Neck agreed, without looking up from the game. "We are to leave the next morning, but there is no reason we need have an early start."

"Why not attend?" Raife leaned back, one hand over his chair and the other on the table beside the chessboard as he waited for Neck to decide his next move.

"Playing for guineas?" Lorry brought a chair over and straddled it to watch the game.

Miss Edgewood entered the library holding a book, and stopped at the threshold when she saw them. "You must forgive me. I have taken to treating the castle as my own again."

Perry dropped the vouchers on the desk and went over to her. "And you must continue to do so. Did you wish to return a book?"

"Exchange it, actually." The corners of her lips turned up when she glanced at him, and he returned the smile.

If he was not mistaken, she was growing more comfortable around him, and the idea pleased him. At least there was not the cloud of antagonism that had plagued them when they had first met. She pulled her gaze from his and turned to skim the titles on the walls that held shelves of books. It was not a proper library, not really. But a man might live out his days here with enough to read if he were as willing to peruse a book on sheep husbandry as he were a novel.

Perry stood at her side and read some of the titles on the shelf, but his mind was on the ball and the delight he would soon read on her face when he told her about it.

"We have received an invitation to the oast house ball that Mrs. Vernon said we should expect. Shall I include you in our number when I return an affirmative?"

She took a step backwards and held her book up to her chest, glancing at the shelves of books as though she could hide there.

"Oh no, you must send my regrets. I have no training in how to go about in society. I have never been to a ball before."

Perry stared at her in surprise. She could not be serious. How could a young lady not wish to go to a ball?

"But surely that is not an objection to be considered. Your manners are not wanting, and it will be nothing but pure amusement. You can have nothing to fear in attending a ball."

She gave a quick glance at his friends, who after having

stood and bowed, returned to their game. He could not be sure if her glance was from interest in the game, interest in his friends, or fear of intruding. Raife talked to Lorry while Neck considered his next move in the plodding match. Despite his intrepid reputation in all manner of sports, he was not bold in the game of chess.

"No, truly. I cannot think of it." Miss Edgewood shook her head, as though to add finality to what she was saying. Without turning her face to his in the way he was coming to expect, she added, "I beg you will excuse me. I wish to find a book about cooking. Perhaps I will assist Sarah in the kitchen one day when we return to the cottage."

She took two steps away then turned back, a pained expression on her face. "Although, after tasting my almond cakes, you might doubt that any skill could be achieved in the kitchen by me."

"Your cakes were very good," Perry rushed to assure her. He wasn't sure how to make her more secure about her abilities in general; he only knew he wished to try. "I have no doubt in your ability to create something fine."

He released her from the conversation to search for the book she desired, but his thoughts were still on her refusal to attend the ball. For some reason, the idea of Miss Edgewood staying behind at the castle while he and the others were attending a ball made him uneasy. It was wrong. And the idea of attending a ball without her felt curiously flat.

Miss Edgewood spent a good deal of time looking at the titles of the books on the shelves before selecting two. She hugged them to her chest and walked by Perry with a shy smile in his direction. The question of how to make her feel more at ease had begun to tug at his mind.

He leapt up from the seat he had taken while he waited for

her to choose a book. "I hope you will feel at ease to sit here in the library and read."

She glanced over at the gentlemen gathered around the chessboard, then back at him. "I thank you. I will go to my mother's room"—she looked stricken—"that is to say, I will go to the yellow sitting room and read there." She curtsied and left the room.

Perry watched her go, then turned back to find Lorry studying her as well. When she exited the room, Lorry folded his arms. "She said no? We shall have to change her mind, won't we?"

"What are your intentions toward Miss Edgewood?" Perry had not intended to ask that, and it brought Neck's head up from the game to look at him, and even caused Raife to dart a quick glance. He attempted to keep his tone light, but he was not sure he succeeded, especially when Lorry raised his brows.

"You are quite up in arms over a girl who is not a blood relation, but you need have no fear on my account." His tone was insouciant, and he didn't hold Perry's gaze but turned back to the game. "Careful, Neck. Don't you see that move will cost you the game?"

His assurance lacked conviction but Perry would give Lorry the benefit of the doubt.

Dinner that night was both calmer and more enjoyable with Miss Edgewood there. She remained almost tongue-tied in their presence, but it made Perry feel more worldly and less like an innocent himself. It was an enjoyable sensation. All three of his friends went out of their way to pull her into the conversation—Lorry and Neck to tease her and try to get her to blush, of which they had no small success—and Raife, surprisingly, with a great deal of consideration for a man who was rather known to not suffer fools gladly.

"Have you given any more thought to the ball?" Lorry

asked when the servants carried in dessert. "I have a great longing to see a Kent oast house. I've never seen one. Besides, it will be as dull as ditchwater if you don't come."

"There will be plenty of other charming ladies present. You won't miss me," Miss Edgewood replied with a wry look that Perry could almost believe was flirtatious if she were capable of such a thing. He would rather have that look directed at himself.

"Ah, but there you are wrong," Lorry countered, dipping his spoon into the syllabub. "We shall pine away. The entire evening will be ruined for us if you do not come."

"Miss Fife will never consent to coming, and I cannot go without a companion," Miss Edgewood replied, looking down at her plate.

She had scarcely touched her meal, and Perry wondered how comfortable she was with their collective dinner, unused as she was to company. No one must ever know that she had sat alone with a table full of bachelors without even her companion present. It would ruin her, even if they were far from London society. How could he convince her to come?

Perry was struck by an epiphany. "Did you not say that Mrs. Vernon looked upon you quite like a member of the family? Why do you not allow her to serve as chaperone?"

She considered this as she took a bite of potatoes and chewed thoughtfully. "It would answer, but what...what does one wear to a ball?"

"Something in silk," Lorry responded with aplomb. "What do we know about lady's gowns? Silk, I say. Although were you to wear sackcloth over your head, you would still be the most charming lady in the room. You need not worry about what to wear."

Miss Edgewood turned a charming pink as her eyes sank to

her plate again. "I have a silk gown." She looked at Lorry. "Very well. I will go, then."

Perry was torn. Relieved that Miss Edgewood had consented to come at last, but suffering more irritation than he could justify to himself that it was Lorry who had convinced her.

CHAPTER THIRTEEN

Mr. Wilmot's words had reassured Marianne and provided her with the final encouragement she needed to take the momentous step into society. Had he not said it did not so much matter what she wore? It meant that even if the silk gowns she'd found in her mother's wardrobe did not prove to be the height of fashion, she would not be shunned by the other guests.

Of course, Mr. Wilmot was being kind when he said she could wear a sackcloth over her head—*it need not come to that!*—but Mr. Wilmot was a gentleman of the ton. As such, he must know what was acceptable and what was not, and he would not steer her wrong. Of course, she still needed to comport herself correctly at the ball, but she would worry about that when the time came.

Happy to have at last made a decision, she took a bite of her dinner and glanced up. Mr. Osborne was staring at her with those intense gray eyes of his that made her feel as though he wished to read her mind and understand its inner workings. Of course, she was being fanciful. She only hoped he would appreciate what a big step it was for her to attend a ball.

When Mr. Osborne had mentioned the ball earlier, she was for the first time in her life filled with a desire to go. Countless times in the past, the Vernons had invited her to accompany them, but she always felt they had done so out of duty. Besides, there was nothing exciting about going to a ball if it was only to dance with Robert. But being proposed the same option by a gentleman she had not grown up with, and having it reaffirmed by his friend, was all the encouragement she needed. Yes, she was terrified, but she would go.

After dinner, and out of a sense of duty, she went to see how Miss Fife was faring and received the usual complaints. Her companion was not able to move around as she would like; the food was cold by the time it reached her; no one came to see her; there was little to keep her amused.

"Well, if you wish to be assisted into the drawing room, you will please tell me," Marianne replied, wholly unmoved by her companion's complaints. "I can request that the servants bring you there."

"Yes, I believe that would be preferable." Her companion sighed, then looked at Marianne as though she were seeing her more clearly. "You are flushed. Now, you must not think about staying up late with the gentlemen. You should not allow those strange men to make improper advances, especially when I'm not there to protect your innocence."

Miss Fife's sudden foray into a lucid sense of responsibility shocked Marianne into protesting, "I would never do such a thing."

However, she had better come clean about her plans if such lucidity were to continue. "I've come to tell you that I will be attending a ball three nights from now. As I know you won't be able to accompany me, I will send a note off to request Mrs. Vernon's chaperonage, and I am sure she will be all too happy to agree."

"Mrs. Vernon is a fat hen. She will drive you mad with her clucking."

Miss Fife was jealous of Mrs. Vernon and thought the woman had an unnatural hold over her. Marianne knew that, but still had to bite her cheek hard not to laugh. Mrs. Vernon had always been kind, but Miss Fife's assessment was not completely amiss. She escaped as soon as she could.

Now back in her room, Marianne opened the wardrobe that held her mother's clothing. Her mother had been fashionable for her time, and some of the gowns there were pretty. She selected one, shook it out, then laid it across the bed before doing the same with another. She focused her efforts on the ones made of silk cloth, and in more interesting colors than what she usually wore.

She didn't know why she had never thought about having these made over into something that would suit her. She and her mother seemed to have been of the same size, and the gown she pulled out next was a pure, deep yellow, which might prove becoming on her. It was most certainly made of silk, so she could not err. It had no extra flounces on the bottom that she often saw the young ladies wear on Sundays. Rather, it was straight and would hug the body, right down to its train. When Marianne tried it on, the gown was a couple of inches too long. Her mother must have been taller than her, but she didn't think anyone would be looking at her feet if the dress tended to pool on the floor. Besides, she could not bring herself to alter one of her mother's gowns, especially with such an inexperienced hand.

She walked forward to the mirror, careful not to trip on the excess fabric, and turned one way, then another. The gown also had long, tight sleeves that were different from the puffier sleeves she had noticed on the gowns other young ladies wore. This bodice, too, was gathered and loose rather than fitted and sewn with darts, and she hoped the fact that it was silk made it acceptable still. She supposed she should speak to Miss Fife about the ballgown, but she recoiled from the idea of asking her advice for anything. Miss Fife had never been the least bit helpful.

In the days that followed, Miss Fife made camp in whatever room Marianne was in, which meant she saw little of any of the gentlemen. It did not take them more than five minutes to discover they had pressing business elsewhere. Never before had Marianne been constrained in such a way—or forced to endure so much of Miss Fife's presence—so it was with great relief that she welcomed the day of the ball, making good her escape hours before she actually needed to dress.

The first order of business was to style her hair, which she performed with practiced efficiency. When that was completed, she examined the effect for so long in the mirror her brows lowered into a grimace, suddenly filled with doubt that it was good enough. Her hair was plaited in the usual way she wore it, which was heavy around the face and not very interesting. She knew better than to ask any of the maids in the household for assistance, because it had already been established that they were not skilled at dressing hair. Such a thing had never before been a requirement.

She pulled on her gown, excited to be wearing a pretty silk dress of her mother's. In her concern over the length of the gown, she had missed the fact that it perhaps did not fit quite the way it should. The bodice sagged in the chest area such that it left room for pockets of air. Despite that, she admired the color on her, a break from the faded shades of blue and gray she often wore.

Now determined to improve her hairstyle, Marianne returned to the wardrobe and sifted through everything to see if she could find some way of dressing up the braids. After tugging out various accessories, she found a piece of gold lace that was nearly the color of the dress and that must surely be an improvement if she could find a way to work it in. Immediately she went to work, pinning it to the plaits in her hair. When she had finished, one of the ends of the lace poked up and refused to stay attached. But it was more elegant than she'd ever worn it, and it would have to do.

Upon exiting her room at the appointed hour, Marianne heard the sound of men's voices at the bottom of the stairs. She approached the stairwell and descended it, wrapped in her cloak for fear of revealing everything at once. She had the pleasure of seeing the gentlemen's eyes widen as she reached the ground floor.

Embarrassed by their attention, she hurried away, murmuring, "I must see Miss Fife before I go."

The spinster looked up from her favorite chair in the yellow sitting room and smiled, more gracious now that she was in her familiar surroundings.

"Am I presentable?" Marianne asked, although what she really wanted to know was whether she was beautiful. It was rare of her to ask Miss Fife for anything. Experience had taught her she would receive little consideration in return. However, she was so nervous to step into the unknown world of polite society and formal balls she could not help but crave the reassurance.

"Very nice. Is that Mrs. Vernon still to accompany you?"

It was faint praise, but she would take what she could get. "Yes. The carriage is waiting for me. Enjoy your evening."

Marianne stood for another moment, pausing for anything Miss Fife might add to send her off with a glimmer of hope, but her companion only turned back to the picture book on her lap.

Heart beating, Marianne hurried out of the sitting room into the main hall, smiling as she passed the gentlemen, and exited through the door that Charlie held open for her. She hadn't dared to wait for their compliments—or worse, for their reproaches.

Charlie then opened the door to the carriage for her, and she entered and took the rear-facing seat across from Mr. and Mrs. Vernon. Robert was to go separately on horseback.

"Heavens, child. What have you done here? You must allow me to…"

Mrs. Vernon leaned forward and pulled at the lace in Marianne's hair to try to adjust it, but she had woven and pinned it so tightly into the plaits of hair it was impossible to remove. "I suppose…it is acceptable like that. It's original, I daresay, but that need not matter." She turned worried eyes to Mr. Vernon. "Does it now, Mr. Vernon?"

"*Hum.* What?" Mr. Vernon turned his gaze to Marianne. "You look very nice, my dear."

A vague sense of foreboding filled Marianne's breast as they rode toward Cliff's End. Perhaps the gentlemen had dropped their jaws because she looked like such an odd duck. Perhaps it was not from admiration as she had hoped. She was beginning to suspect the style she had thought would become her was not achieving its desired effect.

The feeling did not entirely disappear as they rode but was replaced with a nervous excitement as they pulled up to the oast house at last. This was a rectangular brick structure with parallel series of conical kiln roofs, and it was the only one in the villages nearby. Marianne had never been inside, but there must be plenty of room for a crowd of no small size to gather.

The door to the carriage was opened, and they exited amidst a large gathering of people in the near darkness. Conversation mingled with the stamping and snorting of horses, and people streamed into the door of the hall, stopping to sign the subscription book or hand in their vouchers for those who were not members.

"You have your voucher?" Mrs. Vernon asked her.

Marianne responded by pulling hers out of her reticule and holding it up. Too nervous to speak, she followed the Vernons into the brightly lit ballroom that had not settled into formal dances yet, but echoed with mingled sounds of conversation, laughter, and music.

So this was what a ball was like.

Marianne removed her cloak and handed it to a servant near the entrance, following the Vernons to a small receiving line that held the Belford family. Sir John was a hereditary knight, and they were the most distinguished family of the area. Mrs. Vernon had explained to her that when they hosted the public ball, which they did once a year, it elevated the event to something of a more refined nature that anyone might attend without fear of rubbing elbows with the lower order.

Mrs. Vernon turned to speak to Marianne and when her gaze lit on what Marianne was wearing, now without the cloak, the good woman could not help her reaction. Her eyes widened, and she breathed in suddenly.

"Your gown—" She managed to get the words out before the line moved forward. They would be presented to the Belfords next.

"It was my mother's. It's silk," Marianne added, as if that would justify what she was now coming to fear had been a ghastly mistake.

Mrs. Vernon whispered something into her husband's ear and then turned to smile and curtsy before Sir John and Lady Belford. Their daughter, Miss Amelia Belford, who Marianne recognized from church but with whom she'd never exchanged any words, stood on their far side.

She smiled and greeted Mr. and Mrs. Vernon, then caught sight of Marianne and choked back a laugh. She covered her lips with her gloved hands, then cleared her throat and looked away. When Miss Belford turned back to face her, her color was heightened but her expression had returned to something neutral.

"How do you do, Miss Edgewood?" Amelia was tall and thin, and looked down at her from this vantage point.

Marianne was surprised that she even knew her name. She wanted to say something interesting in this first encounter outside of church, but Miss Belford's reaction had made such a thing impossible. It was hopeless even to muster a smile.

"Very well, I thank you."

She looked ahead into the rapidly filling ballroom, now conscious that she had made a gross error in judgment in having chosen to wear one of her mother's dresses. It must be out of style, or the wrong color—or something. Or perhaps it was only that the fit was not what was ideal. She still didn't know exactly what she had done wrong. Could she leave? Even as she wondered it, the crowd herded her from behind toward the ballroom with the others. Besides, how would she get home?

As she stepped beyond the receiving line, Miss Belford looked toward the entrance, completely ignoring Marianne as the sound of Mr. Osborne and his friends filled the hall.

"They've come," she whispered to her mother.

Marianne clutched Mrs. Vernon by the elbow. "I am not suitable, am I?" she asked softly.

"Never mind that, my dear." Mrs. Vernon patted her hand. "I should have seen to your wardrobe much earlier, but I did not wish to encroach upon Miss Fife's role. She has done you a disservice by letting you leave like this."

"Miss Fife only saw me wearing my cloak," Marianne mumbled in a perfect state of misery. "However, I cannot say her help would have made much of a difference. She seems to know even less than I do about what clothing is appropriate for various social occasions—if such a thing is possible."

Robert was on the other end of the ballroom, and he started toward them as soon as he saw her. His mother cast a satisfied gaze over the apple of her eye.

"If ever you and Robert should make a match of it—and I must tell you that my husband and I would be in complete support—we shall see to all things pertaining to your wardrobe."

Never before had Mrs. Vernon made such a direct allusion to her hopes that Marianne might join their family by making a match with their son, but she did not have time to examine that bit of information, as Robert had arrived in front of her.

"Very nice, Marianne. The color becomes you. However, it might be too large." He cocked his head to the side and studied her. "Yes, I am sure it is. And what is that thing in your hair? You'd best remove it."

"You need not tell me that now." Marianne's shame partially morphed into anger. "When Miss Belford started snickering, I gathered I was not quite up to snuff."

"Never mind her. I shall dance with you for the first dance, and no one will notice your dress. If a girl is claimed for the first dance, she must be considered interesting."

The blood drained from Marianne's face. "Robert," she whispered urgently. "I thought I would be fine with dancing, since I learned the steps when I was younger. But I've never done such a thing in public, and now that I'm here I am sure I don't know them well enough."

"Don't be a goose." Robert turned to Mrs. Vernon. "Mother, tell her. Dancing is easy." His application had the reverse effect.

"Perhaps you ought not to attempt it," Mrs. Vernon murmured.

"Nonsense." Robert fell silent, frowning, as Mr. Osborne and his friends walked toward them.

Mr. Osborne was first in line, and he bowed formally before her as though they had not yet seen each other that day. "Miss Edgewood, I hope you will do me the pleasure of dancing with me."

"I've claimed the first dance," Robert interjected, his surly tone matching his scowl. Marianne glanced at him, comparing his address to Mr. Osborne's. Although she had never before noticed it, Robert did not show to advantage.

Mr. Osborne barely glanced at Robert before saying, "Very well. I will come find you for a later one."

She looked at his three friends, two of whom were facing the floor where couples had begun to congregate, and Mr. Raife studying his nails. She was afraid to voice how unsure she was about her appearance—and about her dancing abilities—so she simply nodded and mustered a smile.

"I will. Thank you for asking me."

When he left, Robert grumbled something to his mother that Marianne could not hear, and she could only be grateful that Mr. Osborne had invited her to dance at all. Her appearance must not be so very disastrous then.

Shortly afterwards, the music began, and Robert brought her to the floor for a country set. To her immense relief, she discovered she was able to remember the steps and therefore danced better than she had initially feared. In those early years after her parents were gone, Mrs. Malford had suggested that the servants teach her some basic steps so she'd have something to take her mind off her grief. Sarah and Annabel knew the country dances, and they had Charlie serve as her partner.

It ended up being her saving grace for what was required of her at a ball. As Robert led her off the floor following the dance, Marianne exhaled from the exertion, pleased to have acquitted herself well. She could not have borne it had she made even more of a stir than the one her appearance caused. Robert bowed to her and said she'd done well, just as he knew she would, before telling her he must find his next partner. Marianne stayed on the sidelines, as invisible as she could make herself, wondering at what point Mr. Osborne would come to claim his dance.

The next hour began what was the most uncomfortable experience of Marianne's short life. There were whispers and stares, muffled laughter, and there were arch comments from young ladies and men alike as they passed her by. Somehow, in her misery, she was always conscious of where Mr. Osborne stood in the room, and his face seemed to grow more severe every time she looked at him. He must be dissatisfied with her appearance, or worse, ashamed of it.

A couple moved from her side to join the next set, and she found herself exposed on the sidelines. Mr. Wilmot spotted her and came to take a place at her side, turning to watch the crowd with her.

"I see you've found a ballgown. In silk."

Goaded, Marianne flashed her eyes at him. "Now we both know that one cannot wear a sackcloth over one's head and avoid utter disgrace as long as it's silk. Everyone is laughing at me."

Mr. Wilmot shrugged. "Let them laugh. What are they to you?"

He leaned in more closely than made her comfortable and

murmured, "Gentlemen are not staring at your gown. Trust me." He glanced down at her neck in a way that caused heat to race up her spine and radiate from her cheeks. "Don't give a thought to what those cats say."

He left, and Marianne stared at his back, her eyes naturally seeking those of Mr. Osborne's until she wished they hadn't. He was glowering at her again.

Her mother's slippers had begun to come loose, and Marianne needed to make her way to the retiring room to tie them back up again. She shuffled forward quickly, now alarmed because the silk ties that held her slipper in place were sliding down her leg so that she could only keep the slipper on her foot by arching her toe upward.

With the door to the retiring room in sight, she teetered forward, crossing Mr. Osborne's path with Miss Belford at his side. Just when she felt the eyes of the room on her, Marianne stepped on the front of her gown and began to fall.

She tried to catch herself, her arms flying in circles, but her sleeves were too tight for such movement. She fell flat on the ground with her hands first, and then elbows and knees, smacking the floor with such force it brought tears to her eyes. The sound of giggling reached her, and at the same time she felt a hand on her arm.

"Allow me to assist you, Miss Edgewood. You've had an unfortunate fall."

Mr. Osborne stated the obvious, but she could not tell if he meant to come to her aid out of consideration for her or perform what any gentleman would view as his most fundamental duty. She knew only that he was highly displeased with her, because she had never seen him look so unapproachable.

If embarrassment could melt a person, she was the tail end of a tallow candle that had burnt itself out. Her knees and hands stung, but that was no match for her injured pride. She gave a swift curtsy and shuffled the rest of the way to the retiring room, her slipper clutched in one hand and her stockinged foot mercifully hidden by her overly long hem. She might fix her slipper, but she would never repair her mortification.

CHAPTER FOURTEEN

Perry watched Miss Edgewood's disastrous foray into society with dismay. It should have frightened him away—he who had spent his entire life on the outskirts of the ton, attempting to find his place in it, endeavoring to be worthy of the regard of first his titled uncle, and then his friends, who were superior in social standing. He had worked hard so that he would not stand out in any way. His mission was to be so exemplary as to remain unnoticed. That was the best one could hope for amid the fickle ton. It took someone of a much higher social standing, or someone with a stronger stomach than he, to handle sudden disapproval. Society could turn on a man like the tide.

He should have wanted to run from Miss Edgewood for fear that she would drag him down with her into the social abyss. After all, what was that floppy scrap of gold lace in her hair? What was that dress that even he could tell was years out of fashion, and loose besides?

Her dancing was unexceptional, which was a boon, but that spectacular fall in front of him and the queen of local society—Miss Belford—who, for some mysterious reason, seemed to seek his attention out of all his friends? That fall was an unmitigated disaster. Miss Belford did not laugh outright. Such a thing would have been beneath her. But her tightly controlled expression and lifted brows showed her thoughts clearly enough. He should want to run from all claims of connection to Miss Edgewood.

What was inexplicable was that...he did not. He did not wish to run from the vulnerable, exposed, and defenseless Marianne Edgewood.

Instead, he helped her to her feet, feeling the heat of her embarrassment through the long sleeves that hung flat on her arms. He murmured something—he could not say what—then released her so she might take refuge in the retiring room. He wasn't sure whether she would have the courage to make a reentrance after that, but he would keep his promise to dance with her. This was how she could hold her chin up high in society.

Perry excused himself from Miss Belford, allowing Lorry to take the prime spot in his stead. Instead, she turned to Raife and centered her attention on him. Perry wasn't surprised. Women and men alike seemed drawn to Raife's cool manner—men wishing to ape him, and women, to conquer him. Perry shoved that mystery out of his mind as he went outdoors to get air.

The front of the oast house was no longer teeming with people and carriages, but a few grooms who were clustered in various groups in the cool night air, looked up at his appearance. When they saw their services would not be required, they turned back to their cards and conversation. Perry walked a ways, struck by scenery different from London, Oxford, or Harlow, where he had grown up. It brought home to him like nothing else that he was now the owner of an estate in Kent, and that this was his new social scene should he decide to take up residence here instead of renting the castle out.

After all, he had already begun to work on the necessary repairs to make the place habitable. And there were plenty of projects such as the smithy and the apiary to bring income to Brindale again. The idea that he remain for a much longer duration to oversee these projects was no longer unthinkable. Miss Edgewood's affection for the place was making an impression on him.

Marianne was making an impression on him. He was always aware of her presence in a way he was not with other women, and he could not say why that was. She certainly had little to recommend her apart from her beauty, and would not elevate his social standing in any way. On the contrary, she would likely lower it.

As to character, she was, at times, as timid as a mouse and, at others, fiery in a way that would leave him with little peace. But the attraction was there—a physical pull he could not deny. She had lips he could imagine—had imagined—kissing. And her need for protection called up every male instinct in him to be the one to shield her. The day they drove on the cart together, when she was squeezed between him and Lorry, he was conscious of each time their legs or arms touched. He began to anticipate when the carriage would throw them together. And he couldn't help but think she was moving closer to him than she was to Lorry.

But what obsession was this? Perry came to a sudden standstill, his breath making a light cloud in his exhale. It was a cold spring night, and the sky was filled with stars twinkling in the black sky.

Was attraction a force that so abandoned reason? Because there was absolutely nothing linked to reason that could explain what was quickly beginning to consume him—that he could not stop thinking about a woman who was everything contrary to what he had always wanted. It was truly as though Cupid had a wicked sense of humor and had aimed at him when he was near Miss Edgewood, skewering them both with one shot. At least...he hoped she had been struck as well and that some of his feelings were returned.

That was all the reason he would get, he feared. He should turn away now, but that was the vexatious thing about having a heart that beat for another: he did not wish to.

Perry headed back toward the oast house. He must be there when she exited from the retiring room, and he must remind her of their engagement to dance. It would be the best thing for her, he decided, to dance again after her fall. To allow her color to return to normal and to blend back into the crowd. He quickened his steps in case he might have dallied too long outdoors and left her to fend for herself inside. Marianne would not find herself friendless if he had any say in it.

His reentry into the hall went unnoticed, and he found that he had been right. Marianne was back in full view, but she was speaking to Vernon. When he studied her face, she did not appear to be happy with what Vernon was saying. Perry didn't care if another gentleman had claimed her attention. He would go rescue her. After all, he had promised her a dance.

He took two steps forward before he saw her frown meant for Vernon lighten, then turn into a full smile when Lorry— who had grown weary of not being Miss Belford's favorite— came over to join her. Perry hastened his steps before Lorry could cut him out.

"Excuse me, gentlemen. Marianne, I believe this dance is promised to me." Perry had not specified for which dance he had requested her hand, but she had already danced with Vernon, and Lorry could very well wait. He saw the eyebrows of all three raise, and only then realized his gaffe.

"Miss Edgewood, I mean to say."

The strains of a minuet filled the hall, and Marianne hesitated before setting her hand on his arm. Victorious at having snatched her away, he bowed to his friend and Vernon.

"Mr. Osborne," she whispered as they walked to the floor, tugging at his arm to bring him closer. "I am not certain I am able to dance this. I know only the country steps."

"Miss Edgewood, trust me. You must dance this if you hope to regain your standing at the ball. Only...are your slippers tied correctly?" He looked around at the set, conscious that they would lose their place if they didn't quickly take their position, and pulled her forward.

He felt her nod at his side. "Yes."

With that confirmation, he led her inexorably to a place where they might be the next in the set, determined to show Miss Belford and every other person present that Miss Edgewood belonged among their society and was worthy in their eyes.

The couple in front of him, who should have closed the first set, came to a halt when the woman grunted in pain and said in an angry whisper, "Not yet dancing, and you have already stepped on my foot."

The gentleman, in seeming mortification, led her to the sidelines, opening up for Perry to escort Marianne into the set, which he did so at once. He was eager to have this done with and restore her reputation. It might be true that she was not dressed in the height of fashion, and she might have suffered an unfortunate fall, but everyone would see she was worthy.

Marianne stood woodenly next to him while the music called his steps forward and he circled the gentleman across from him. As he danced the gentlemen's steps before they each claimed their partners, Perry attempted to catch her regard and reassure her with his own. Her eyes were wide, her gaze fixed at some point in the distance.

At that precise moment in the music, he held out his arm, so she might take his hand and join in the steps of the dance, except she did not. She stood frozen and gave a tiny shake of her head. Heart sinking, he insisted, putting his hand out again. Marianne had grown pale. She turned on her heel and left the floor, with him standing in the middle of it.

"Miss Belford, you are able to step in now, are you not?" Raife's quiet voice came from behind Perry before he felt Raife's hand on his shoulder. He turned and gave way as Raife and Miss Belford took up the positions he and Miss Edgewood had vacated.

He knew he should say something to save the moment, but he could think of nothing. He was on the sidelines now and the dance had taken up again as though nothing were wrong. People hardly seemed to notice that she had run off, now that the set was complete. But he saw more than one amused pair of female eyes look at him, before hiding again behind their fans. At some point, he would have to go find Marianne, but he instead marched in the opposite direction. He was too angry he had been dragged into her humiliation. If only she had persevered with the dance!

It was not until Perry had walked around the edge of the floor and found a place in a secluded corner, where his heartbeat returned to normal, that he could admit to himself that he had been wrong. He was to blame for pulling Marianne into a dance she warned him she could not do. He hadn't believed her. Her country dances had gone off almost without fault, and the minuet was reputedly the first dance young ladies learned. Although...in her peculiar upbringing, she hadn't had a normal childhood, had she? How would she have learned any dance at all?

He needed to go find her.

"Miss Edgewood has had quite the unfortunate start for her entrance into society." Neck came to take his place beside Perry, who had been on the point of seeking her out. "I don't believe I've ever seen a more disastrous beginning, and I have seen some young ladies who have had little enough charm to recommend them."

"It's not charm that's lacking," Lorry said, as he came up on Perry's other side, making his discomfort complete. "True, that dress of hers is a monstrosity. But if I had the dressing of her, I would turn her beauty to advantage. I'd wear her on my arm with pride."

"She's not a straw damsel," Perry retorted, goaded beyond his usual circumspection in answering his friends. "She's a lady destined to become someone's wife, not mistress. You will not wear her on your arm in any form whatsoever."

"Oh, come now," Lorry protested, causing Perry to glare at him in warning. "Do not pretend she is under your protection. *You* don't plan to marry her, and mistresses are not in your line. She's more like a barque of frailty to tuck away than she is a wife. After all, I could hardly take her into society, now could I?"

"This is my warning, Lawrence. Stay away from her." Perry turned abruptly, but not before seeing that Raife's eyes had missed nothing even as he performed all the steps of the minuet without one mistake.

Lorry's comments were offensive in the extreme, but Perry couldn't exactly call out a man who was staying as a guest in his own home. Such a thing was not done. It was good his guests were leaving the next day. How could he have thought for a minute that Lorry was his friend? He wasn't even entirely sure about Neck. Raife had surprised him on this trip, though. If only he could be sure he was authentic.

Perry's mother, bless the woman, had tried to warn him about his friends, but Perry had been so grateful for their welcome into their circle he'd turned a deaf ear on her counsel. She had been right, however. Lorry was the worst, but even Neck had his moments. He would as soon provoke a duel as bet on the downfall of another and laugh at the man whose misfortune made Neck's own purse fat. Raife had surprised him with a steadiness of character Perry had not discerned in him before this visit, but what caused him to be so constantly in Neck and Lorry's company—he who could choose his society with a snap of his fingers?

Why am I trying so hard to impress people I don't even like? He was done with adapting himself to fit others. After this visit, Perry would do no more than give them a civil nod in passing. However, after Lorry's not-so-veiled threats regarding Marianne's honor, he would do well to watch him until they had safely seen the back of him.

Where was Marianne now? He needed to apologize for having made things so much worse. Had he the least sense, he would have realized she was not ready for such a public dance where the steps were performed with everyone watching. In his eagerness to restore her reputation, he had shown himself a fool.

Perry looked around at the main hall which was now full. Servants carried in trays of food that could be eaten with the fingers and drinks that he had found to be overly sweet. The mix of noise and colors, and the heat, overwhelmed his senses, making it hard to think straight.

"Are you, by any chance, searching for the unfortunate Miss Edgewood?"

Perry turned to find Miss Belford at his side. It did not seem from her tone or demeanor that she reveled in Marianne's downfall, which was something. In fact, she sounded almost compassionate. In another lifetime, he would have forgotten all about Miss Edgewood—after all, she was not his charge, was she?—and he would have attempted to flirt with Miss Belford, whose situation was more promising. He didn't.

"I am looking for Miss Edgewood, yes."

Miss Belford inclined her head toward the door. "She left with the Vernons moments ago. I'd say you might still catch her if you try, but are you sure she will want to see anyone just now?"

Perry didn't answer but bowed and strode toward the door. He stepped outside and saw much the same scene that he had come upon earlier, with grooms and drivers lounging about. After all, the evening was still too young for people to be calling for their carriages. Above the murmur of conversation, the noise of carriage wheels reached him from a distance. The coach was already turning from Cliff's End toward the coast. He was too late.

The sound of hoofbeats came next, and he turned back in time to glimpse Vernon ride by. Although he was sure Vernon had seen him, the man ignored Perry and followed in the direction of the carriage.

CHAPTER FIFTEEN

When Marianne fled the floor, she ran straight to Mrs. Vernon but was not required to explain herself. Mrs. Vernon had witnessed enough to take pity on her, and as it timed well with the Vernons' own desire to return, she and the squire accompanied Marianne home right away. Robert followed on horseback, and he made sure to swing down and open the carriage door for her when they arrived, so he might remonstrate her as he led her to the castle.

"You know you should not be staying here at Brindale alone. I've told you time and again, and now look at what happened tonight. You allowed yourself to be persuaded to dance with a gentleman who had all eyes focused on him as the newcomer, when you would better have done to have danced a second time with me. I could have softened the blow of tonight's unmitigated disaster. And what's more, you'd have had a certain protection with me as your betrothed if only you would see we are well-suited. But you've been unforgivably obstinate."

"Don't scold," she had told him wearily. "My heart cannot take it."

He fell silent, but his disapproving look followed her into the castle. His disappointment did not weigh on her as heavily as Mr. Osborne's did.

Marianne needed a full night's sleep to restore her body and soul, but she did not get it. Just as she was dropping off to sleep, the humiliation of the night's events would rouse her again and cause her breath to quicken even as her throat closed in. It seemed that dawn would never come, and when its purplish light finally did bring the features of her room into relief, her only wish was for many more hours of night because she was not nearly well-rested enough to face the day. Nor did she wish for time to drag her inexorably to the point where she must face Mr. Osborne and the other gentlemen, who were certainly laughing at her—or disgusted by her.

She lay on her side, staring with dull eyes at the washstand in the corner. What had come over her, to set aside her practice of avoiding all formal gatherings and agree to attend a ball, when she had long known that such a thing wasn't for her? Life had taught her early on that the only refuge to be had was found inside Brindale and the people who lived in it, even if they were considered inferior by others due to their status as servants. Sanctuary was not found with uncles who lived at the opposite end of the world and then died without warning, or in mingling with Kent's upper crust. She had been too flattered by Mr. Osborne's invitation and lulled into thinking she would acquit herself well. Vanity, which she had never thought to be one of her besetting sins, had led her to wish for Mr. Osborne's approval, and to think for the first time in her life that she might have a chance of gaining it. How wrong she was.

The memory of falling on her face sprang up again in her

mind, causing Marianne to roll over and bury her head in her pillow, wishing she could die. And then! Oh, and then—there was the mortification of not knowing how to dance the minuet. She had told him she could not. Why had he insisted? And why had she not remained staunch in her refusal, but instead thought she might somehow be swept along by the crowd and able to perform complicated steps she had learned a decade ago? The reality hit her like a dousing of cold water the moment it was her turn to move in the steps of the dance, but her feet stayed frozen to the ground. The crowning addition to her misery was the sight of Mr. Osborne's livid face as he curled his fingers to summon her again, as inflexible as though it were their first encounter and he was looking down at her from his massive horse.

Then she had run.

Marianne sat up in bed. There was no point in reliving the tragedy that was her life. She could not be sure if there were any whispers about the fact that she was living in a house with gentlemen. Mrs. Vernon's presence provided her with a certain degree of protection—even more so than Miss Fife's. However, as she had gone from almost no reputation in society to now an unfavorable one, she could take no risks. She did not need anyone else. She had been perfectly content living her life in the castle with just the servants to talk to, the garden to tend, the rooms to live in, and the books to read.

She was *perfectly happy.*

Tears slid down her cheeks. It was still dim in the room, but there was no sense in staying in bed. Marianne dried her tears, dressed in one of her usual gowns that was the right length, and pinned her hair up. As soon as she was certain her face had retained no trace of her distress, she reached for the door and pulled it open, nearly stumbling over a large burden that lay at the threshold. She gave a sharp intake of breath when her foot came into contact with something soft.

"*Ouch!*"

To her astonishment, the large bundle moved, and it was Mr. Osborne looking up at her. He blinked as though shaking off sleep, then scrambled to his feet when he registered her presence.

"What are you doing here?" she demanded in a loud whisper, torn between surprise and embarrassment. And...something else. Something that felt like a refuge.

Now standing before her, he adjusted his coat so it was straight, but his neckcloth was untied. "I...I thought it prudent to see to it that your sleep was not disturbed in any way."

She stared at him, attempting to decipher what could have led him to think her sleep might be disturbed. Part of his neck was visible, and she stared at the bare skin, her mouth agape.

His movement to hastily retie his neckcloth shook her from her stupor at the same time that a blush heated her cheeks, and she remembered his unfriendly face from the night before. His punishing eyes. It was all she needed to stir her emotions from embarrassment to temper.

She placed one hand on her hip. "You need not make yourself uncomfortable on my behalf, sir. As you know full well, my door has a latch. I was in no danger. And who could hurt me here? I am living in a house full of gentlemen, and I am guessing there is not one of you who is not armed."

The way he closed his lips and looked at her oddly sent a bolt through her middle. He seemed to be aware of a circumstance she was not, but it didn't feel like the same danger as she had faced at the cottage.

"Besides"—he reached down and grabbed the cloak he had used as a bedroll—"I wish to speak with you."

Tears of humiliation pricked the backs of her eyes, and she

blinked them away. "What could you possibly have to say to me? After last night, I think we both know it is best I find my own way as soon as possible and avoid society at all costs, including yours."

She moved forward quickly and he hurried to keep up, his cloak now tangled in his legs.

"Do wait." Mr. Osborne stopped her with a gentle touch on her arm. "I don't want you to avoid me. I merely wished to apologize for insisting that you dance last night. It was wrong and misguided of me."

Marianne faced forward, not looking at him. She did not remember anyone ever apologizing to her who was not a servant.

"Your apology is accepted, of course," she said, moving forward again. "But it does not lessen my humiliation, or my determination to move back to the cottage." She descended the stairs at a quick pace, and he was forced to keep up with her.

"I understand. But I do not think you should dwell too much upon what you call humiliation. Truly, what need is there to care about society in a small village? If this were in London—"

She rounded on him. "*That* is why you do not belong here. Of course you do not care. You plan to lease this castle out to strangers. But Brindale is my home. This village is my home, and I have nowhere else to go. There is nowhere else I want to go."

Silence fell after her impassioned words, and she heard only the sound of her breathing. He stared at her without speaking in that odd way of his—that keen scrutiny as though he were trying to read something in her. For the first time, his silence led her to guess that he might be wishing to tell her something but had not made up his mind to do so. It made her drop her gaze and speak with quiet resolve.

"It is best that I move back to the cottage as soon as possible, no matter what danger there might still be. In truth, I don't think there can be much."

She glanced up at him. "As soon as I have a male servant there, I will go. We have not heard of any other disturbances, and you have already sent the carpenter to repair the shutters. I will be sure to bolt every window and entrance before I go to bed. I will see to it myself." Her words came spilling out, and she couldn't tell if she was trying to convince him of the wisdom of her idea, or if she was challenging him to contradict her and beg her to stay.

Sounds came from the direction of the kitchen, and soon the door opened. Sarah walked by carrying bread into the dining room. After murmuring a good morning and darting a glance at her mistress, she curtsied and continued on her way, leaving them in peace.

"It is not because I wish to rent out the castle that I think you need not worry about village society." Mr. Osborne exhaled and looked at the ceiling. "I just think they are more forgiving here, and therefore you need not worry overmuch. And...I like you, Miss Edgewood—Marianne."

Shock stole her voice, along with any notion to flee, and he planted his feet farther apart, folding his arms that were still wrapped in the cloak. "If I may?"

Was that what he had been struggling to tell her? *No, surely not.* Though she focused all her attention on him—blinking to catch some subtle clues as to his meaning—his words did not become any more sensible. What did he mean that he liked her? Did he mean that his opinion of her had not changed though she had publicly disgraced herself? As he did not assist her comprehension by clarifying his words, she was forced to ask.

"What do you mean that you like me?" Her voice squeaked

at the end, proving just what a timid, spiritless creature she was.

Mr. Osborne looked again to the ceiling and exhaled as though searching for divine inspiration to answer an impossible question. "By that I mean that I like to talk to you and look at you"—he paused—"and that I would like you to call me Perry instead of Mr. Osborne." He frowned and tucked his brows together as he thought some more. "It means that I think about kissing you—and would do so if I could."

Her face burned scarlet then, and he hastened to add, "Not that I mean to do it, so you need not worry. I will behave as a gentleman. But that is what I meant when I said you need not dwell much upon what village society thinks. Because such prejudices against those who do not fit into the mold are not universally shared."

Marianne looked down, a warmth settling in her breast, which warred against the nervous breathlessness coming from what she had just heard. *He liked her enough to kiss her?* She had not thought of such a thing, but now that the idea had taken root, she discovered just how much she would like to see what that was like.

It didn't change her position, however. Had he not said that as a gentleman he could not kiss her? He had probably meant those words as a kindness—a balm to her heart to let her know she was not so repulsive after all. In truth, the words did help her—especially as someone who had no intentions of marriage. So there was no need for her to feel so empty at the thought that he would not attempt it. And it was good to know she was not universally found distasteful.

A suitable reply escaped her, and she kept her gaze glued to the floor. "I must tell Miss Fife that we will remove to the cottage as soon as it might be arranged." She curtsied and hurried away, putting as much distance between them as she could.

But his declaration had not left her unmoved. It would take everything in her to fight the temptation to build a castle of dreams on his words. She marched toward Miss Fife's room, numb with bewilderment from the morning's revelations.

"*Perry*," she whispered, discovering that his name slipped effortlessly off her tongue.

CHAPTER SIXTEEN

Perry watched Marianne flee from his declaration. He could hardly blame her for having done so. It had not been particularly smooth. His mind was befuddled thanks to the stiff neck and uncomfortable night spent tossing and turning on her doorstep. He had been incapable of thinking in any kind of coherent manner, much less expressing some new and revelatory feelings he was only discovering himself.

Despite how exhausting the night had been, he had done right to camp out in front of the door to her room. It might have a latch, but that was easily worked around. And at some point in the middle of the night, he had been awoken by the sound of Lorry's door creaking open. Light spilled out into the corridor, and Perry had sat partly upright, leaning on an elbow and peering at the source of the disturbance. He caught Lorry's gaze and sent the man a pointed look, freezing him in his steps. Lorry raised his hand as if to acknowledge a hit, then retreated back into his room. Perry wondered if he would mention it when they met today, or if it was better left alone—much like their friendship, he had come to realize.

Not knowing what else to do with himself, Perry headed into the dining room, hoping breakfast would wake him up. Before he stepped into the room, it crossed his mind that perhaps Marianne had come here instead of going to Miss Fife, but the hope turned out to be an empty one. He went over to the sideboard and turned a cup over on its saucer as Annabel hurried in with a steaming pot of coffee in one hand and tea in another.

"Good morning, sir. May I?" She held both aloft and he nodded at the coffeepot, allowing her to fill the cup. "Mrs. Malford is making the steak and potatoes. The bread is freshly baked."

"Very good." Perry sat, facing the northern window where he had a glimpse of the sun's reflection on the pond and the corner of the stables above that. The forge was not visible from here, but he must see about that today along with hiring Marianne's footman if she was determined to go. For now, he would enjoy his coffee and the silence, grateful he could be alone with his thoughts.

What good had it been to divulge his feelings to Marianne if he was not yet brought to the point of a declaration? All he had done was succeed in embarrassing her, if her reaction gave any indication. He remembered Robert Vernon's glance his way last night, and the proprietary look that had gone with it. Had the man made any inroads into her heart? The way she defended the village this morning made him wonder if indeed the village was another name for her childhood friend. It might take only a single event outside of her comfortable surroundings for Marianne to suddenly paste virtues on a man who did not possess them, simply because he was familiar.

Then Perry was left to wonder if those virtues were indeed

present in Vernon, but hidden from him by some vein of jealousy. He stood to refill his cup. *Ah, these wonderings are futile.*

The door opened, and instead of the maid returning with the breakfast, Raife entered and lifted a hand in greeting. He went over to the sideboard and helped himself to tea, then took a chair across from Perry. They sat in silence for a few minutes.

"You'll have to keep me abreast of your gentleman poacher." Raife raised his eyebrows above his cup.

Perry glanced up and nodded. "I will. Likely by letter, as I'm not sure how soon I will be back in London."

"I'd guessed as much." Raife met Perry's surprised look with a smile. "Once a man has an estate to oversee, the clubs and gambling begin to pall. If he is a man of sense, that is to say."

Perry thought about this, and shook his head. "Neck has property."

"I said a man of sense," Raife clarified.

Perry chuckled, then as the silence stretched, his thoughts turned in a more sober direction. "I will be honest with you. I'm finding I have little in common with Lorry and Neck."

He looked up, assessing how Raife took the news. "In fact, I can't think why I seek their companionship at all." He left unsaid the part where he wondered why Raife did either.

Charlie entered, followed by Annabel, and they placed dishes of steaming meat and potatoes on the sideboard. Annabel had a sack of plums she emptied into a bowl. Then, after loading plates for the gentlemen and verifying that they needed nothing further, the servants left the room.

Raife appraised the contents of his plate before lifting a fork. "I suppose gambling at The Cocoa Tree and parading as part of the Four-in-Hand Club has been at the root of our friendship, but I've grown weary of such sport myself."

"The 4HC? I had no idea you'd even belonged. I've never seen you wear the yellow striped waistcoat," Perry said.

Raife gave an exaggerated shudder. "Ghastly."

Perry laughed, feeling an odd kinship with Raife, whom he had always thought a touch above him. He came from an old family and old money, which meant he did as he pleased and frequented those who pleased him. Perry had always suspected that Raife tolerated him because of Neck and Lorry, but now he was not so sure. There was a depth to him Perry had overlooked in his eagerness to set him on a pedestal.

They ate breakfast, and Perry began to shrug off sleep. "I wonder how long Neck and Lorry will remain abed," he mused.

"I will not stay long enough to find out, I'm afraid. I'm having my valet pack my things now. I told them last night I planned to make an early start of it."

"You won't be making the journey back together then?" Perry pushed back and folded his arms over his now-satisfied belly.

"My sister will have her lying-in soon, and I want to be there to welcome my nephew, if she is right in her predictions," Raife said. "If I travel with them—with their stopping for any number of days at whatever inn catches their fancy—I might be celebrating my nephew's first birthday instead."

He stood. "My groom will have made the carriage ready by now, so I will bid you farewell."

Perry got to his feet as Raife came around the table, and they shook hands. Raife stayed for a second longer. "I'll be at Overmere should you wish to send news of any sort."

Perry shook his head, now confused. "News? Of what?"

"If I knew, it would not be news, would it?" Raife smiled in his enigmatic way, opened the door, and left.

Perry could only surmise Raife had guessed the direction in which his interest lay, which then led him back to wondering whether he would be successful in wooing Marianne. His intentions may not have been clear even in his own mind when he'd spoken to her that morning, but they were becoming crystal clear as the minutes ticked by. The sight of her caused his heart to beat, and he wanted to clear any obstacle that might give her alarm. He felt a kinship with Marianne when it came to navigating the difficult world of polite society, and the urge to offer her his protection was impossible to resist.

And then there was the castle he had inherited. Rather than act as Brindale's lone proprietor—although it was indeed what he was—Perry had started focusing on the estate improvements that would win her favor. Unlike his previous attempts to earn his uncle's or friends' approval thinking it would cause him to have self-esteem, his attempts to win Marianne's were simply to bring her joy, something of which she'd had precious little in her two decades on this earth. Oh yes, he was in deep where Marianne Edgewood was concerned.

He did not bother waiting for his two other guests to wake up, but set about on estate business. He was more than ready to turn from entertaining to the task of improving his estate. The first thing he did was pen a letter to Mr. Mercy to request he come pay a visit. He wanted to speak with him on the urgent business of hiring another footman for the cottage. If Marianne was truly determined to return to the cottage, he would make sure she was well-protected by a footman who was burly enough to bring down an opponent in a boxing match.

In the end, the letter was not needed because Mr. Mercy appeared, bringing the promised beemaster with him, who tugged what looked like a promising load of brood boxes containing more than one hive. Perry went over to the modestly dressed older man, conscious that the sight of a restored apiary could only bring joy to Marianne, besides adding to the estate's profit. He accepted the garb needed to protect himself from any errant bees that were unhappy to have been disturbed and stood back a ways to watch the beemaster set up the hives. He asked questions to understand the art, should he decide to multiply his colonies and sell them for profit.

After the beemaster finished, and they had seen him off, Perry invited Mr. Mercy into his study, crossing paths with Neck and Lorry, who looked the worse for wear after having stayed up far into the night. They had finished the last of the French Burgundy days ago then made do with the English wines and spirits. Perry didn't have time for them just now, but he needed to be a good host until the end.

"Good day to you. You'll be wishing for something to eat, I imagine." He paused and spotted Charlie coming from the drawing room and signaled for him to come over. "My footman will see to it that you have a proper meal."

He wanted to ask when they would leave, but such a thing would be so rude as to be unthinkable. It was already after two o'clock, and he feared that if they did not start out soon, they might wish to remain for days, something he fervently hoped to avoid. He had been graced with their company for long enough. It was one thing to endure someone's companionship when one could slip away at any point when time alone was needed. It was quite another to be the one who provided for the guests' comfort and who must be ready for their every whim. *Including protecting innocent damsels from their unwanted attention.*

"Some sustenance will be just the thing. Lorry and I have decided to race to our first posting house, although we've agreed there is to be no cheating, is that not so, Lorry?" Neck declared, to Perry's relief. He needn't have worried that they would try to extend their stay. "Shame Raife left so early. It would have made for a more interesting bet."

Perry waved them into the breakfast room, feeling more gracious now that he would soon see them no more. "It sounds like great fun. Have a servant come to fetch me if you are ready to leave before I have finished."

He then ushered Mr. Mercy into the small study that had once belonged to Mr. Edgewood, appreciating the quiet here. He liked this room and wondered that Marianne rarely seemed to go into it. It was not one of the rooms she tended to speak of as though it had personality. Perhaps she did not wish to disturb its memories.

The steward caught him up to date on the progress of the carpenters and roofers, who had finished the timbers but were still waiting for the right professionals to repair the clay tiles. Perry told him of his desire to rent out the smithy and received a look of approval in return. He was coming to appreciate his relationship with the steward, who was cautious at beginning new ventures, but hardworking and willing to follow Perry's lead when he wished to take some risk. It was a gratifying experience to be the recipient of such respect.

After learning that Mr. Mercy had a suitable candidate for footman and that he would be able to employ the fellow by the next day, as it was his nephew—who, funny that Mr. Osborne had asked, was skilled in the pugilist arts—Perry had only to discuss his remaining piece of business.

"I am looking to add to the estate such simple ventures as will bring about the greatest return. I think we might raise some basic livestock beyond the pigs, if you can find me a man to care for them. And the garden that Mar—that Miss Edgewood has been tending to might bring in a profit if she is willing to sell the flowers and herbs to be made into cosmetics and tinctures. I will have to speak to her."

He was conscious of the jolt of excitement that shot through him merely at bringing up Marianne's name in conversation. *You are being absurd*, he tried to tell himself, but his heart wouldn't listen.

"Miss Edgewood is indeed skilled at gardening, especially in tending her mother's rose bushes," Mr. Mercy said. "If she is amenable to the idea, I say that you have hit upon the very thing."

He and Mr. Mercy stood and, with this, concluded their business in perfect agreement as Lorry pounded on the door to the study.

"Still in there, Oz? Come see us off."

More welcome words could not be heard. Perry entered the main hall and managed to have a genuine smile for Lorry and Neck. They might not be ideal friends, but they shared a few years of memories together. And he would think of them fondly...once they were gone.

In another quarter of an hour, the castle was quiet. Muffled sounds came from the kitchen, or perhaps somewhere else in the house. The afternoon was now advanced, and he wondered at the fact that he had not seen Marianne since their conversation that morning. He wished to tell her that he had found a footman to keep her safe but feared to force his presence on her if she needed time away from him to think. He was also eager to share all the improvements he was bringing about in the castle. Maybe she would look upon him more favorably when she knew.

He sat in the ugly drawing room, which had strangely begun to grow on him, as dark and outmoded as it was. He put his feet up on a stool and laced his fingers together in quiet contemplation. Now that he was intent on wooing Marianne, maybe he should go about it in a more suitable manner and not bash her over the head with threats of kissing that were immediately retracted. He groaned at the recollection and smacked his own head.

What little peace he'd had that was not destroyed by this rumination was cut up by the sounds of a carriage drawn by four horses pulling into the estate. Perry stood and walked over to the window, leaning to the right of the honeycomb panes so he could see outside more clearly. The glass was blown in cleaner lines on the edge of the window, he'd discovered.

He squinted at the sight of a liveried footman, who seemed oddly familiar, then shot a glance at the crest on the carriage. Curiosity turned to apprehension as Lord Steere stepped down from the coach and lifted his head to scrutinize Brindale Castle. His uncle had come.

No sooner had he rid himself of his friends than his uncle would arrive with set expectations of being entertained and catered to. Perry remained frozen for a moment, staring at the unwelcome sight through the window before coming to his senses. He had no choice but to go and greet his uncle and make him welcome, even if it was the last thing he wished to do. Groaning under his breath, Perry exited into the main hall and plastered a welcoming smile on his face before opening the front door.

"You've come, Uncle," he said as he strode outdoors to greet him. "I did not expect to have this pleasure. What has brought you to Kent?"

"Surprised you, boy, did I?"

Lord Steere handed his hat and cane to the new footman, who had hurried forward. "As you might've guessed, handing the keys to Brindale Castle was your test. I wanted to see if you were fit to step into my shoes at Mulgrove Estate. Granted, there's not much I can do regarding the title," he said, walking toward the front entrance, "but there are many pieces of land I can choose to will to someone else should I find your style of management not up to snuff. I wanted to see with my own eyes how things fare here."

Perry was well aware he needed to win his uncle's approbation, but it didn't make the words any easier to hear. Was simply trusting him with the task too difficult a thing to do? He forced his tone to be conciliatory.

"Please come inside. Shall I offer you some brandy?"

"A small glass would be welcome after my journey, but I'm eager to have a look at the land I handed over to you." He scowled at Perry. "Not that I regret it, mind you. This was not such a large estate that I would suffer if you ran it into the ground, and I'm a man who knows what he's doing. Still, I've come to look over your management."

Perry kept his tongue between his teeth, applying every ounce of self-control he possessed so he could appear as though his uncle's surprise visit were a pleasure. Once they entered, he sent Charlie to bring some brandy to the drawing room, while Brindale's newer footman Albinus hurried to bring Lord Steere's belongings into the room Lorry had just vacated. Perry pulled the newest maid aside and asked her to see that the room was cleaned and fresh sheets put on at once.

"Dismal drawing room here, isn't it?" Lord Steere took a seat, the paunch of his *embonpoint* spilling over onto his pantaloons. "I don't know why you didn't start with renovations in this room."

Perry looked around, now feeling quite the opposite. The drawing room was spacious, and a coat of paint in a fresh color would more than likely lighten the room sufficiently. "This was not the most urgent of things that needed to be done. The roof on the north side had a leak."

"You did not mention it in your letters." Lord Steere's eyes brightened as the footman arrived with a bottle and two glasses.

"I didn't wish to burden you with mentions of all that needed to be done. You were quite explicit in saying that this was my affair to deal with. But the roof was in need of urgent attention, and that was where I put the first bulk of my funds." He accepted the glass from the footman, who had learned by now to serve him very little.

As his uncle took the refreshment, they spoke of the changes Perry had already put into effect. Then, as soon his uncle had finished his brandy, he stood.

"Well, we're not likely to have many more hours of daylight left. Why don't we get started on the outdoors first? You can show me what you've done so far and what you plan to do. I trust you've been using your time well."

Perry stood, realizing what a close call he'd just had. If his uncle had arrived when his friends were still at Brindale, he would have assumed Perry had not taken his ownership of the estate seriously. Perhaps he had not at the time he'd invited them, but he did now.

He hoped his uncle would be impressed with what he had done, but doubt made him fear it was not enough. Everything was so new. Yes, the timbers were fresh, but the clay tiles had not been installed. The apiary was in its beginning stages, and it needed to be left completely alone for the hive to get settled. There was therefore nothing to see yet. He had still to speak to Marianne's blacksmith about renting out his smithy, and he'd only just spoken with the steward about getting the livestock project up and running.

"Right this way," he said with an optimism he did not feel, leading his uncle out-of-doors. He decided to show him the stable first, which was well kept and was one of the nicer outlying buildings. They could then visit the apiary, and he could explain what he was doing there.

"Where is the young miss who had been living here before you inherited? What have you done with her?"

Perry walked forward without missing a step, but his insides froze. He didn't like the way his uncle had referred to her, as though she were a dog in need of a new home. Lord Steere must form a good impression of Marianne. It was so early in his courtship, Perry couldn't quite spell out the reasons, even to himself. He just knew it was necessary.

"As a matter of fact, Miss Edgewood was bequeathed the cottage on the edge of the estate. I helped her to move her belongings there." He was about to say more but his uncle interrupted him.

"A cottage? That was not in the attorney's report. There was no mention of an outlying building other than the stables and house adjoined to it."

"That's because her portion had been sectioned off before the property came to you. But I assure you, it is hers." Perry continued forward, desiring to protect her at all costs.

Lord Steere resumed the walk, frowning. "I shall want to have a look at that document of hers. So she's living there now, is she?"

Perry pinched his lips together before shaking his head. He would have to tread carefully. "There was a break-in at the cottage, and I had her brought back to the castle as a temporary measure. She has been occupying the master bedroom in the southern wing, which is why I didn't put you there."

"My boy, I hope you're not doing something foolish like developing feelings for her." Lord Steere turned to Perry and studied him. "She's been raised in the country, and it's not for a gel like her to become the wife of a baron. You'll need to look much higher when you make a match."

Indignation rose in Perry's breast, which led him to speak with more honor than truth. "Sir, I'll have you know that Miss

Edgewood is perfectly respectable. She has had a genteel education and is a lady in every sense of the word."

A loud series of grunts and squeals interrupted the rest of what he would have said, and Perry turned toward the sound, his jaw dropping in dismay. Coming up from the field toward the stables was Marianne, wearing one of her oldest dresses, her hair half undone, but that was nothing compared to the filth that covered the front of her dress and extended right up onto her face. Her mouth was set in determination as she pushed the ornery Buttercup in the direction of the pighouse.

"I swear, Buttercup, if you do this to me one more time, you'll be 'rashers of sindg'd bacon on the coals' by morning."

CHAPTER SEVENTEEN

Marianne couldn't believe Buttercup had escaped again. The new footman had come running to tell her, having learned the hard way that he was no match for the large pig. She discovered the sow in the eastern lawn and had pushed and shoved her back toward the pighouse, but that effort on the slippery hillside had only caused Marianne to glide out of control and fall face-first in the mud...much in the way she had done on the dance floor. Only this time it was with less embarrassment because there was no one to see her.

"I swear, Buttercup..." she muttered.

Marianne had stayed out of sight the whole of the day. She did not desire to be there when the gentlemen took their leave, learning from Sarah that Mr. Raife had departed first, and that Mr. Wilmot and Neck-whatever-his-name-was had not yet surfaced by noon. That made her more determined to remain invisible.

She had not ceased to ruminate over Mr. Osborne's declaration that morning, which she still had trouble believing could be meant for her—had trouble thinking of him as Perry, despite the thrill of being given such intimate use of his name. She had not expected him to feel anything toward her, inconsequential creature that she was. Although she had sometimes allowed herself to wonder whether those light touches coming from him were entirely accidental, not once had it occurred to her that he might feel a degree of attraction toward her.

She'd thought of him as an interloper, a foe, someone to battle against. In hindsight, she had been deceiving herself, convincing herself he meant nothing more to her than any other stranger. But she could not fool herself for long. The particular attentions he paid, and his coming in the guise of a rescuer, had softened something in her heart.

After she'd left him on the stairwell, Marianne went to see Miss Fife, who had not attempted to try to walk, likely enjoying the way the servants were forced to wait upon her. They were under orders of both Marianne and Mr. Osborne to do so, and Miss Fife seemed in no hurry to lose her privileged position. In order for Marianne to ease her conscience for the increasingly belligerent spirit she harbored toward her companion, she spent a full hour with her before claiming tasks outdoors which could not wait.

She kept least in sight, meeting no one until she crossed paths with Mr. Mercy at the stables, who had said he'd just finished his meeting with Mr. Osborne. The steward gave her the good news that Mr. Osborne had overseen the hiring of a footman for her, and he was to begin work the next day.

Mr. Osborne again. The feelings he evoked were stronger than she felt capable of examining, and she was glad to be leaving the castle the next day. As she went through her tasks, she thought about when and how she should return to the cottage, testing in her heart how it would feel to be there again. She would not need to importune Mr. Osborne any longer, which could only be a good thing. Surely, if she stepped away, he would forget those feelings he'd expressed. Did she want him to?

These and all other thoughts fled the moment she'd discovered the pig's whereabouts and she tried to wrestle her the long distance back to her pen. She wrinkled her brows as she gave Buttercup another shove, her thoughts still on Perry. With a pang, she wondered if he would indeed forget her.

The sound of someone clearing his throat broke through the mist of her cogitation, and she froze in place. Her heart thumped at the thought of having Mr. Osborne witness her second disgrace, and she turned slowly to confirm her fears. It was worse.

Not only had Mr. Osborne witnessed how truly unfit she was for society, a gentleman stood beside him who, if the age and slight resemblance indicated correctly, could be none other than Lord Steere, although she had not been informed he intended to visit. Mr. Osborne had an unfortunate habit of not apprising her of visitors. If he had warned her of his uncle's, she would have taken pains to be more presentable. The irritation of that thought gave her courage, and Marianne lifted her chin.

"Uncle, may I present Miss Edgewood. She is the only person at Brindale who has any success with Buttercup. That is, the uh...the pig. Miss Edgewood, may I present the baron, Lord Steere?" Mr. Osborne's voice was tight with what could only be disapproval.

Holding herself stiffly, she curtsied. "Good day, my lord."

"Not always successfully, I see," Lord Steere replied in a dry voice. Unlike Mr. Osborne, who occasionally revealed a hidden well of humor, the baron appeared to have none.

Marianne stood for a moment, unsure of how to repair the situation. In the end, she decided not to try.

"If you'll excuse me, I will finish my work and see to the menu for dinner. I understand from Mr. Mercy I cannot return to the cottage until tomorrow."

When she dared to meet Mr. Osborne's eyes, she found his gaze understanding and almost apologetic. Maybe he didn't disapprove of her.

"I would not wish you to do so tonight, at any rate. Without a man to see to your safety, I cannot recommend your leaving the castle."

She nodded, suddenly recalling her immediate task. "If you'll excuse me then."

She discovered Buttercup hiding next to the old smithy. The pig was suddenly docile, though whether it was shame at having put her mistress in such a predicament, the threat of bacon, or the hope of a meal, Marianne could not be sure. She opened the gate to the pighouse and Buttercup went in willingly enough. She closed the gate and left without a word.

The slight lift from earlier in the day as she thought over Mr. Osborne's declaration was now dissipated. Her spirits plunged again, reminding her of how she felt since he'd come to take possession of the castle. It appeared she was to suffer one reminder after another that the life she had known since birth was no longer hers. And as if that were not enough, she was doomed to remain on the outskirts of polite society.

Marianne returned to the castle with heavy steps, and Sarah, having spotted her from one of the windows, came running out. Mrs. Malford must have done the same from the kitchen window, because she exited from there at the same time. Both came toward Marianne, and without heeding the mud, they each put an arm around her, Mrs. Malford clucking affectionately and Sarah promising to bring hot water and get her cleaned up in a trice. Marianne could not remain disconsolate at such displays of affection. Truly, Mrs. Malford and Sarah were more like family than they were servants, even if she could not say such a thing to them. What more could she ask for than such kind devotion?

She allowed them to ready a bath for her in her parents' room, and Sarah washed and brushed out her hair, then plaited it as best she could. As Marianne pinned it up and dressed, she decided she needed to leave the castle for a walk before dark. She was too agitated to sit idly after her humiliating encounter. Perhaps she'd go for a walk into the village— or to visit Robert? But no. Strangely enough she did not want to see him just then.

Struck by an idea, she turned to Sarah. "I wish to visit Joe Dobson and bring his children some food. Do we have anything in the kitchen?"

"Yes, miss. If ye'd like, I 'ull go with ye." Sarah turned her clear gaze toward Marianne, and it prompted a rush of affection—a sense of how pretty Sarah was, made more so by her loyalty and steadfastness. The feeling pushed Marianne to follow her impulse and step out of the mistress-servant relationship.

"Sarah, do you ever wish you could marry?"

"Me, miss?" Sarah looked down. "'Course, I do. I've always dreamed of having children of my own. But maids are not to marry, miss. Not unless they'm looking to be dismissed. I've no wish to leave my position."

Marianne nodded in silence, the newfound confidence between them dying at birth. She knew maids could not marry, but why was that? Who had made that rule? She sensed that Sarah did not feel comfortable saying more, and she did not wish to pry. Marianne stood, seized by a rebellious desire to thumb her nose at the rules.

"Let us go, then. I believe we have time enough before it

turns dark. I will lace up my boots, and if you can gather things from Mrs. Malford, we may set off."

A short while later they left, Sarah carrying the basket under her arm that contained bread, cakes, and even a bit of soup that Sarah had made herself. Although Annabel was the designated undercook, Sarah had learned to cook from her own mother and Mrs. Malford never resented her presence in the kitchen when she asked to use it. Marianne had grown grateful for that skill when they were alone in the cottage. In no time, they turned onto the muddy lane that led to the smithy.

"Miss Edgewood! Mith' Tharah!" Joe's children dropped the pebbles they were playing with and came rushing over to them, grins on their faces as they eyed the basket. A hissing sound came from inside, that of hot metal being dipped into cold water. Joe came out next, wiping his hands on his apron, and the children stepped respectfully back.

"Miss Edgewood, 'tis always a pleasure to greet ye." Joe bowed to Marianne, but...did her eyes deceive her or did his gaze linger on Sarah? Did he also recognize her virtues?

Marianne could not be sure whether it was the hope of love in her own heart that awakened the desire that love might be found elsewhere, or whether she were truly looking at a potential match. But here he was, a widower with two children, and Sarah was eligible. Why could this not work? She peeked at Sarah, wondering if her offer to come sprang from deeper feelings toward the widower, but she could read nothing in the maid's face.

Although it had been Sarah who gathered and carried the items, including her own soup, her maid remained silent. Marianne took the basket that Sarah handed her and said, "We've brought some of the extra food from our kitchen."

"I'm right grateful." Joe's eyes lit up with his smile, and he shot a surreptitious glance at Sarah before returning his gaze to Marianne. "What can I do for ye? Is there something that needs repairing?"

"Nothing is broken. It was just an excuse to see the children," Marianne replied. She left off that she was also hiding from home. How was she going to face Perry's uncle at dinner tonight?

When her maid continued to remain silent, she added, "Sarah made some soup that she thought you might like. I imagine there is not much in the way of warm meals here?"

"Little enough." Joe's glance in Sarah's direction was longer this time, but seemed shy. It was broken by the approach of his two children, whose curiosity had overcome their reticence, and who inched over to the basket. They seemed thinner to Marianne.

"Why do I never see Art Reacher working here when it's his smithy?" She had meant for the words to be light, but she thought the smith's behavior most unjust, and it showed in her tone.

Joe's face hardened. "That's a question ye 'ull have to ask him yerself—if ye can catch him."

His sudden familiarity caused his eyes to widen in dismay. "I hope ye'll forgive me, miss. I was meaning no disrespect. I bin out of sorts thinking on Art." He left the rest unsaid: *I'm to be his assistant and work for wages that can barely put food on the table, but I'm doing all the work myself.*

Joe would not say it, but she had learned from Mrs. Malford, who was in tune with servants' gossip, that he had fallen behind on his rent after his wife died and had built up a debt he could not pay. Now he was working as little more than a slave. There were many things that were unfair: her losing her castle and her uncle's last-minute betrayal, Sarah's inability to marry and have a family, Joe being forced to work for meager wages. All of this was unfair, and there was absolutely nothing she could do about it.

After staying a few minutes to talk to the children, Marianne and Sarah headed back to the castle, the afternoon light fading. She idly wondered if Robert would come to call soon to see how she fared after last night's debacle. It was not that she longed for his visit, but when she had been at the cottage for those few days, he had taken to visiting daily. He had not come to the castle once since Mr. Osborne had first arrived.

She supposed it was jealousy and wished she could have a more natural friendship with Robert. She had never thought of him in a romantic way—not once—and did not suspect that his feelings regarding her were anything approaching love. They had always felt more proprietary than amorous. And yet, he was her first and only friend in the village, pre-dating her parents' deaths, and that was hard to dismiss.

"Miss Edgewood."

They were at the crossroads to Cliff's End when Marianne was pulled from her reverie by someone calling her name. She turned to find Amelia Belford walking her way with her maid. They rarely crossed paths in the village, and whenever they did, they did not exchange greetings. She could only suppose that Miss Belford had done so now for one of two reasons. One of them was to gloat.

Miss Belford was flushed and slightly out of breath, as though she had run to catch up with her, and her maid was still several steps behind.

"Miss Edgewood, I have been meaning to call at Brindale."

And there was the other reason. Miss Belford knew that there was a handsome and eligible bachelor residing at Brindale, and as she could not call on him for his own sake, she needed the excuse of Marianne to call.

Marianne could not ask her, in the abrupt manner she

wished to, the reasons for her proposed visit. She had not the courage. She could not smile either as she replied in a dull voice.

"That is kind of you."

Miss Belford had now come face-to-face. She stopped and looked at her fully before glancing away. "I have not been a friend to you the way I should have."

Her declaration surprised Marianne into silence. She did not know how to respond and didn't rightly know if she believed her sincerity, but Miss Belford's words offered like that could not help but soften her.

"You are kind to say that." *Oh goodness, no wonder I have no friends. Can I not think of anything more original to say?*

"So, I wished to ask if I could visit you at the castle? If you are amenable to the idea." Miss Belford's expression did seem sincere, as though she hoped Marianne would say yes.

"Of course you are welcome, but you must know that I reside in the cottage on the eastern wall of the estate." There was no point in telling her the history of the break-in and her move to the castle while four gentlemen were residing there. The Vernons would not tell, and neither would her servants. She would only risk public censure if it came out.

Besides, that was the other reason she suspected Miss Belford's offer of friendship, so she may as well warn her now. "That means you will not have an occasion to see Mr. Osborne when you call."

Miss Belford surprised her by waving it off. "Never mind that. It was you I wished to see. I am sure I will meet Mr. Osborne again at some assembly if he continues to stay on at Brindale."

Marianne was nearly speechless. It seemed Miss Belford was neither gloating nor using her for her own ends. At last she managed a curtsy and something that might be taken for a smile.

"Very well. You may come when you wish."

She turned with Sarah to go, running through the conversation in her mind. What a surprising turn this was. She didn't know if she could trust Miss Belford, but she supposed that it didn't matter anyway. It was highly unlikely that she would actually visit.

CHAPTER EIGHTEEN

After Lord Steere had expounded on the dangers of frequenting the society of women with no education in the arts of young ladies, he thankfully left the subject alone and was taken by the work Perry had effected on the inside of the castle. He was particularly struck by the wisdom of Perry's using his resources to replace the rotting beams in the northern part of the castle, and dismissed his worry that the tiles had not yet been replaced because they were waiting for an order to come through. In the meantime, the masons had put the old tiles back in place with temporary plaster in the holes and cracks as a stopgap to keep water from pouring in until the tiles could be replaced with new. His uncle was delighted with his industriousness, and Perry had to own that such praise coming from an uncle he respected was a source of pleasure.

He could not wait to see Marianne at dinner. He hoped she would come down, despite the humiliating encounter from earlier that afternoon. Her face had not revealed much when she was made aware of their presence, but as he was coming to know her, he was sure she had suffered embarrassment over the event.

It had pained him that his uncle had seen her at her worst and frustrated him that his uncle had already formed his opinion in her regard. But it had not changed Perry's own feelings for Marianne. Knowing she might be incapable of placing her best foot forward at all times due to shyness or pure maladroit touched a tender chord in him and made him want to defend her. She had been on the outskirts of society for too long.

When the dinner hour came, Marianne presented herself in the room adjacent to the dining room, wearing the same dress she had worn when they first met. It was the faded gown with blue trim, which he thought suited her, but one glance at his uncle let him know that he did not feel the same way. It was not the first stare of fashion—far from it. It was not even the second stare of Cliff's End.

He quickly strode over and held out his hand so he could bow over hers. His uncle would learn that he esteemed her despite the warnings. As he did so, he faced away from his uncle, who was most likely frowning, but was rewarded with a smile from Marianne.

"Shall we go in?"

He turned when he heard a commotion in the hallway, which proved to be Miss Fife being carried in a chair between Charlie and Albinus. *Ah, yes.* He had conveniently forgotten about Marianne's companion. At least this should prove that everything was aboveboard with her staying at Brindale. The introductions were made, and they followed Miss Fife's chair into the dining room.

When the first course had been served, his uncle led the conversation. "So you've grown up at Brindale, Miss Edgewood." It was a statement, not a question.

"Yes, my lord," she replied. She was back to eating like a bird. No wonder she was so petite.

Miss Fife picked up her spoon. "Marianne's father inherited it from his godmother, and when he died, it was bequeathed to his brother. The Edgewoods were relations of mine. Second cousins, to be exact. I have always thought..."

The spinster, having launched into the conversation, continued in this strain, to Lord Steere's growing astonishment. Perry wanted to laugh. His uncle had apparently led a life sheltered from such females and could not quite credit his ears that a lady's companion should take the reins of a conversation in such a way and gallop off with it.

When there was a pause for breath, Lord Steere turned back to Marianne. "And what have you done for education?"

She opened her mouth to reply, but Miss Fife was too quick. "I have been teaching her the art of conversation, my lord, and other matters that are pertinent to the daughter of a gentleman."

She took a bite of soup, prepared to charge back in, but Lord Steere was not an innocent maiden, subject to a garrulous companion from whom she could not escape. Nor was he a young society buck who would flee from it. He glared at Miss Fife and came as close to a bellow as the dinner table would allow.

"Woman, if you speak out of turn again, I will have you bodily removed from this room and ban you from entering it again. Mind, I gave this castle to Peregrine and I can take it back again. Do not think I have to put up with your inanities."

Although the former statement was not precisely true— Perry hoped—he had to admire the deft way his uncle had dealt with her. Miss Fife turned red, opened and shut her mouth a couple of times, then set her spoon down, her brows almost meeting in the center of her forehead. Lord Steere turned back to Marianne.

"I asked about your education. I have yet to hear your reply."

Marianne glanced at Miss Fife. "I have had little education as a lady, my lord." She stopped when Miss Fife gave an angry huff. "I am well read, and I am a woman of honor. Those are my qualifications."

"Sewing? Dancing?" Lord Steere fixed her with his gaze. She shook her head. "French? Pianoforte?"

"None of those." Marianne lifted her chin, and Perry was proud of her. A woman of honor trumped all. His uncle was blinded by society's dictates.

Perry had been of the same ilk until he'd arrived at Brindale. He could not put his finger on what had changed him in the meantime. It must not be what, but rather who.

When Marianne and her companion were finished with dinner, she murmured an excuse about needing to pack her things for her return to the cottage the next day. Miss Fife bid Perry good night with great distinction, then sniffed and looked away rather than address Lord Steere. He was wholly unmoved. At Perry's command, Charlie and Albinus removed Miss Fife in a chair then brought the port and two glasses, setting one in front of each of them.

Lord Steere took out a box of snuff and helped himself to some of it before directing his gaze Perry's way. "You said Miss Edgewood was gently bred. You said she had the training of a lady."

Perry had been prepared for this. "In character, she is genteel in every way."

"Herding swine and sharing their filth?"

His uncle's irony was cutting, and it sent a rip of rebellion through Perry. He was not a religious man, but an unexpected memory of a biblical studies class at Oxford came to his rescue.

"Does Proverbs not speak of a wife"—he caught himself—"a *woman* of noble character as seeing that her trading is profitable and working from dawn until dusk? Miss Edgewood has kept Brindale running for ten years, starting from when she was a girl. And if she was herding the pig, it was because no one else is capable of doing it, and she didn't want to have one of Brindale's commodities threatened. It says such a woman is worth far more than rubies."

"Don't quote your biblical jargon to me, boy. That won't bring credit to the Steere name when you are baron one day. Tell me truthfully. Are you considering taking a foolish step in her regard?"

Perry had held his uncle's gaze, but now he broke away. "I... I don't know."

"*Hmph.*" The baron sipped at his port, then set the glass down. "At least you are honest. It is a good thing she is moving out tomorrow, as I will leave again two days hence, and you will do better without the temptation. I can't dictate what you do, much as I would like to. Just give me your word that you will not take an irrevocable step without careful consideration."

His uncle placed his hands on his waistcoat and leaned back in his chair, his eyes on Perry. "Remember how hard you've worked to get to where you are."

Perry nodded, not ready to give any promises. Fortunately, Lord Steere was in the mood for talking and did not require one. "My brother did you no favors when he married your mother."

At all times, Perry was respectful toward his uncle but brooked no nonsense when it came to her. "Not a word against my mother, if you please."

The baron softened. "Very well. She turned out to be a better bargain than I had given him credit for. He was the one who ended up ruining your future for you, eating through his entire fortune save for what had been set aside for your mother. When you're caught by the pretty face of a merchant's daughter, it's not so easy to be welcomed back into society, as he soon found out. If he had but listened to me..."

Lord Steere shook his head and sipped his port. "In the end, he spent everything he had trying to regain his position among the ton."

"He would better have done to have stayed home with Mama and made peace with his life." Perry would not be moved on this. His father had been wrong, and Perry had watched his mother suffer for it.

"He wished to pave the way for you," his uncle said, equally unmoved from his position. "That is what caused him to try so hard to reintegrate in society."

Perry looked up in surprise. Could his father have had such an altruistic motive? Memories flitted back to him of his father's infrequent visits and how Perry had tried to get his father's attention to no avail. He shook his head, meeting his uncle's gaze.

"I think he did it for himself."

Perry suffered a check. *And you are like him.* Why had Perry tried so hard to insert himself into society, putting up with the rejection and derision at school with as good grace as he could muster, then accepting the dubious friendship of London society men who did not treat him with true friendship—except Raife. That had been a surprise. He was more kind than Perry would have supposed from him. However, even without this unexpected display of goodness on Raife's part, Perry had been ready to accept anything at their hands.

Never again.

The next day, Perry had Beau saddled and wasted no time in going off to see Joe about the smithy. He knew Marianne would be pleased when she found out and suspected she would be even more so than she had been with the apiary. He hoped to be back in time to oversee her move into the cottage.

He found Joe sitting outside of the smithy, his shoulders slumped and his arms over his knees. When he saw Perry, he leapt to his feet and bowed.

"Mr. Osborne, what can I do for ye?"

Perry stepped forward and looked around for the two children he remembered from his visit with Marianne. Not knowing exactly how to broach the idea he had in mind, he asked, "Where are your children?"

Joe's shoulders dropped again. "My little Beth is out of sorts. Ant'ony is caring for her, but he's a mite small for the task."

"It's not easy raising them on your own," Perry observed. "Where is your house situated?"

"About a quarter of a mile from here, which is why I keep 'em about the smithy whilst I work. I keep a better eye on 'em that way." Joe straightened himself with the will of a man used to difficulties in life. "But ye did not come here to talk about my children. How may I serve ye?"

Perry nodded, figuring it was better to plunge right in. "I'd like you to come and open up the smithy that's been sitting unused at Brindale. I believe you'll find the forge in good working order, though I'm a poor judge of such things. There is a house next to it which is yours if you want it, though it will need a little work. But I believe it can be put in good order.

There are no tools, but I assume you have what you need? I think you'll find the rent reasonable."

Joe's eyes widened in astonishment. Then almost immediately, they grew hooded as a sense of despair seemed to overtake him. "That sounds grandly, but I cannot accept. I owe Art Reacher too much money, and he 'ull claim it if I leave. I've 'naink set by."

"How much do you owe?" Perry asked.

"Five guineas." Joe shook his head at the impossibility of the amount. "I 'us to pay off a guinea a year, but I cannot—not with how little I earn."

"I'll advance you the sum," Perry said without giving it a thought. "If you think you might attract customers this far outside of Cliff's End, then you should be able to pay me back without too much of a problem. You'll be working for yourself and not on slave's wages for Art Reacher."

"Ha!" Joe let out a huff of air in a dry laugh. "As for customers, it's been s'long Art's worked at the smithy, most 'ull stay loyal to me."

He dropped his hands at his side, perhaps stunned by his windfall, then exhaled loudly as he raised his eyes to Perry. "Sir, I can scarce believe my luck. I accept, and I'm right grateful."

Perry grinned, happy to be the bearer of good tidings and delighted at the idea of surprising Marianne. He would let her discover Joe's new position herself.

"I'll have Mr. Mercy come by to see you today if he can. He'll arrange for the loan to be paid off and for the rent of the cottage and the smithy. Like I said, I think you'll find the terms reasonable." He gave a nod and left Joe, finding that his step had a certain extra lightness to it.

Perry directed Beau back to Brindale, deciding as he entered the castle grounds that he would go to the cottage first to make sure that nothing was out of place. If Marianne was to move in today, he wanted to be sure there was no danger. Nothing that could cause her concern. As he rode through the opening in the trees, a gentleman stood at the door who turned at the sound of Perry's arrival. Robert Vernon.

"Osborne," Vernon said by way of greeting. "It appears Marianne has not moved in yet. I expected to find her here."

"She's still at the castle. She'll be moving in today." Perry looked up, examining the shutters of the house. "I came by with the intention of going around the house to make sure there was nothing amiss. I don't want her to suffer any worries once she moves back in."

"Mighty solicitous of you," Vernon replied. "It is my opinion that she should not be living here alone, and my mother shares the sentiment. On the grounds of our long-standing connection, we invited her to live with us, but she refused." He shook his head. "I cannot understand her refusal after what happened here."

Perry did not share his disappointment. He could only feel relief that he would not have to go to Vernon's house to exchange a few words with her.

"We can hardly force her to accept something she does not wish to do. She is of age, or very nearly will be. Besides, I have arranged for her to have a footman, which is why she will be able to move in today. She will not be unprotected."

"Marianne may well be reaching her majority, but she's an innocent. It is my object to have her reconsider what she's about. Perhaps I will help her move her things."

"I don't think that will be necessary," Perry said, then paused, not wishing to be too transparent. In truth, he'd rather not have Vernon around today so he could have her to himself. "None of her furniture has been taken back to the castle, so there will only be her trunk."

He tied Beau to the iron ring attached to the wall and tipped his hat. "I will just have a look around the property."

Nothing had been disturbed that Perry could see, and when he rounded the cottage, Vernon was no longer there. He hoped he wouldn't come back, but Vernon had not exactly promised he wouldn't. Meeting with the man unexpectedly only fueled a desire to see Marianne. Perry didn't like the idea of men hanging about her. There was a fragile side to her, and he didn't want her to give in too easily to Vernon's pressure. As soon as he returned from the cottage, he went straight to her room and knocked on the door.

She opened it at once and smiled at the sight of him. "Good day, Mr. Osborne."

"Please, call me Perry," he insisted. He had told her she could and there should be no objection. After all, she called Vernon "Robert" and he wasn't about to take second place to him.

She dipped her head, averting her eyes. "Very well, Perry."

He looked past her into the room. "You are preparing your trunk, I see. I will help you bring it over as soon as you are ready. Have you met your new footman?"

She nodded. "It was excessively kind of you to hire one for me. Mr. Mercy brought Jack to meet me this morning, and he is running errands for Sarah in the village until it is time for us to leave."

"You may ask me for anything you like, Marianne. If it is in my power, I will assist you."

He held out his hand and saw a look of hesitation before she placed her own in his. Hers was warm and tiny, and at its touch his heart began to pulse a steady rhythm. How he wanted to do so much more for her. Everything. He lifted her hand up to his lips and pressed a kiss on it, breathing in her fresh scent.

She didn't speak, but he saw its effect in the way her breath quivered. On his right, the door to the room where his uncle was staying opened, and Lord Steere stepped into the corridor.

"Let us know as soon as you are packed." Perry's voice came out harder than he'd intended from the jolt that came from the interruption. He hoped his uncle had not seen anything that would cause him to ask questions Perry was not ready to answer.

Marianne nodded in mute response, and he turned to join his uncle as they walked down the stairs.

CHAPTER NINETEEN

After Perry had gone, Marianne stared at the hand he'd kissed. His insistence that she call him by his Christian name struck a tender chord in her heart. The only other person she called by his first name was Robert, excepting the servants. Adding another person into that circle made her realize how lonely she had been until now—how isolated.

She cradled her hand to her chest and closed her eyes, breathing in and out. His kiss touched her on another level, because she was now certain he felt something in return that went beyond words. He had lingered, raising his eyes to hers before his uncle's appearance had broken the spell and he pulled away.

Her hand tingled, and her insides were warm, causing her to smile and cover her mouth before a laugh escaped her. Here was her proof that his declaration had been true when he spoke of developing feelings for her—at least, she thought it was proof. As vulnerable and as little protected in society as she was, Marianne hoped she was reading his feelings correctly. She hoped he did not think to propose an unworthy offer, or believe she might surrender her innocence for one. Her heartbeat sped in panic at the thought. After all, he was a London gentleman, and she did not know his breed. If only there were someone to advise her!

The memory of the way he had slept outside of her room flitted through her mind. No. He had done that to keep her safe. If he'd possessed ill designs on her, he would never have made himself so uncomfortable just to protect her. He must love her. And when she examined her own feelings, she could not deny that he had penetrated the fortress of her heart, allowing her to feel something in return. How could such a thing be possible—she, who thought she would never rely on people again?

Marianne returned to packing her belongings and soon let Jack know her trunk was ready to be carried down. Her surprise upon entering Miss Fife's room and finding her companion ready, with her things packed, was soon diminished when she learned that Sarah had come to assist her. Miss Fife had not yet taken to walking again. The necessity of waiting upon her while her foot healed was inconvenient enough that Marianne was tempted to send for a doctor to rule out anything serious. She might thereby remove the excuse from her companion's lips that she was incapable of doing anything due to a twisted ankle.

Mrs. Malford sent a message through Charlie that she wished to see Marianne before she left and also promised that she would send a hearty tea tray to her mother's sitting room to partake of before she left. When Marianne entered the kitchen, Mrs. Malford waved for Annabel to come and handed her the spoon she had been using to stir the sauce bubbling in the pot.

"There ye are, Miss Marianne. I was cleaning out the stillroom when I found yer mader's dishes and tools for her perfumery and cosmetics. I wondered if ye mightn't wish to take 'em with ye." She brought Marianne over to a tightly woven basket on a table in the corner of the kitchen.

Marianne's breath hitched. It had been many years since she had discovered something new of her parents'. "Thank you," she murmured.

In silence, she looked over the pile of porcelain bowls and funnels, the wooden mortar and pestle, lifting the latter to her nose and sniffing. It still smelled like roses. How she wished she knew how her mother made such things. As she lifted a wooden plank away from the basket's woven side, the edge of a bundle of papers caught her eye. She carefully slid it out of the basket and read its contents. Her mother's neat handwriting listed:

To prepare Eau de Cologne
Essence of bergamotte, 3 oz.
Neroli, 1 1/2 drachms
Oil of rosemary, 1 drachm
Cedrat, 2 drachms
Lemons, 3 drachms
Spirit of wine, 12 lbs
Spirit of rosemary, 3 1/4 lbs
Eau de mélisse de Carmes, 2 1/4 lbs
Mix, then distill in balneum mariae, and store in a cold cellar. Used as a cosmetic, and made, with sugar, into a ratafia.

Ottar of Roses
Steep a large quantity of the petals of the rose, freed from every extraneous matter...

The page was filled with various recipes for perfumes and

cosmetics, and Marianne eagerly read the precious script of a beloved hand. It was almost as though some divine force was reminding her she was not alone. That she never had been. She looked at Mrs. Malford, who was watching her with fondness as Marianne acquainted herself with the contents of the basket. The cook had known how much this would mean to her.

"Thank you, Mrs. Malford. I will treasure this."

"I don't doubt ye will." Mrs. Malford patted her hand. "I told Sarah, ye must ask me for anything ye might need whilst yer at the cottage. We're not far."

Marianne smiled and hugged the basket to her chest. "I will have some of the tea you prepared, and then we should be going if we want the cottage made ready before nightfall."

Upon entering her mother's sitting room, Perry jumped up from the seat he had taken next to his uncle. "We were waiting for you to pour the tea. Shall I take that for you?" He reached out for the basket and she handed it to him.

She turned to Sarah, who was standing by the tea tray. "Has Miss Fife had any tea sent to her room?" She did not offer to have her companion brought to the drawing room, knowing that Miss Fife only exasperated Lord Steere.

"She has, miss." Sarah dipped a curtsy, which Marianne suspected was more for Lord Steere's benefit than hers since she herself did not require such formality. "If ye 'ull excuse me, I'll prepare a basket with what Mrs. Malford set aside for our kitchen."

Marianne nodded and sat, pouring the tea and handing a cup to Lord Steere, then another one for Perry. She served herself last.

"How came it to be that your uncle bequeathed the cottage to you?" Lord Steere reached over and filled his plate with ham, cheese, a roll, and some of the cakes that were on the tray. "Were you aware of it?"

Marianne sipped her tea, suddenly plunged into the unhappy memories of the day she had learned that the castle was no longer her home.

"I was not aware. The attorney who came to inform me of his death brought the map with the property carved out of it, which he said had been set aside for me."

"*Hm.*"

Lord Steere made no further comment, and Marianne could not discern a motive for his question or whether he was displeased. She doubted he had asked out of compassion over her having been cut out from inheriting the castle itself. She remained silent as he and Perry spoke of other matters pertaining to the estate, and even things regarding the barony that did not concern her at all. At last, Perry stood.

"Miss Edgewood, I will have the cart readied so I might bring you to the cottage." His demeanor was formal, but his clear eyes met hers with such tenderness she could not help but respond with a smile. When he left, she found Lord Steere looking at her shrewdly.

"Miss Edgewood, I hope you will know your place." His benign smile held a hint of severity that caused Marianne to look at him in surprise. He was displeased somehow.

"My place?" she asked, at a loss. The only thing she could think of was that her place was here at the castle, but surely he did not mean that.

"Your place regarding the difference in station between my nephew and yourself," he replied. "He is in line for the barony, a great estate far from Brindale and with some visibility, not only in Essex but also in London. You have grown up here, have no accomplishments and are not fit to move about the ton. You must not think that my nephew has any serious designs upon you. My preference would be that you had inherited something not on the grounds of the estate, but rather at some distance to avoid any temptation you might present. As it stands, we cannot change the facts. But you would do well not to set your sights too high."

All of the day's joys were whisked away in an instant, and Marianne set down the teacup with great caution lest he see it tremble. Her gaze fixed on her lap, she answered in a quiet voice, "I do not have my sights set too high, my lord."

At her words, Lord Steere nodded, satisfied. "I'm glad to hear it. You seem like a very nice young lady, and I'm sure you will have a fine life here with some local chap." He took a large bite of the ham, seemingly content to focus on his meal now that he had said his piece.

Marianne stood. "I am sure you will excuse me. I must see that everything is ready for my departure." Lord Steere's mouth was full, so he waved her along with his fork, and she left the room.

The disappointment wrought by Lord Steere's disapproval was a crushing thing to bear, and Marianne attempted to put it aside until she was alone and could sort through how she felt. She went upstairs into the main hall where their belongings for the cottage were placed in a pile near the open door of the front entrance.

Outside, Perry was waiting for her in the cart. She would still call him Perry because he wished it. But must he be a mere friend to her—like Robert was—and nothing more? It seemed too difficult, now that her heart was engaged, to stem the feelings that rose up. If she truly worked at quashing any sentiment other than friendship, she might be able to maintain an indifference to him in her heart. But it would take continual effort on her part and would be impossible if he showed signs of tenderness on his.

Jack and Albinus came to pick up her trunk and carried it between them as Sarah followed, holding both her and Miss Fife's belongings. Miss Fife limped to the cart, clutching Charlie's arm and was helped into the middle of the bench on the cart so that Marianne would be deprived of sitting next to Perry again. He nevertheless came and assisted her onto her seat, smiling at her with a deliberateness that spun her into doubt again. Did he not agree with his uncle on her suitability? And if he did not, could he withstand his uncle's influence?

Once settled in the cart, Marianne faced forward. What a remarkable thing it must be to have a gentleman one admired single you out—for a lady to be chosen out of all the other women in London, or even here. But she must be misunderstanding his looks and his words. She was just a green girl with no knowledge of society.

Perry flicked the reins and the cart moved forward, and after a short while they were at the cottage. Their arrival coincided with Robert's.

It appeared Marianne was to have Robert's daily visits again. She was not sure how she felt about them any longer. It was good to have a friend, but it was hard not to compare him to Perry now that she knew what it felt like to love. Her heart had never once fluttered in such a way with Robert. As Perry helped her down from the cart, his gaze was fixed on Robert and his mouth pulled down into a frown.

The servants made quick work of bringing all their belongings in as Marianne went over to greet her friend.

"You've come to see me. You haven't been coming to the castle."

"Too busy there," he said, with a glower in Perry's direction.

After a brief nod of greeting, Perry went inside and began to open the shutters in the drawing room. He was making everything welcoming inside, ensuring that all the shutters were opened and she had everything she needed. She wished she could be with him talking as he performed these actions.

"I must say, I'm glad you're no longer living in the castle. It was not right, as I've told you. Not while single gentlemen were in residence there." Robert tugged her hand, pulling her attention back to him.

"Not this again, Robert—please. The castle has always been my home. I cannot think of it the same way you do. Everything was properly done in the eyes of society, even if"—she glanced over at the cart and saw that Jack had already helped Miss Fife into the house—"even if Miss Fife is not much of a companion. But you should trust my integrity, if nothing else."

"I do, but you don't know what it's like to be overpowered by a gentleman. You're an innocent." His gaze was intent upon her as though he wished to give her a sample of such a thing.

Marianne glanced toward the house. "Mr. Osborne would never do that. You don't know him."

Robert stepped closer, and it made her long to move back. His presence had never intimidated her in the past, but even before the dance, he had taken to stepping close to her while facing her, which felt too intimate. His breath had the remnants of lunch on it.

"You don't know him either, Marianne. It's time you think about moving to Grinnell again before you get too settled in here. And there's the foal we can look after—"

"Robert." Marianne spoke in a sharp voice—stronger than she ever had before—and set her shoulders squarely in front of him. "You must not speak to me about this again, not if you want us to remain friends. I want to make my home here. I will not be persuaded to change my mind by your words."

He glared at her, and she saw the disappointment, the hurt

—and it was the look of hurt that softened her. She placed her hand on his arm.

"Forgive me. I know you want what's best for me. You must give me the space to make my own way. We've long been friends, have we not? I don't want to lose that."

Robert shifted to the side and fixed his regard on some distant spot. "I see I have been pressuring you too much, and it's had the reverse effect. I will give you the space you ask for. In fact, I won't come for a while. Perhaps then you'll remember what a good friend I am and reconsider what it means to have me in your life."

Marianne still had her hand on his arm, as though to soften her blow, but his words made her give a soft, pleading laugh.

"Don't stay away too long, I beg you. I am only asking you to be my friend without there being the condition attached to it that I remove to Grinnell. Can you do that?"

He glanced at her, still turned away, his arms folded as though pouting. "Very well. I think I will not stay any longer just now."

Then, in one swift movement, he turned and leaned down and gave her a kiss on her cheek, right close to her lips. Her mouth dropped open, and she darted a glance at him in time to see a dull flush on his cheeks.

"Good day, Marianne."

Still stunned, she watched him go over to his horse and climb up. It had been awkward, and a little endearing, for she had known Robert her whole life; it was not his habit to show affection. But it had been enough to convince her, if she had needed such a thing, that she would never return his regard in the way he hoped. She could only wish that he find someone who would.

By the time she had reached the cottage interior, Perry had opened all of the shutters and was in the process of picking up the broken pieces of glass still lying on the floor of the sitting room. He glanced at her quickly, then looked down again.

"I regret that I did not think to have the glass repaired before today. I'll see that the window is covered until I can find a glazier to do so."

She hesitated on the threshold of the room as Sarah entered and set down a small pile of books she knew Marianne would like to read. She left again quickly, and Marianne studied Perry's face. He didn't meet her gaze, and his voice sounded stiff to her sensitive ears.

"Mr. Osborne, what is it?" She no longer dared use his Christian name, not when he was glowering at her like that.

He looked up and quirked an eyebrow at her. "Mr. Osborne, is it now?"

"Well, I hardly dare…" When he merely stared at her and said nothing, she attempted to explain. "When you look at me like that."

"Like what?"

"Like you're displeased with me."

"Ah." Perry dropped his gaze to the stack of broken glass in his hand and got to his feet, setting the pile on a nearby table. "I'm not displeased with you. I'm displeased when I see Vernon kissing you." He placed his feet apart and folded his arms. "Do you welcome his kisses?"

Marianne's eyes widened. Could it be that he was jealous? Oh, if only that were true! A warmth settled in her breast, and it made her smile, which she tried unsuccessfully to hide. Perry glared at her.

"I'm glad you find something to smile about."

Still giddy, she laughed and shook her head. "I don't welcome his kisses." She was rewarded by a glimpse of his lightened brow. He stared at the floor, the corner of his lips tilting in a smile, before lifting his gaze to hers.

"I am happy to hear it."

Their eyes held for a moment before Jack came into the room, carrying a blanket, which he set on the armchair Miss Fife tended to use. He went back out of the room and returned shortly supporting Miss Fife on one arm.

Perry came and stood beside Marianne. "Jack, after you've settled Miss Fife, see to it that the broken windowpane is covered, will you?" He was nearly as close as Robert had been, but she found she did not want to escape from his presence.

"I must take my leave," Perry said to her. "My uncle is only staying until tomorrow, and I should not abandon him to his solitude for too long."

"I understand." She peeked at him, then lowered her gaze, her heart still light at the thought of his being jealous of Robert. He needn't be.

"Thank you for your assistance."

He hesitated as though he wished to say something else, or stay longer, but he simply bowed and took his leave. Marianne remained frozen for a minute, prey to a whirlwind of emotions. She feared that despite Lord Steere's warning, the feelings she had developed would not be quite so easy to dismiss simply because a stranger had ordered it. And what was she to do about such a thing?

In an hour, the house was restored to order with the only visible change from before being the cloth on the windowpane. Miss Fife declared that she would have a rest, and Marianne took out the basket with her mother's things, prepared to go through them again when a knock came on the door. Jack went to answer it.

"Miss, there is a Miss Belford here to see you." Jack reappeared at the entrance to the doorway, and in a moment, Miss Belford and her maid came into view.

Marianne stood. "Thank you. Please show Miss Belford's maid to the kitchen and ask Sarah to prepare tea for us."

She went over to Miss Belford and curtsied. "You have missed Mr. Osborne, who was here helping me to settle in. He left not long ago." She wasn't entirely sure why she brought him up if it wasn't simply to test Miss Belford's motivations for coming.

"How kind of you to invite me in," Miss Belford said. She waited for Marianne to invite her to sit.

Marianne, who was regretting her choice to wear one of her oldest gowns on the day of Miss Belford's visit, finally came to her senses.

"Please, do have a seat. I believe the tea tray will come to us soon. As you might guess, we have only just settled in here at the cottage."

Miss Belford looked over at the broken window pane, and a crease appeared between her eyebrows. "What happened there?"

Marianne followed her gaze. "We had an unfortunate incident shortly after I moved in. There was an attempted break-in. That is what caused my companion and me to move back into the castle until we could be sure that the cottage was protected."

She was deliberate in her mention of her companion. No need to cause further risk to her reputation.

Miss Belford's brow creased with concern. "How terrifying. I am glad to hear you had somewhere safe to take shelter." She paused and, with delicacy, asked, "What makes you sure the cottage is safe to live in now?"

Marianne gave a bleak smile. "I am not entirely sure of it. But now we have our footman at least, which was something I did not have the last time. I feel safer with him here. Mr. Osborne saw to his hiring."

"He is kindness itself," Miss Belford said, and Marianne darted a glance at her. Did she have her sights set on him?

Miss Belford took a breath. "Miss Edgewood, I wished to apologize to you. I was not compassionate toward your plight at the ball."

"Oh." This was the last thing Marianne expected, and she did not know how to respond. Miss Belford went on.

"I am by no means a saint, but I don't think I'm cruel, either. I don't know why I've never made an effort to befriend you before, except that perhaps it was Mrs. Vernon's explanation of your circumstances that seemed to hint at your not being interested in local society."

Marianne frowned, wondering why Mrs. Vernon would say such a thing. "That is far from the truth. Brindale is my home, and I do care about local society. I am merely...a bit shy, I suppose. I did not dare to go to balls or assemblies." She gave a bitter smile. "And now I suppose we both know it is for the best."

Miss Belford shook her head. "This was the other reason I wished to visit. A ball or assembly is an intimidating thing when one has no female friends there in support. I am hoping you will attend another ball, as soon as we have had a chance to become better friends."

Marianne lifted her eyes to Miss Belford, surprised. "I would like that. That is...if I might have help with my wardrobe. I do not dare attempt it again without assistance. Left to my own devices, I seem to only produce disastrous results."

Miss Belford sent her a warm smile in return. "Of course. It is what I like above all things. Please then, call me Amelia. And feel free to visit Loden any time you wish. You will always be welcome there." She was seated close enough to reach out her hand in friendship, and Marianne clasped it in return.

The warmth that had lingered after her exchange with Perry only grew at this further evidence of the possibilities for friendship—for extending her heart past the walls of Brindale.

"Please call me Marianne. I should probably not confess this to you, although you likely know it already. I have never had a friend—well, except for Robert Vernon." She went pink at this admission.

"A male friend is well and good, but it cannot replace female friendship." As Sarah brought the tea tray into the room, Amelia lifted her brows and sent a warm smile. "I believe my offer of friendship has not come too soon."

CHAPTER TWENTY

It had only been two hours, but the castle seemed emptier without Marianne in it. Perry went around the estate and checked the house next to the smithy, which had been made ready for Joe Dobson's arrival. He went to inspect the apiary, from which he could now hear faint buzzing. He would ask Mr. Mercy to see to hiring someone to begin harvesting the honey.

The clay tiles arrived at last for the roof, and the steward would have them put up before more spring rains arrived. They had been fortunate in the weather. Now, Perry rounded the northern tower of the castle and came upon the pond. He must have it stocked with carp, as much for the sport as for his table. The more he could use the estate to his benefit for profit, the quicker he could bring it to self-sufficiency. The largest project, he had yet to begin, and that was the livestock. But he would do that soon enough.

His uncle was content to spend the hours looking over his correspondence and putting his accounts in place, so Perry did not need to entertain him on his last day. He went riding and gave Beau a decent run, but by nightfall he was still restless. Even the excellent dinner and his uncle's discussion of estate business over port was something to be endured rather than enjoyed. He kept thinking about Marianne by herself in the cottage—or rather, not by herself but with servants and that unpleasant Miss Fife. How could she bear the woman?

His uncle bid him good night at eleven o'clock, saying he wished to retire early to prepare for his journey the next day. Perry was glad of it, because it meant he could be left alone with his thoughts—thoughts that turned rather compulsively around the subject of Marianne Edgewood.

He told himself he merely worried that she was in some sort of danger over at the cottage. After all, that poacher or smuggler or thief, whoever he was, might have returned if he knew of her circumstances and thought her weak prey.

A half-hour of useless rumination brought him no peace, so he decided to take a walk on the estate. Slipping on his cloak, he opened the door to the fresh night air. His steps directed themselves toward the cottage as though they had a will of their own, and he told himself he was going merely to see that no one had disturbed her peace.

The estate was dark in the front, but not yet shuttered, and a flash of irritation shot through Perry. How could he protect her when she wasn't willing to close the shutters of her house? Now, he had good reason to circle the cottage and make sure no one was lurking there. From the look of it, everyone was already asleep inside, but as he rounded the corner of the house, he saw signs of life. The drawing room shutters were open as well, but this time candlelight was discernible from the inside. Not wishing to frighten whomever was in there, he crept over to the edge of the window and looked in.

Marianne was seated alone in the drawing room. A book

was on her lap, but she was looking off into the distance, her thoughts clearly elsewhere. He stood for a moment as though bewitched, his breath coming quietly in the rustling sounds of night. She did not move. What was she thinking of? Was it of him?

With Marianne so near, he fought the temptation to speak to her. It would be completely inappropriate in these circumstances and at this time of night. As the seconds ticked by, however, the desire became too strong. He was simply here to ensure her wellbeing. He would only ask her if she was all right.

He had to make his presence known but rejected the idea of knocking at the front door and waking the household, only to tell them that all was well outdoors and there was no danger. He tapped on the window softly, and thankfully her quick glance toward the sound did not show fear, but rather curiosity. When she spotted him, her face broke out into a smile, and she set her book down and hurried over to the window and opened it.

"Perry, what are you doing here?"

"I did not wish to alarm you, but I could not rest until I had taken a turn around the cottage to make sure there was nothing to disturb your peace." He paused for a moment. It was awkward conversing with her in such a way.

"May I come in?" He would not stay long.

"You may. I will go open the front door." She began to close the window, but he stopped her.

"There is no need. It will be a simple thing for me to climb in over the windowsill." He turned and pulled himself up to a seated position on the ledge and swung his legs over into the room. "I should not be in here this late, but I promise my goal was merely to ensure your safety. Is your companion still awake? Your servants?"

"No one," Marianne said. "Should I make us some tea?" Then she laughed, as though it had just occurred to her that serving tea to a gentleman caller at midnight might not be quite the thing.

She did not show any consciousness of their being alone together. He was not sure if it was from naïveté or because she was so comfortable in his presence that she knew she need not fear anything from him. He hoped she knew it.

Perry shook his head, glancing at the empty teacup on the table by her side. "I do not require tea, and it looks as though you've just had some. I came... Well, the clay tiles for the roof should be coming any day now, and I wanted to tell you about the hives, too. I've started to hear the bees moving there." He was blathering on.

She gestured back toward her own chair and the one next to it. "Well, do sit then and tell me."

Marianne cleared the book off the chair next to hers. He sat, reasoning that it would do no good to sit farther away to maintain a proper distance, only to have to shout to be heard and thereby wake the household. The obvious solution was to sit at an intimate distance and speak in quiet tones. As they settled in next to one another, he was struck by how natural such a thing felt—as though he had always spent quiet evenings at Marianne's side, discussing the day's events.

"Have you noticed the new hives at the apiary yet? I asked Mr. Mercy to find me someone who can begin harvesting the honey and looking for ways to sell it." Perry leaned toward her, his elbow on the armrest.

"What excellent news that Brindale is to have honey again. I'm sure my father would be so pleased. You've brought good changes to the castle, Perry." She lifted her bright blue eyes to him and smiled with approval—the reaction he had been hoping for.

He looked away. She must not see by his fidgeting that his heart had started to tap out a faster rhythm. If she noticed that, she might see the longing in his eyes. And if she responded to his longing with even the least bit of encouragement, he was afraid he might not be able to continue keeping a gentlemanly distance. And honorable intentions were at the forefront of his mind for this impromptu call.

"Well," he said, dropping his gaze to his feet as the corners of his mouth turned up. When he had mastered the wave of desire that had come over him, he looked up at her. "And you will soon see fresh tiles put on the roof in the northern corner. Honestly, the whole of the roof should be redone and the affected walls replastered, but I must see to the urgent needs of the castle first."

"I understand. I always felt like I was weighing what was most necessary when I was mistress of the castle. It was not an easy task." Marianne sighed, and clasped her hands in her lap. "I cannot claim to be happy with my uncle's decision, but the cottage is far easier to manage than the castle was."

The fire popped, setting Perry's pulse racing. At first, he feared it was a gunshot. Marianne also jerked at the sound, sending her teacup crashing to the floor.

She shot to her feet before bending to pick up the broken pieces. "How clumsy of me." Perry bent down at her side to help her retrieve the broken porcelain, his head nearly touching that of Marianne's.

"*Ouch.*" Marianne pulled her hand away and stared at her finger, which now had a thin cut that was starting to bead with drops of blood.

"Here, give me those," Perry said. He took the broken porcelain from her hand and set it gently on the table. Then he helped her to rise, cradling her hand in his to examine the cut. Pulling his handkerchief out of his pocket, he wrapped it around her finger, then gave her the excess cloth to hold. They were facing each other and standing closer than they'd ever been. It was suddenly hard to pull away.

His breath became a little unsteady when he looked into her eyes and found her gazing back. Her lips parted, and she did not pull her hands away from him.

They stilled, neither moving, as the room grew warm and a mild buzzing in Perry's ears blocked out all sounds. He should leave. It was folly to remain here. What had prompted him to enter her sitting room at midnight? He tried to hold on to the threads of proper decorum, but then she drew a breath, lifting her collarbones, and she swayed into him. His rationale for leaving fled, and he cleared his voice to make sure he could still speak.

"All day, I couldn't help but wonder—" He lifted his hand that was not holding on to hers and twirled the piece of hair in his finger that had fallen next to her cheek. "I cannot help but wonder, Marianne, if you would welcome *my* kisses."

She leaned even closer, her eyes closing as his fingers moved to her face. Her cheek was of a softness he had never known, and he didn't think he could pull away if he tried.

"I would." It came out as no more than a whisper.

Needing no further encouragement, Perry bent his head down, the difference in their height helped by the way she lifted up on tiptoe and tilted her face to his. He pulled his other hand away and framed her face with both hands, touching his lips to hers. Her lips were heavenly soft, and they parted at his touch.

His heart beat so loudly he could hear nothing but the roaring in his ears. At first, he was conscious only of the sensation that came from their kiss. Then, Marianne placed her hands timidly on his arms. And just when the longing grew to feel her arms around his waist, she leaned into him more fully.

Every thought fled in the wake of sensations that had long lain dormant. Perry lost all reason, all control. With a sound deep in his throat, he slid his hands from her face and put them around her back and pulled her to him, cutting all distance between them.

Upstairs, the sound of a door opening shattered the thick fog around his consciousness, and Perry pulled away, breathing hard. He looked at Marianne, alarmed—the delightful sensations from a moment ago turning into the sinking feeling of having behaved without honor toward a woman who deserved so much more.

Her eyes opened slowly, and she blinked. She didn't seem to realize the precarious situation he had put her in—she merely looked dazed.

"Marianne, I must go."

She blinked again as though to clear her head and licked her lips, causing a pang to cut right through him. "I should not be here. This was most foolish of me. I beg you will forgive me."

Her smile was as soft as her words. "There is nothing to forgive, Perry."

She was more gracious than he had deserved. He seized her hand, knowing he must flee before someone appeared, although he had not heard anyone descend the stairs. "You must trust me. I will not dishonor you again."

Perry bent down and kissed her hand, then climbed back over the window. "Fasten the shutters securely," he ordered. She nodded, and he dropped to the ground, heading toward the castle as the sounds of closing windows and shutters behind him reached his ears.

As he walked back, the cool night air further brought him to his senses—of which he had completely taken leave the moment he asked to enter her drawing room.

His boots crunched on the path and the occasional twig, as his heart both relived the delicious feel of her lips and the horror of what might have happened had the kiss not been interrupted. He most certainly must never do such a thing again—he could not. He would make sure of it.

CHAPTER TWENTY-ONE

When Marianne had finished closing the shutters and windows, she went over to the broken porcelain and picked up a remaining piece from the floor and set it next to the others. Then she sat and brought her hand, still wrapped in Perry's handkerchief, to her cheek.

The door opened and Sarah stepped in. "Miss, yer still awake. Oh, that's what I heard, annit? Ye've dropped your cup."

"I did indeed. I am sorry to have woken you up." Marianne feared she looked differently, and she soon had her answer.

"Yer flushed, miss. Are ye feeling ill?" Sarah had gone over to retrieve the pieces and paused with the broken porcelain in her hand, studying Marianne's face with concern.

Marianne had a sudden desire to tell Sarah everything—that Mr. Osborne had kissed her and that she loved him, and that she might be getting married after all. She stared at the maid for an instant, unable to respond. But a split second's reflection caused her to reject the idea. They were not friends, as much as she almost felt they were. They were servant and mistress, and Sarah had no obligation to remain loyal to her should life take her on a different path.

Marianne shook her head. "I think it was merely from the night air when I closed the windows. Please do not worry about me. I am ready for bed now, and I hope you will return to bed as well." She stood and looked at the fire, which had died down to embers.

Sarah nodded, seemingly ready to accept her words. "I 'ull jest bring this to the kitchen then. G'night, miss."

Marianne climbed the stairs to her room and undressed for bed, where she spent a long time turning in the dark, reliving Perry's hands on her cheek, his strong arms pulling her close as though she were the most treasured thing in his existence. She relived the feeling of his lips on hers—*oh heavens*. Just the memory brought heat to her cheeks. She could not believe that he liked her well enough to want to kiss her. Since her parents had died, she had never once known what it was to be the focus of someone's attention—the apple of someone's eye. And now she was his.

The next morning, Marianne woke early and breakfasted, ready for the day. She wanted to be prepared for when Perry would return to see her. He had said he would not make the same mistake again. Did that mean he was preparing to ask for her hand in marriage? In recent days, she had increasingly hoped he might indeed have feelings for her, but could not be sure, even with the assurance of his words and gestures. After last night, Marianne was now certain of his regard for her. Surely he would come to see her, now that they had shared an embrace. She wondered if he would look at her in that special way again and perhaps this time, talk of love.

When he did not come by noon, her heart beat with impatience. He must have been occupied with estate business. Perhaps Mr. Mercy had come by. Perhaps he was even now at the apiary with the man who would harvest the honey. She had to go and see.

"Sarah, I am going for a walk," she called out when she reached the kitchen.

"Yes, miss. My cousin 'ull be by this afternoon to clean the chimneys. Jack and I 'ull see that everything be done proper."

"Thank you." Marianne tied her bonnet, anxious to leave before Miss Fife made a reappearance. It had taken all her patience to sit and have breakfast with her and make stilted small talk, when all she wanted was to be left alone with her thoughts.

At the apiary, she saw the evidence of healthy beehives, and the humming sound reminded her of happy days with her father. Perry's investment in the castle and estate only made her heart grow more tender toward him.

Perry was not to be found there, nor was Mr. Mercy. She put her hands on her hips, chewing her lip, before deciding to visit the stables. Perhaps she would meet him there—at least, she hoped. She did not dare to go directly to the castle. The transition had been a subtle one, but it no longer felt like hers. Marianne had not quite reached the stables when she heard someone calling her.

"Miss!"

The blacksmith, Joe Dobson, set down a crate and walked over to greet her. His face was lit with a hopeful expression that transformed his features. He had also entered farther into the estate than he ever had before, beyond even the stables.

"Joe," she said in surprise. "I am very glad to see you, but... What are you doing here?"

"Mr. Osborne didn't tell ye?" Joe folded his arms with a broad smile. "He's leased out his smithy for me to work on me own terms. And he loaned me the money to pay off Art. We're to live in the house attached to the smithy."

"Why, that is wonderful!" Tears sprang to Marianne's eyes at such unexpected, yet good news—such proof of Perry's goodness. "How clever of Mr. Osborne to come up with a solution. Why did I never look upon the forge here as something that could be opened up again and put to good use? Are the children here?"

"They 'ull be along later today. Mrs. Wilmington is watching 'em whilst I move our things." He rubbed his hands and looked around. "Is Sarah staying with ye, miss? I wished to thank her for the soup she made. I haven't tasted 'aink quite so good in a long time."

"She's at the cottage right now. That is where we live, and if you follow the path there eastward, you can't miss it. I'm sure Sarah will be happy to know you've found such a good situation for yourself." She glanced at the small house where he'd be staying and saw signs of change. "I'll come by when Beth and Anthony are here to welcome them to the estate."

"They 'ud be mighty glad of it, miss." Joe bowed and went over to retrieve the crate he had been carrying. There was a spring in his step she had not seen since before he had lost his wife, and it had been enough years that she almost did not remember it at all.

Heart light, Marianne decided to put off all excuses and go to the castle to see Perry there. He was such a good man. Surely he would not be shocked by her visiting? She had to trust he would not.

At the door to the castle, Marianne hesitated, wondering whether she should knock or go directly in. With a nervous intake of breath, she decided to knock. After a minute the door opened, and Charlie stared at her in surprise before grinning.

"Come in, miss. Never did I think to see the day when ye'd be knocking at yer own castle."

She smiled at him. "Good day, Charlie. I've come to see if

Mr. Osborne is receiving." She untied her bonnet and turned to go into the drawing room.

"Mr. Osborne left Brindale this morning, miss." He took her bonnet from her. "Shall I inform Lord Steere that ye've come? He's not gone yet."

Marianne drew her brows together and turned slowly to face Charlie. "Mr. Osborne has left? Do you mean he has ridden to the village? Perhaps I should come back later."

"No, miss." Charlie punctuated his words with the shake of his head. "He's left Brindale. Said not to expect him for a week or more."

Marianne swallowed, her throat suddenly dry. "Did he... did he leave word for me?"

"Ah, yes, miss. How stupid of me to forget." Charlie handed her a sealed letter. "I was to bring this to ye today."

Marianne broke open the seal, turning away from Charlie so she could read the words in private.

Dear Marianne—

Forgive me for this short letter, but I am writing it in haste. I have decided that I must leave Brindale without delay. I have not behaved properly toward you, and I feel I must go away for a time so I can set all to rights.

Yours,

Perry

Charlie waited, but Marianne was incapable of saying anything further. She looked up blindly, her gaze fixed on the dark staircase that was familiar to her but no longer home. He did not behave properly... Did that mean he regretted their kisses? He was going away to set all to rights? What did he mean by that?

"Shall I inform Lord Steere of your arrival?" Charlie asked again.

That shook Marianne out of her stupor. "No. There is no need to disturb his lordship."

She drew a breath and turned toward the door. After the previous discussion they'd had before she left for the cottage, a conversation with him was the last thing she wanted. The sound of the door to the library opening informed her that it was too late for her to leave unnoticed.

"Miss Edgewood." Lord Steere waved toward the drawing room. "Please. Come sit with me so we might have a few words. I will be leaving Brindale shortly."

Although Marianne could think of nothing they could have to say to one another, neither could she think of anything in the way of excuses. She nodded and followed him numbly into the drawing room. She still could not fathom that Perry had left Brindale without coming to see her after what they had shared. He must be going for some good purpose. She hadn't thought him the type to kiss her if he did not have any serious intentions toward her, but now she could no longer be sure.

"You came to see Peregrine, I am guessing." Lord Steere gestured for her to sit, then took the armchair across from her.

Marianne wanted to dissemble—after all, it was none of his business—but her brain was not sharp enough to do so. "I did."

"Well, you must know that he has left Brindale for some time. He surprised me when he informed me of it this morning, for it was not planned. But since I am leaving myself, he did not fear I would suffer an inconvenience by it. I must own that I am gratified he has heeded my wishes concerning his future."

He paused to look at Marianne and did not seem put out when she kept her lips firmly closed.

"When he returns to London, as I encouraged him to do, he will see that there are women more suitable to fill the position of wife to a future baron. And I think you will agree with me as well, when you find a local gentleman farmer who will not cause you to suffer any discomfort by having to perform in high society. Trust me when I say you will thank me for it when the day comes."

Marianne stood. "You have made your position clear, my lord. Good day."

Lord Steere looked up in surprise, his brows drawn together. He swiveled in his chair to face her. "Ah, you're going, then? I would like a tea tray sent. Have the goodness to order one, would you?"

She didn't bother to answer as she turned to leave. He would soon discover that no tea tray had been ordered and would have to bestir himself.

The sun streamed bright through the honeycomb panes of the window, giving the drawing room more cheer than usual. Was it her father's playful presence trying to pierce the spirit of misery that had enveloped her? She had trouble believing it so. One outgrew such fancies, she supposed.

Marianne exited into the hall, hoping she could hide the sinking of her heart from the servants who knew her too well. She forced her shaking limbs to move toward the exit, when she stopped suddenly, struck by a realization. The baron might take his frustration out on the servants if he did not receive a tray of tea, and she did not want them to suffer from her fit of pique.

In the kitchen, Mrs. Malford was kneading pastry dough, but one look at Marianne caused her to stop and wipe her hands on the kitchen towel. "Miss Marianne, what is it?"

Marianne attempted a smile and shook her head. "Lord Steere has asked for tea. Can you send Annabel up to pour it? I, myself, cannot stay."

Mrs. Malford studied her face for a moment. "Mr. Osborne has left the castle for a time. I believe ye know it?"

Marianne nodded. "Charlie told me."

"Before he left this morning, he came into the kitchen and said that ye are to view the castle as quite yer own in his absence."

Marianne raised her eyes to Mrs. Malford, her heart a degree lighter for the first time since she had heard the news. He would not have said that if he didn't have consideration for her, would he? The lift of encouragement brought her lips up in a smile.

"Thank you, Mrs. Malford. I will visit the castle as he suggested, then. Perhaps I can be of some use to him."

CHAPTER TWENTY-TWO

The next two days moved at a slower pace than Marianne had thought possible. Any progress she determined to make in the cottage or garden never seemed to come to fruition. She found herself sitting and staring off into the distance, unable to find the motivation to do anything.

Sarah proved worth her weight in gold as she carried on her tasks without complaint of the little help she had. The maid directed her cousin to see the chimneys swept, and Marianne was relieved to see the kind way in which he spoke to the climbing boy he had brought with him. The process took only one day, and Marianne sent him to Mr. Mercy for payment. The steward had promised to act for her in estate business.

She also had the satisfaction of witnessing Joe's first visit to the cottage, and his first encounter with Sarah. Marianne was sitting on a bench in the hall, trimming the wicks on new candles, and she could see the front entranceway through the narrow glass panes on either side of the door. Sarah was the one to answer his knock, and she stepped outside to talk to him. Marianne saw her duck her head shyly as Joe likely thanked her for the soup she had brought him. They spoke for long enough that Marianne was convinced of his interest in the maid. It would not be long before he saw Sarah's potential as a spouse, and her worth, both for his sake and for his children.

For Marianne, it would mean she would have to separate from Sarah, who was irreplaceable. But what kind of friend would she be if she denied Sarah—and Joe—the happiness they deserved? Indeed, if Sarah were no longer under her employ, they could perhaps be friends.

"You should speak to your maid," Miss Fife said, as she limped by Marianne, leaning heavily on her cane on her way to the sitting room. She stopped and stared at the front door, then returned her gaze to Marianne.

"If a common serving girl thinks she can stand outside talking to men who come calling and have flirts as though she were the lady of the house, she will be good for nothing. You must nip that in the bud now."

That was one of the drawbacks to sitting in plain view. She had to endure Miss Fife's distempered comments, which had become constant since the spinster had been forced from the comfort of the castle.

"I don't plan to say anything to her. And I will take it kindly if you would not either. Sarah is being kind to Joe, who is a widower with two children. The world could use a bit more kindness." She looked pointedly at Miss Fife, who did not appear cowed by the unspoken rebuke.

Marianne fell silent again. For the hundredth time, she wondered what Perry was doing and why he had left. She had yet to take him up on his offer to treat the castle as her own and wasn't sure why. Perhaps she was afraid the castle would seem empty without him and did not wish to go back to it and feel his loss.

The memory of his kiss had dulled with time and with his departure. There was little in the way of hope or excitement to keep the memory burning brightly. Not only did she not know when he would return, a nagging internal argument persisted that he did not feel for her the same way she did for him. There was enough evidence to the contrary, but she had become used to steeling herself against disappointment.

"You are sitting there idle. You should be up doing something." Miss Fife had not budged from her place, bringing Marianne back to her surroundings. The oppressive atmosphere became too much for Marianne, and she stood.

"I have been meaning to visit Robert. I may as well do so now." It was not ideal after the way they had left things, but perhaps Robert was ready to come to his senses and treat her as he had before when he'd been a mere friend.

"He should be Mr. Vernon to you unless you have an understanding. You are too old to be calling unrelated gentlemen by their Christian names who are not your husband." Miss Fife sniffed and limped forward again, headed for the sitting room.

"You are probably right," Marianne said in a tone of indifference. She went over to pluck her bonnet from where she had tossed it and began to tie it on. Perhaps Mr. Mercy would help her find a different companion as soon as she came of age.

Miss Fife *was* right, she supposed. If she called Robert by his proper name, he might think twice about pressuring her into marriage. But it was too difficult a thing to change now. Funny that Robert had not attempted to visit her again, and she supposed he had taken his promise to heart to give her space. Without Perry...without a friend here at Brindale, she would have to rely on Robert for company and hope he had dropped the idea of marrying her. Besides, she could see the foal, who must be much stronger by now.

In a short while, she was directing Sweet Nips into the

stables at Grinnell. Robert was inside, and his face broke out into a grin when he saw her.

"Marianne, you've come to your senses and paid a visit at last. I didn't dare come again after you sent me packing."

This was said in a playful tone that could not give offense. It sounded much like how they were with each other before the idea of marriage had marred their relationship. He pointed into the stall and she led her mare over to peer in. Cassie was feeding from her mother, her coat glossy and her legs strong.

"Ah, she's turning into such a beauty." Marianne stood at his side companionably as Sweet Nips turned to the hay in a feeder on the stall next to them.

"Here, let me take your nag. Josiah, come unsaddle her and rub her down." Robert handed the horse's reins to his stable hand and gestured for Marianne to follow. "My mother will want to see you and have a tray of tea made up. I believe Cook has been baking this afternoon."

True to his word, Mrs. Vernon began addressing Marianne before she had fully entered the drawing room in a torrent of words that did not allow for an answer.

"Oh, my dear. I have wondered when you would come to see us. You must have been fully occupied at the cottage, turning it out proper. I hope you've been safe there. I heard about that horrid break-in, and it makes me lose sleep thinking of what might become of you. As you know, you are always welcome to come here."

She walked over to the bell pull. "I will call for tea."

Marianne smiled. "The cottage has been very quiet, and I believe with our footman, we are perfectly safe."

She took a seat at Robert's side, full of relief at being back in familiar surroundings. She had been too hard on Robert. He had only wanted what was best for her, and he would soon come to see that she was not the wife for him.

If Perry proposes marriage, he will have to reconcile himself to the idea, at any rate. The thought came suddenly, causing Marianne's heart to beat at the idea. She thought she had dampened that hope since he'd left. At least she was trying to.

The footman entered a short while later bearing a tray, laden with a wide variety of foods and sweets. Marianne helped herself when invited and spent a most agreeable hour discussing all matters of friendly local gossip, smiling and laughing more than she had in the last two days. After an hour spent in the Vernons' company, she felt a good deal better and was almost able to forget about Perry's absence and the fact that he had left without giving a clear idea as to his return.

"I'll walk you out," Robert said, after Marianne expressed she thought it time to be going back. "I can even ride back with you."

"Thank you." Marianne said, more kindly disposed toward him than she had in a while. He had been her only true friend since childhood. They had ridden together and played with hardly a cross word between them in all those years. Surely they could move past the idea of a marriage she was certain wouldn't suit either of them.

They entered the stables and Sweet Nips gave a soft whinny at the sight of her. Marianne went over and stroked her neck. "You may not be a sweet-goer, but you are a sweet thing."

"Where is Josiah?" Robert grumbled. "He is never where he's wanted. Mary, your nag is irritated on her back. Did you notice that? It must be the saddle. Go get a blanket from the storage room, will you?"

"I hadn't noticed, but thank you. I wouldn't want her to suffer." She headed away from the entrance to where the storage room was, on the aisle that led off to the adjoining carriage house.

As she advanced, she passed a wooden crate on the floor with pieces of wood, including the unused spokes of a wheel. In their midst was one more polished than the others, and it had the jagged pieces of an end that had been broken off.

She stopped, her breath suddenly cut off at the sight. She reached out, taking the stick in her hand. Near the broken bit was a polished metal band with blue decorative markings, and the other end was the foot of a cane.

"Find it?" Robert's voice reached her in the dim aisle.

Marianne returned to him slowly, carrying the cane. As she walked up to Robert and held it up for him to see, his features changed from confusion to recognition.

"What's this, Robert?"

"How should I know?" He turned back toward Sweet Nips and rubbed her nose. "Looks like a cane to me. Or it was at one time. Not much good for anything anymore."

She went directly up to him and lifted her face, so he would have to look at her fully. "Tell me this. Did you use this to break into my house?"

"Of all the harebrained things to say. Why ever would I do a thing? I can just come and knock on the front door if I want to see you." He still wouldn't look at her.

Marianne's heart was thumping violently. "You did, though, didn't you? You scared me out of my wits. Why did you do it?"

"You shouldn't be living there." The words came out in an explosion, and he turned to her, his brow lowered. "You're not meant to be setting up house when you're a chit of a girl. You should have seen that for yourself after living in a castle full of single gentlemen, but you're too stubborn."

"And so you thought you'd convince me by terrifying me?" Marianne's voice matched his now. She seethed with indignation.

"It's not so big of a deal. You're making a mountain out of a molehill." Robert left her and strode toward the storage room with Marianne trailing behind.

"It's a matter of honesty. How can I trust you about anything if instead of coming to my aid, you decide to render me more uncomfortable? You didn't even have the courtesy to find me a footman when I told you I needed one."

Robert grabbed the blanket and slid it under one arm, before going over to the bar that held the saddle which he took with both hands. He put the blanket and saddle over her horse and tightened the girth before turning to her.

"If you had come to stay with me, you wouldn't need a footman. You would have had mine. And if you agree to marry me, I will do anything you say, Marianne. I'll hire any servant you want. I'll—" He reached out to seize her hands.

Marianne yanked her hands away and grabbed the reins to lead Sweet Nips over to the joss block. "I will never marry you, Robert. You should have believed me the dozens of times I have repeated it. I will never love you."

She gave a signal to her nag, who seemed to sense her discontent and for once, moved at a faster pace than usual toward the stable exit. "And I never want to see you again."

CHAPTER TWENTY-THREE

As Marianne rode toward the cottage, she wiped tears from her face. As much as she sniffled and tried to control her emotions, she could not. They overpowered her, and despite the recent encounter with Robert, she couldn't help but blame it on Perry.

Where was he? She missed his presence in her life, and in his absence began to doubt whether the feelings he had declared for her were true. If they were, would he not have left something more concrete, more promising, in his note? Why did he have to leave at all?

Robert's betrayal only drove home how alone in the world she truly was. One thing was certain. Robert had not only been heedless of her needs, he had betrayed her thoroughly and was not welcome in her life again. She felt some loyalty to Mrs. Vernon, but considering that she would not likely be able to visit her without being importuned by Robert, she considered the relationship to be finished.

She would not wish to tell his mother what he had done—and with his father being the magistrate? His was a punishable offense. Mr. Vernon would never be able to live with his own son committing such a crime. She would not betray Robert to his parents, thereby stooping to his level. If they wanted to know what he had done to deserve her disfavor, he would have to be the one to tell them.

She had continued to keep her horse in Brindale's stables, although such a favor had not been specified in writing. What would happen should she ever be at odds with Perry? Or if he did end up renting out the castle as he had once declared he would do, would she even be allowed to use the stables? The level of doubt regarding Perry's affection for her began to creep upward again. Her doubts and hopes were in constant fluctuation where Perry was concerned. Inside the stable, Marcus helped her to unsaddle her mare, and she thanked him before leaving for the direction of the cottage.

In the drawing room, Miss Fife was sitting in her usual chair. "You've returned. It is nearly time for dinner, do you not think?"

Her voice was once again sweet and not the captious tone she had used of late. The constant movement must be hard for someone her age, and Marianne made the decision to be more gracious with her companion for whatever time they had left together.

"I will see whether Sarah has anything on hand." She paused and turned her gaze to Miss Fife. "Have you attempted to walk again without a cane to see whether your ankle is better? It seems it has been enough time for it to have healed."

"Oh, I could not possibly attempt it again. I tried to put weight on it this morning, and it was agonizing," Miss Fife replied with such emphasis Marianne decided she did not have the energy for the argument.

"I suppose we must have the doctor call, since it does not

seem your foot is healing as it should." She turned toward the door, preferring the company of Sarah in the kitchen.

The maid was humming as she stirred a soup that smelled delicious. A loaf of freshly baked bread sat on the rough wooden table. She turned when she heard Marianne come in.

"You seem happy," Marianne observed with a smile. Her spirits could not help but lift at the sight of her. "I don't suppose it has anything to do with Joe Dobson coming to Brindale? I saw the two of you outside talking for quite a while."

Sarah blushed. "Oh, miss. Do ye not mind? Joe, he..." She stopped and put her hands to her face, covering her cheeks.

Now Marianne was curious. "What? Do not tell me that Joe has made you an offer of marriage already?"

Sarah pulled her hands away. "How did ye know? 'Tis exactly what he did, and us having so little time to be acquainted, apart from the visits when I was with ye, and the times Mrs. Malford sent me to him with a basket of food. We did find it easy to talk then."

Marianne laughed. "I would not be surprised if Mrs. Malford knew what she was about when she sent you. What answer did you give Joe when he asked?"

The maid raised apprehensive eyes to her. "I said as I'd have to speak to ye first, miss, but that I should like it above all things."

Marianne smiled. "On the matter of marriage, you don't answer to me. You answer only to your own heart. And I hope you will tell him yes. Beth and Anthony need a mother, and I think Joe would be much happier to have a wife—especially if the wife is you."

Sarah lifted the corner of her apron and used it to wipe her eyes. "Well, miss, I did say as he 'ud jest have to wait if I *did* marry him until I found someone who could take good care of ye in my stead."

Marianne took Sarah's hands in hers. "No one will ever replace you. But I would be very unhappy if that should stop you from marrying him as soon as you may desire. Perhaps in the meanwhile you can continue to come during the day and work here."

The next morning dawned bright, calling for Marianne to put off her disappointments and begin turning the cottage into a well-run home. However, this lofty ambition deserted her by the time she had eaten her breakfast. Her thoughts turned continually around Perry, and she simply removed to the drawing room to indulge in them. She knew she was waiting in expectation—in hopes of hearing the sounds of a horse riding up, hoping it would be only one gentleman.

Despite the lethargy that had come over her, last night had been mostly agreeable, free from worry that they might suffer a break-in. She had been able to temper her disappointment in Robert Vernon with her happiness for Sarah. Miss Fife, she tried to avoid unless strictly necessary.

She was not entirely able to do that at the moment as Miss Fife entered the room with the help of Jack, whom she seemed to regard as her personal servant. Marianne was not convinced her foot truly bothered her, and she was resolved that Miss Fife would at least help with some of the mending of the curtains. She herself had never learned to sew but that was something Miss Fife could do if she was determined to sit there.

"You have promised to help hem and mend the curtains. May I fetch your sewing box for you?"

Miss Fife sighed. "I suppose so. You will find it on the writing table in my room, I believe."

Marianne stood, already anxious to escape from her presence. How could she bear the remaining two months until she reached her majority and could take control of her own life?

She went into her companion's bedroom, but did not see the sewing box on the small desk. There was a stack of papers on the smaller table beside the window, and without seeing anything resembling the sewing box elsewhere, she went over to it. As Marianne lifted the papers, a letter slid out, catching her eye. It was her uncle's handwriting—unmistakably his, though shakier than usual.

She slid the letter out, her breath catching. She had corresponded with her uncle for ten years. It had been regular even if it had not been frequent. The front of the letter was addressed to her, but she was sure she had never read it. The shock of it caused Marianne to turn it over and open the flap where the broken seal was to look at the date. It was days before her uncle had supposedly died. She skimmed her eyes over its contents greedily.

Dear Marianne,

I am coming to the end of my days, I fear, and I wished to take a pen to write to you before the illness makes such a thing too difficult. As you will soon learn, it is an illness that causes a wasting disease, and I have yet to see any Englishman get up from his sickbed once he has caught it. I have no expectation that I will be any different.

There is a particular matter that weighs upon my mind, and I feel I must explain it to you. I have never been a wealthy man. I believe you know this. However, I always thought I might leave something behind that would set you up in the world, and I have made investments to that end. Two months ago, my man of business made a ruinous investment with my money, along with that of several other gentlemen.

One of those gentlemen, the baron, Lord Steere, invested a significant sum upon my recommendation and encouraged others to do the same. In exchange for his bringing in other investors, I signed a promise that the original sum of his investment would be returned to him, even if the venture did not prove profitable. As you can guess, it did not. As a result, I found myself indebted to Lord Steere, and I could not allow my reputation as a gentleman to suffer—not even after my death. I hope you can understand such a thing.

This is why the baron was given the deed to your beloved castle. I have managed to carve out the cottage as your own property, with a small bit of land attached to it. Forgive me, my niece. I have not been the uncle you needed. There is a reason I am still a bachelor—I was never meant to be responsible for a child. I have written in my will that the remaining assets in my name, amounting to close to two thousand pounds, also be given to you. It will take time, perhaps up to a year, for the attorney to tie up all these loose ends, but he will contact you when he is ready.

As for your companion, Miss Fife, of whom you have spoken much over the years in something of a lament, I suspect—no, let me not dissemble—I know she is not what you have needed in your tender years, but I felt it beyond me to provide someone more suitable, especially from such a distance. It was far easier to allow her to stay in her position since your laments did not speak of outright abuse. When you are twenty-one, I am sure you will do as you see fit. You need have no obligation to her.

Here, the writing became shaky and barely legible.

My dear Marianne. I have not been a perfect uncle, but I do send you my love. I hope you will manage to find a way to remember your poor old uncle with some affection.

Yours most devotedly,
    Joseph Edgewood

Marianne's breath grew unsteady, and she dropped the letter to her side as she stared through the window, attempting to still her whirling thoughts. A sharp noise of something hitting the floor made her jump. It was Miss Fife's cane.

"I knew it when you did not return right away. You were going through my things." The spinster strode forward with more energy than Marianne had ever seen and attempted to snatch the letter from her hands.

"This is mine." Marianne put it behind her back, then pushed past the companion to leave the room. When she was at the doorway, she turned to face Miss Fife. "How could you? How could you keep this from me? Open *my* letter?"

"You have not reached your majority. It is my responsibility as your companion to judge what is best for you to read and what is not."

Marianne's heart burned in anger. Anger for all the years of loneliness, for the deceit, for the betrayal—of Robert, of her uncle she had once thought but now understood was really Miss Fife's. "You may pack your things and leave."

"You cannot live alone here. It would be scandalous!" Miss Fife screeched. "And you cannot do anything without me, for you are not yet of your majority." She moved forward, but Marianne held her ground.

"I will not live here alone. I will leave, and I will take the servants with me. You will have to cook your own food and light your own fires until I am of my majority and can call upon the magistrate to forcibly remove you for trespassing."

Marianne shook from fury and the shock of the past days'

revelations. "But there is one thing of which I am sure. I will not spend another day under the same roof as you." She spun around and quit Miss Fife's room at too rapid a pace for her to follow.

After her unfortunate encounter with Lord Steere, Marianne had held off from going to the castle out of a delicacy she could not explain to herself. It was almost as though returning when Perry was not there would in some way make it as though he had never come to Brindale in the first place. As though she had never met him or lived through the experience of being loved—of being kissed. Brindale had lost some of its allure as a secure fortress for her heart. She was coming to see that when it came to love, her heart was vulnerable wherever she went.

Now that she had to be anywhere but in Miss Fife's presence and could not go to Robert, the stones of the castle called to her. Its cavernous drawing room, filled with her father's presence, called to her. The yellow sitting room of her mother, filled with her sensible peace and organized stack of books, called to her. Mrs. Malford's motherly affection beckoned. Marianne strode out of the cottage and onto the leafy path to the castle.

Instead of knocking on the front door like a stranger, she went to the kitchen and opened the door there. She expected to see Mrs. Malford busy, preparing the day's meals, but found her instead sitting at the kitchen table, her hands folded on the rough wood in front of her.

"What is it, Mrs. Malford?" Marianne turned to see Annabel pulling dried herbs from their stalks, but the maid looked away as though she couldn't bear to meet Marianne's gaze.

"Oh, my dear." Mrs. Malford's eyes filled with tears, and

she patted the place beside her. Marianne sat, her heart filled with foreboding.

Mrs. Malford had not called her "my dear" since her parents died. After that time, she had always been careful to elevate Marianne to her proper place as a gentleman's daughter. Despite the cook's deep affection, she never allowed herself to be too familiar.

"You are frightening me." Marianne tried to laugh, but it did not come out. She swallowed the lump in her throat.

Mrs. Malford turned to Annabel and gestured for her to leave them, which the maid did at once. She then turned to Marianne.

"Forgive me for my familiarity, Miss Marianne, but I'd long suspected Mr. Osborne to have some intentions towards ye— and that ye returned his affection."

Marianne felt the heat creep up her neck onto her face. She had not realized she had been so transparent, even to the servants. Thankfully, she was not forced to confirm the cook's suspicion because Mrs. Malford spoke again, meeting Marianne's gaze with a significant one of her own.

"Mr. Osborne has not yet come back to Brindale, but he's gone and sent a butler to run things here."

Marianne could not contain her sharp intake of breath, her heart leaping at the words. If Perry had sent a butler ahead, it meant he would soon be returning for her.

"But is that not good news?" She tried to smile through her confusion. "If he has sent his butler, then it means he's planning to return to Brindale for good."

"Oh, miss. I had thought so, but the butler told me as he 'ud come to prepare for the arrival of the new Mrs. Osborne." The cook grabbed her hands and squeezed them tight. "Mr. Osborne has gone and taken a wife."

What? Marianne gaped at Mrs. Malford, unable to reply. A

piercing bolt of pain shot through her chest as the implications dawned on her. After everything Perry had said to her, he married another woman?

His uncle must have prevailed upon him to give up his suit. Or Perry had himself had a change of heart. He had left the castle's bewitchment and realized that to bind himself to such a poor specimen of a wife was folly. Even now his friends must be congratulating him on his lucky escape after witnessing her performance at the ball.

She had been imprudent to let down her guard and allow him to enter into her affections, but she would not be so naïve again.

CHAPTER TWENTY-FOUR

Marianne stumbled out of Brindale, swallowing hard to keep the tears from falling as she hurried along the path to the cottage. It was only now that she admitted to herself she had been holding on to the memory of Perry's kiss as her one last hope.

Betrayed by first Robert and then by Miss Fife—both of them, selfish—she had held out hope that Perry could be relied upon. That his love was solid and true. She had thought him good, and...that his courtship was honest and coming from a place of love. Now she was coming to realize just how naïve she truly was. Only a stupid, foolish girl would believe the false kisses of a rake.

She stopped on the path to catch her breath, leaning against the trunk of a tree and staring at the beige stones of the castle across the pond. No, she was neither stupid nor foolish to have trusted that there was good in people. If some chose only to look out for their own interests, they would have to live with themselves. It did not mean she needed to harden her own heart.

After a few minutes, a slight breeze dried the tears on her cheeks while she pondered what to do next. She could not live under the same roof as Miss Fife, who was not likely to leave unless there were no more servants to wait upon her. And she could not live in the castle while Mr. Osborne—as he must be to her now—prepared for his wife's arrival.

She blew out in a sharp exhale, then began walking again. She might not have the ready solution she could hope for, but perhaps if she stayed with Mrs. Malford in the servants' quarters while Miss Fife left the cottage, she might be able to return to her house before Mr. Osborne returned to his.

That was what she would do. Marianne continued to follow the path until she came to the clearing in the trees where the cottage came into view. She stopped, the sight of a fashionable horse and curricle parked there catching her by surprise. Its markings looked like Amelia Belford's conveyance.

As she came to this conclusion, Miss Belford herself exited the house with Miss Fife following her, the spinster moving now in the easiest way and waving her hands in excitement as her petulant voice reached Marianne. Amelia turned and smiled when she saw her.

"Amelia," Marianne said, going forward. She could never have imagined just how happy she could be to see a woman she had thought indifferent her whole life.

"Marianne!" Miss Fife addressed her in sharp tones that revealed her ignorance of Marianne's true character once she had set her mind. "I insist you come inside at once and stop running around the grounds unchaperoned. Whatever will Miss Belford think of you?"

Marianne ignored her. She would never be under that woman's thumb again. "Amelia, would you care to come inside? I beg you will forgive me for my casual way of welcoming you." She turned to Jack, who had rounded the cottage. "Jack, kindly care for Miss Belford's horse, will you?"

Amelia glanced at Miss Fife, who was hovering about, waiting to intercept them. In a smooth gesture, she wove her arm through Marianne's. "It is such a beautiful day. I thought we might take a walk about the estate if you did not mind."

"Lovely." Marianne started forward as Miss Fife sputtered behind them. Marianne rather feared she would attempt to follow and was glad she did not. There had been enough unpleasantness for one day.

They walked in silence until they were some distance from the house, and Marianne released Amelia's arm. "You have come at a most providential time. I have just dismissed my companion, but I foresee a problem in encouraging Miss Fife to leave. And I do not reach my majority until June. I suppose I fear the gossips if it is found out I am living on my own. Perhaps you might advise me."

Amelia had listened in silence. "Can you not return to Brindale Castle in the meantime? Our servants have heard that Mr. Osborne has gone away, so it should not be improper."

Marianne could not speak of what was so close to her heart and merely shook her head. "Please do not press me for details, but that is not something I can contemplate."

She attempted a smile to lighten her heavy words. Perhaps Amelia would help her to keep her mind off of Perry's new wife. She needed a distraction more than anything right now.

"Ah." Amelia looked ahead and did not attempt to reason with her. They came to the eastern edge of the pond that was created from the remnants of the moat. Ducks paddled from the reeds at the edge, leaving ripples in the water. The silence and companionship restored Marianne's heart. Then, as though she had come to a decision, Amelia smiled and turned to face her.

281

"I will invite you to come and stay with me." When she saw Marianne's surprise, then hesitation, she added, "You need not fear my parents. As much as they present an image of reserve, they will accept my sudden appearance with an unexpected guest without blinking an eye. I will merely explain that you find yourself between companions, and that I offered a space in our home until that could be sorted out."

Marianne's surprise only increased. "You would do such a thing for me? Your parents would? When I am all but a stranger?"

"Everyone is a stranger until they become a friend." Amelia smiled and glanced back in the direction of the cottage. "Here, let me support you against that dragon of a companion you have while you pack your things, and you can tell me all about her treachery as we drive away."

Marianne was tempted to slip her arm back through Amelia's but she did not dare. She was not accustomed enough to female friendship to resort to easy gestures, but some of the pain of betrayal dissipated as they turned toward the cottage.

It had taken Perry longer than planned to return to Brindale, and every extra day increased his anticipation to be back in what he had come to regard as his home. He rode in advance of the rest of his party, but only for the last leg of the journey. He wished to be alone when he arrived to make sure everything was perfect.

As he pulled in at last through the grounds of his estate, a grin came to his face, and he rode directly to the front entrance. Albinus exited the castle as he swung down from his horse, and he handed him the reins.

"See that Marcus takes care of Beau, will you? Has Dawson arrived?"

"He has, sir. I believe ye 'ull find everything to yer satisfaction." The footman bowed and led the horse away, while Perry went inside to find the butler. He did not have to go far.

"Sir." The butler greeted him with a bow from the front entrance. "I trust your travel was satisfactory. Where is Mrs. Osborne?"

"She is traveling in easy stages but will be here in another hour or two. Be sure that Mrs. Malford has a proper dinner ready to welcome her."

"Yes, sir."

Dawson continued to stand for any additional orders, while Perry hesitated, hat in hand. He soon came to a decision, "Matley will be arriving later today. As he is not here yet, see to it that hot water is brought to my room right away. There is something I must attend to."

Dawson nodded and hurried off as fast as his stateliness would allow, and Perry climbed the stairs, clutching his portmanteau in one hand. He could not visit wearing all his dirt, and there was something he needed to discuss with Marianne. He had left so precipitously; he hoped she would hear what he had to say.

Less than an hour later, Perry stood waiting in front of the cottage, his heart thumping in anticipation. Since it was on his own estate, he had come hatless, allowing his hair to dry on the way over. He smelled of soap rather than horses and was glad he had taken the time to bathe, despite how eager he was to see her again. He knocked on the front door, surprised to see that the shutters were closed, though it was in the middle of the afternoon. He suffered a most disconcerting feeling, preparing himself for bad news.

There was no answer, and just as he was about to turn to

leave, he was scared nearly witless by the sight of a grim face making its appearance in the strip of narrow glass next to the door.

Miss Fife. Then came the sound of a key turning in the lock, and he waited while she opened the door.

Miss Fife had never presented a desirable appearance, but now her hair was stringy and falling out of her cap. She trembled and threw herself upon him, weeping.

"Oh, Mr. Osborne, I have been used most ill. Marianne has gone with all the servants, leaving me to fend for myself. I have gone without fires and have bathed in cold water. I've had nothing to eat but dry bread."

Perry could not credit his ears as he disengaged himself from Miss Fife's clutches. "How is this? When did she leave?"

"It has been three days." Miss Fife groaned. "I cannot stay here another night. If you have any honor, you will allow me to come and stay at the castle before I must set off to I know not where."

"Where did she go?" he asked, ignoring Miss Fife's request. Of course, he would take care of Miss Fife, but what if something had happened to Marianne? He had to know where she had gone.

"All I can say is that she is the most duplicitous, conniving creature. I can only guess she has gone to live with that Robert Vernon. You must have noticed they were most particular friends. As her companion, I did all I could to direct her down the right path, but I believe she was bent on ruin. There was nothing I could do."

Miss Fife pulled out the handkerchief she was clutching and used it to good account, blowing her nose with a loud honk.

At Vernon's! Surely Marianne had not transferred her affection to that man! Perry had to call upon him without delay. As unpleasant—this was the only sentiment he would allow himself to contemplate as matters stood—as it would be if he found her to have had a change of heart, he needed to know now.

"I will see to it that you are put up at an inn for the night and will arrange for your transportation once you have informed me where you wish to go. Please excuse me."

Perry strode off, now deeply troubled. He had not admitted to himself how much he was thinking about their meeting and what it would feel like to have her in his arms again. He ground his teeth, imagining her giving her affection to Vernon in his absence. He went directly to the stables where he met Marcus.

"Saddle Beau for me again. I'm sorry ole boy," he said, addressing the last words to the Percheron as he patted its side.

He glanced at the groom. "I must go out again. He did not ride far enough today that he should be winded by a short journey. He's been watered and fed?"

Marcus nodded in the affirmative, and Perry swung up on the horse as soon as it was ready.

"I need you to do me a service, for I am short on time. Inform Dawson that he will have to arrange for a room at the local inn for Miss Fife, who is staying in the cottage. I will figure out what to do with her later."

Marcus nodded again, and in minutes Perry was riding in the direction of Grinnell. He had forgotten his hat, which caused a twinge of regret, when he approached the door to knock. He was not in the proper style, but he could not think of that just now.

A servant answered the door, and Perry thankfully had a card in his waistcoat to hand over. In another minute, Mrs. Vernon appeared in the hall, full of smiles.

"Mr. Osborne, you are most welcome. Please come in."

"I beg you will excuse me, ma'am, but I cannot stay. I came merely to inquire after Miss Edgewood. She is not staying at the cottage, and Miss Fife hinted that she might be here. May I see her please?" It took everything in him to inquire calmly when he wanted to storm through the house and look for her.

"Marianne!" Mrs. Vernon could not have been more surprised by his request. "Why, she is not here. I last saw her several days ago when she came for tea. Robert has not gone to see her since, and it seems there is no more communication between them. He won't tell me what happened."

Perry exhaled. He had steeled himself, preparing for the tormenting news that her heart was no longer his. He had not imagined that she might have gone missing all together. His relief at finding that she was not in the arms of Robert Vernon mingled with his fear that something had happened to her.

"Would you like to speak to Robert?" Mrs. Vernon asked.

Perry hesitated. As much as he was anxious to be off, if Vernon knew something of her disappearance, it would be better for him to learn of it.

"Yes, I would appreciate that."

"Come right this way. You may wait here, and I'll see that he comes." Mrs. Vernon showed Perry into the drawing room before bustling off as quickly as her heavy tread would allow.

Vernon stepped into the room five minutes later, his face already mistrustful. "Osborne."

Perry gave a slight bow and came right to the point. "I am searching for Miss Edgewood. She has gone from the cottage. Do you know where she is?"

Vernon studied him for a minute with a strange look, as though he'd expected something else, before shaking his head. "No. I did not know of it."

Perry's throat was dry, and his heart beat faster as the idea now seized him that some harm had befallen her. "Do you have any idea where she might have gone? Any friends or connections?"

"Marianne has no friends or connections apart from me. I cannot imagine where she has gone."

Vernon's face showed more belligerence than worry, and it made Perry want to grab him by the neckcloth and force some decency into him.

He controlled that burst of emotion as his reason took over. They would find her more quickly if they were both looking. After all, Vernon had said he was her only friend. The urgency to locate Marianne largely outweighed any dissatisfaction he might have at the thought of setting out with Vernon.

"Will you help me search for her?"

Vernon turned his face to the side, averting his gaze from meeting Perry's. "You will have to excuse me. I am busy at present and am unable to be of assistance."

Perry frowned, thunderstruck. "You have something more important to do than search for Marianne?"

"She has made her choice and is no longer my concern."

Vernon still would not look at him, and after a moment, Perry breathed out in disgust and left the room.

CHAPTER TWENTY-FIVE

Marianne had spent two days at the Belford estate without feeling like she was in the way, a fact that did not cease to amaze her. Lady Belford continually saw to her comfort, and Sir Belford included her in the conversations at the dinner table, both of them showing a much warmer side than they presented at church or public events.

Amelia was unrelentingly kind, and Marianne finally let down the walls that had always been fixed in place and accepted that she was truly a friend. If she was not entirely successful at banishing thoughts of Mr. Osborne from her mind, she did enjoy moments of true comfort.

After she had been at Loden for a few days, Amelia invited her into her bedroom after breakfast and had her sit on the bed while she opened her wardrobe and perused its contents.

"Marianne, I've been thinking. I have a gown in a very modish shade of blue, but I find that it doesn't suit me. Would you allow me to try it on you and hem it if necessary? I believe we are of a size in the waist, and it might only need to be shortened."

"That is kind of you." Marianne hesitated. "I know I am unfashionable. Until now I have not cared. I preferred to use my small independence for the needs of the castle...."

"But?" Amelia prompted with a smile.

"But I suppose paying attention to my dress is not a wasted effort. I have all of my mother's old gowns, many of which are made from very fine cloth, and all of which are carefully preserved. She was taller than me, and I think she must have been given more generous proportions in her bosom." Marianne smiled shyly. "At least, it seemed to be so from the one I wore the night of the ball."

"Well, I might be able to help you with your mother's gowns. I am terribly fond of fashion and of sewing. However" —she tapped her fingers on the door to the wardrobe before turning—"why not begin with this gown that will likely fit without much alteration? I have no sisters or female cousins to give it to, and I will not wear it again."

Amelia pulled it out and held it up in front of Marianne as she stood before the mirror. It was of a brilliant blue, unlike her own faded dress, and it had everything she had been seeing on other young ladies—the flounces, the fitted bodice, the puff sleeves with a pleated sheer blue fabric bordering the neckline. In short, it was the most beautiful thing Marianne had ever beheld, and when she tried it on, she turned to look at herself from each angle in the mirror.

"*Ooooh*," Marianne breathed out, unable to speak as she saw how the bright color and fine details brought her features to life.

"It is just as I thought," Amelia said. "A little long, but if you'll slip it off, it will take me no time at all to hem it. Shortening the length will only increase the flounces and make them more charming. After that, we must contemplate what to do about your hair."

"My hair?" Marianne repeated, laughing. She felt like she was being swept along by a tide more powerful than her.

No one had ever cared for her appearance that she could remember. At the time of her mother's death, she already knew how to comb her own hair and dress herself and was not accustomed to getting help from the maids.

"Yes, Marianne. Your hair." Amelia sat down with the dress in her hands before licking the end of a thread and poking it through the eye of a needle.

"You have the most beautiful brown hair, and I thought perhaps if there were some curls instead of plaits, and maybe..." She reached over to the table next to her where a pair of scissors sat and held them up with a snip-snip motion. "Maybe you will let me make just one little cut on each side so we can add curls there too?"

Marianne threw up her hands and laughed some more. "I am in your hands. The truth is, I have always wished to do something different with my hair, but did not have anyone to ask."

"Then let us get to work," Amelia said, bending down over the dress.

Two hours later, they went downstairs, Marianne dressed, for the first time, in elegance from her head to the bottom of her hem. She still wore her old half-boots as Amelia did not wear the same size shoe, but those were barely visible. She entered the drawing room where both Sir and Lady Belford sat, and their exclamations of approval caused Marianne to duck her head with pleasure.

When she had first arrived, after having overcome her initial shyness, Marianne mentioned her surprise that she and Amelia had not yet become acquainted, despite growing up in the same village. Amelia explained that Mrs. Vernon had always been quite protective of her, letting it be known that Marianne did not wish to be invited to any society events. This put the rest of the village off from inviting her to anything.

"She did me a disservice, then," Marianne said, frowning. It sounded as though Mrs. Vernon had been busily working behind the scenes against her rather than on her behalf.

Had she cared so much that Marianne marry her son that she kept her isolated from village society? Maybe she did when she had thought Marianne would inherit Brindale. And Robert must have grown accustomed to looking upon her in a proprietary way, which he continued to do even after she did not inherit.

"I merely expressed my fears of large gatherings when I was younger, but I needed to overcome it eventually. It is a shame that I did not benefit from more interaction with the rest of the village."

"Mother regrets not having tried harder," Amelia had replied. "As do I."

Now Marianne sat on the chair Lady Belford indicated, appreciating the comfort of moving in a dress that was both stylish and a good fit. She had only time to nod in answer to an offer of tea when a knock sounded on the front door. Amelia had set the tea leaves to steep and was putting out the cups and saucers when the footman entered.

"A Mr. Osborne is here to see you."

Marianne gasped loudly enough that all three heads turned her way in time to witness her deep blush. She looked around for a door in the drawing room that did not lead to the main hall but did not see one. She did not want to meet his wife—not until she had had time to compose herself.

Or move to Jamaica.

"Please have him come in," Lady Belford responded calmly,

as though there was no threat of the world caving in, bringing complete and utter devastation.

Marianne's eyes were on her hands when Mr. Osborne walked in, her heart beating as rapidly as a bird's. She glanced up quickly and found his eyes trained on hers. He was alone. She could not bear his regard and looked down again right away.

He must have come with the intention of making a proper social call. But then she wanted to see if he was surprised to find her here. Would he look uncomfortable after what had transpired between them? She would never, ever kiss another gentleman again. Not ever in her life. Not if it meant this torturous, humiliating pain of disappointment. She looked up just as he was pulling his gaze from her and then bowing before the Belfords.

"Will you join us for tea?" Lady Belford asked him.

"Another time, if you please." Mr. Osborne shifted from one foot to the other. "Actually, I was hoping Miss Edgewood might join me for a walk—that is, Miss Edgewood, if you are so inclined?"

The fear of having his marriage confirmed almost caused her to refuse. But the desire to know for a certainty, thereby lancing the wound at once, grew overpowering. After only a short hesitation, she stood. "I am."

Amelia smiled at her then turned to their guest. "Mr. Osborne, the path leading to our gardens is on the left when you exit the house. I think you will find some pretty places to walk there."

He bowed again to the Belfords, murmuring his thanks, and as Marianne reached his side, he gestured ahead.

"Shall we?"

In the main hall, she took her bonnet from the bench where she had placed it alongside Amelia's earlier that morning and tied it on as they exited into the outdoors. It was warm enough that she didn't need a pelisse, and the fabric of her new gown rustling against her legs gave her confidence. They didn't speak until they had rounded the house and were out of the keen eyesight of the servants.

"How have you been, Marianne?"

Mr. Osborne's voice was cautious, and he placed his hands behind his back as he stared ahead. She had a hard time grasping that he would still call her Marianne. Was that how gentlemen acted as a general rule? They kissed women they had no intention of marrying and then continued to use their Christian names?

She opened her mouth to speak but was too full of these private struggles to give any clear answer. "I—"

"I was surprised to find you gone from the cottage when I returned," he said, apparently too impatient to let her finish. "And you didn't leave word."

She stopped and turned to him, eyes wide, her anger cutting through the hurt. "I didn't leave word? You left with barely a word, and I haven't heard from you since."

"But I did leave word," he said, now facing her, confusion evident in his features. "I explained in the letter that I had something I must do, but that I would be back."

"You did *not* say you were coming back." Marianne clutched her hands together in front of her. "You merely said that you regretted the kiss and would set all to rights."

"I did not say that," he protested, his brows furrowed. He put his hand out but stopped just short of touching her. "And I did not regret the kiss."

"Not even when you married another woman?"

Tears sprang to Marianne's eyes, and she could no longer bear the pain and humiliation of meeting him again. She picked up her skirts and ran into the garden, hoping he would not follow her. If he were a gentleman, he would not. She did not want him to see her cry. Such a thing would complete his victory.

"Marianne!"

She heard his swift footsteps behind her until he rounded the leafy arch separating a portion of the garden, and came into view. There was nowhere to hide, and Marianne turned to face the solid yew hedge. He did not care, then, for her dignity.

"Marianne," he said again, coming up behind her.

"Go away." Her voice broke on the words. She sniffed, her nose beginning to run.

There was silence behind her but no sound of him leaving. Then, a handkerchief appeared in front of her, and she could feel the warmth of his arm on hers.

"I'm not going away until you explain yourself, so you may as well turn around and look at me. Here. You need this."

Marianne took the handkerchief because she had no choice, then sighed. "Perry, return to your wife and leave me alone."

"Wife?" Perry put his hand on her arm and spun her around to face him. "What in *heaven's name* gave you the idea that I took a wife in the fortnight since I left Brindale?"

"Mrs. Malford told me," Marianne replied, lifting her gaze to his and suffering the first stab of doubt. "Your butler arrived to prepare for the arrival of Mrs. Osborne. She's there at Brindale now, isn't she?"

She held the handkerchief in her fist, the weak threads of hope already dissipating. "Deny it."

After a stunned pause, Perry relaxed and a chuckle escaped him. He rubbed his hands on his face and looked at her with such tenderness that doubt, fear, and confusion shrieked at her from within.

"I won't deny it, and I should hope she has arrived by now. Mrs. Osborne is my *mother*."

Marianne raised her eyes to his, frozen but with the first tendril of hope piercing the ice of her heart. "Your mother?"

The implications that came from this revelation caused her to go cold with shock. Perry was not married to someone else. In fact, it seemed—she was almost sure of it, or he would not be here—that he still loved her.

She had been steeling her heart and telling herself that she would be absolutely fine on her own. But now it seemed she would not have to be alone anymore. She began to tremble violently.

"Yes, my mother. I went to get her." Perry reached out for Marianne's hands and held them to his chest, covering them with his own.

"You are cold, my dear." He released her hands and took off his jacket to put around her shoulders.

"Your mother." Marianne was still trying to make sense of this shift in events. Her lips were dry, and a shudder went through her from the medley of emotions that hit as the foundations of the castle she had carefully built around her heart began to crumble.

"After I put aside reason and entered your drawing room that night, I left Brindale to plead with my mother to come serve as chaperone for us. I was afraid that if I stayed at the castle with you so close by at the cottage, I might be tempted to visit again."

Perry stopped speaking, and looked off to the side. "And I feared it might lead to my behaving in a way I was not proud of. Somehow, the risk felt urgent since I knew my uncle was leaving. I made up my mind early the next day, conjured up an excuse to Lord Steere, and left as soon as I could."

Marianne had difficulty lifting her eyes to meet his gaze

and managed only the top of his waistcoat. "You were afraid you would be tempted to kiss me and then not marry me because I am not of your standing?"

"What do you mean, not of my standing?" He sounded almost angry. "Marianne, I knew I wanted to marry you. I was just afraid that once I started kissing you... Well, there was a danger that I would not act the part of a gentleman, and that was not a risk I was willing to take. You deserve nothing less than the utmost proper and honorable attentions from me. So I removed the temptation by rushing off to implore my mother to travel over fifty miles to meet my future bride."

"Oh." Marianne was besieged by a whirlwind of feelings that no longer included stabbing grief and hurt. She darted a glance up at him, her teeth catching her lip to keep from offering so transparent a smile.

"However"—Perry lifted his eyes to the sky, an odd smile playing on his lips—"in order to introduce my betrothed to my mother, I believe the natural order of things is that the lady must be asked. And she must accept."

Marianne laughed nervously and wiped her eyes with the handkerchief, then inexplicably covered her face with her hands.

"I do believe that is the natural order of things," she said in a muffled voice.

"Therefore, Marianne Edgewood..." He put his hands on her arms and waited until she looked at him. It took several seconds before she had gathered the courage.

"Will you do me the very great honor of becoming my wife? I once cared most about winning my uncle's approval and my own place in society. But I've come to realize that I don't give a fig for any of those things if I can only win you. Say you'll marry me, because I love you and don't think I can live without you."

She studied his gray eyes, which somehow seemed more blue under the sky. "I will, Perry."

He let out a deep breath he had been holding and smiled broadly. "I am so glad," he whispered as he lifted his fingers and trailed them along her cheek. He leaned forward but waited until she had lifted her face before he touched his lips to hers.

Marianne melted into him, allowing herself to sink into his embrace and be healed, allowing herself to trust. She then continued to cling to him as joy and excitement coursed through her. Perry held her tightly in return and kissed her hungrily, not letting her go until she lost count of the minutes and her surroundings.

At last, he kissed her once more and stepped back, looking as flushed as she felt. He lifted his gaze to the garden around them, then turned to her with a shaky grin.

"Let us sit for just a moment before we return to the drawing room, where I am sure they are expecting some sort of announcement."

He led her to one of the benches that was placed on the side of the path. "I was never more surprised than when I found out you were staying with Miss Belford. When did you become such fast friends?"

Marianne was more concerned with how he discovered it than she was with answering his question. "How did you find out? I didn't tell anyone. Well, I suppose you must have learned it from Miss Fife. She saw me leave with her."

"No, Miss Fife did not inform me," Perry answered in a dry voice. "She sent me on a wild goose chase to Vernon, who was of no help at all. Not only did he not know where you were, but he refused to help me find you."

"Oh, Perry, I have so much to tell you. But first, what happened?"

Marianne rested her head on his shoulder, smiling and limp with relief. The muscles in his shoulder were firm against her temple without the padding of his coat.

"Well, after I left Vernon, I was bent on returning to Miss Fife and shaking it out of her, but Joe Dobson was sent as an angel of mercy to keep me from committing a crime of violence. How do you ever put up with that woman? Never mind that. You won't be anymore."

"I know." Marianne traced her toe in the dirt. "I have already informed her of as much. So Joe told you where I was?"

"Yes. He saw you ride off with Miss Belford and was able to relieve my fears about you having completely disappeared off the face of the earth. I would not like that, you know." He leaned over and kissed her on the head.

"Because you love me?" she asked shyly.

"Because I do," he confirmed. "I don't suppose I can hope for your admitting to returning those feelings?"

"*Hmm.*" Marianne scrunched up her nose but could not refrain from smiling. "As a matter of fact, I am afflicted with quite a similar sentiment, and I believe I have been for longer than I realized."

"Love?" he asked hopefully.

"*Mm.*" Marianne nodded, blushing. She was unable to look at him just yet when avowing the deepest of feelings, even if he had done so first. Still, even facing forward, she was almost certain he was smiling.

She heard the warmth in his voice when he teased, "You must know how relieved I am. Otherwise I might begin to wonder if you'd accepted my suit only that you might become mistress of Brindale once again."

Marianne shot him a glance, wide-eyed. "Do you know, it hadn't yet crossed my mind. Therefore, I think you may safely assume that I am indeed afflicted with a case of love."

"Good. I should hate to suffer alone."

After a few minutes of blissful silence, Perry pulled away to look at her more closely.

"Is that a new gown? And your hair is styled differently. It's all quite fetching. I hardly dared address my proposal to one so elegant as you, but I gathered my courage at last." He nudged her from the side. "Although my knees were positively knocking."

Marianne laughed out loud, something she hardly remembered doing in the last ten years of her solitary life at Brindale.

"Stop teasing, Mr. Osborne, and kiss me."

He stopped teasing—and he did.

EPILOGUE

Perry woke before dawn and attempted to fall back asleep, but to no avail. Today was the day he was to marry the woman he loved—the woman he would never have chosen for himself if he had been able to do so in a cool, rational manner. The woman he would have raged against Cupid over if his logic had been able to prevail. But it did not. And for once, he was glad.

He had a full hour to himself, lying in bed and reflecting on his future. He would marry a woman who reminded him of what mattered most in life. Not a visible place in high society, but a secure place in one's own society. He would protect her from all harm and help her to see that she would never be alone again.

He had begun to care for Brindale and its inhabitants and projects the way Marianne did, but now they would be able to work together to bring the projects to completion. She had let him know about her uncle's letter that Miss Fife had hidden from her and about her unexpected inheritance that they decided would go toward continuing the castle repairs.

Brindale would come to life again under Marianne's care. It was hers. It had always been hers, and now it would be theirs.

It was time Perry began to dress for his wedding. He had just buttoned his shirt when a knock came on the door. Matley had left him to get hot water for shaving, so he supposed it was someone else. His uncle to come give his blessing? Lord Steere had arrived two days before, grumbling that although he could not approve of the match, Perry was his heir and he would do his duty by him.

After the betrothal, Perry had gone to Lord Steere in person to announce his upcoming wedding and insisted his uncle would see that not only was she perfect for him, but that she would make a perfect baroness one day. He was sure his uncle was blinded by appearances, the same way Perry had been. Lord Steere had only harrumphed, but Perry quite thought that after a grand-nephew or two, his uncle would be singing a different tune. He cared about the barony and its continuation above all.

On the other side of the door was his mother. She stepped in and looked at him in approval, then laid a hand on his cheek. "My dear boy. What a happy day this is."

He was glad someone thought so. "Did you spend time with Marianne last night as you promised?"

"I did. She asked me if I thought the color she chose for the wedding would be acceptable, before peppering me with questions about whether I thought her hair might not be quite the thing, or whether her gown fit well enough. Poor girl. For one who grew up in such a fine castle and has much to recommend her in looks and character, she is lacking confidence in her appearance."

Perry stepped back, smiling fondly at his mother. "It is understandable. I was there to witness her first public appearance, which did not go well. Her gown was unfashionable and fit poorly, and she fell in front of many people. I think that must be what is behind her fears."

"Ah. That is reasonable then. But she has nothing to fear today." Mrs. Osborne assessed him, a smile hovering on her lips. "Perhaps I should allow you to finish dressing—"

A knock interrupted the rest of her words, and Perry bid the person to enter. Matley stepped confidently through the door, and upon seeing Perry's mother, bowed.

"When shall I return to assist you, sir?"

"Give us just five more minutes, Matley, will you?" his mother asked in a soft voice.

The valet nodded, stepped back, and closed the door, and she faced to Perry. "I came mostly to have one more moment with my son before he leaves to attach himself to another."

Those words sounded alarmingly pessimistic to Perry, and he couldn't help but protest. "Mama, you know that in my marrying Marianne"—*by George, that's a mouthful*—"we are only adding to our family. You will not be excluded in any way. And God willing, there will soon be grandchildren to dote upon. We shall need you."

This brought a gleam of mirth to his mother's eyes. "And I shall be here. No, I didn't mean this in any sort of morbid way. I only meant to tell you that I have always loved you—this, you know. But I am also proud of you. You might not have been required to struggle for your future once you became your uncle's heir, but you have had to fight for a place in society, and even for your uncle's approval. It has not been easy, and you have risen to the challenge."

She gazed at him with affection. "This, I do not doubt, is due to your character. And now you have chosen the perfect wife for you. You will make a fine husband, and you will make a fine father."

Perry looked down, touched. His mother had always been

supportive, but it meant a great deal to hear it repeated on the day he was about to begin his own family. An unexpected lump rose to his throat, and he only managed to respond with, "Thank you, Mama."

"Well!" Mrs. Osborne's tone turned brisk. "I had best let Matley turn you out in rare gig. And I must hasten to the cottage to see how Miss Belford is faring with our Marianne."

She and Perry had decided that he would go to the church with his uncle, and she would serve as family to Marianne. After all, she would soon be.

"I will see you at the church." Perry reached over to open the door, just as a second knock sounded. He allowed his mother to step through, and on the other side was Charlie with a tray containing some coffee and rolls that would tide him over until their wedding breakfast.

"Don't be late," his mother called out as she walked down the corridor.

The next hour was spent in anticipation that barely tolerated Matley's fussing over his appearance with greater care—declaring it was an important day indeed that saw a man wed—and anticipation that he was able to meet Lord Steere with tolerance for the baron's natural prejudices. It seemed forever before the hour had come when he was allowed to enter the church.

The light filtered through the long, narrow panes of stained glass that had been fixed in the stone church centuries before. They colored the wooden pews and the stone floor, and the effect was almost magical, if Perry were of a fanciful nature. He was not, but knew Marianne would find it magical when she set eyes on it.

The few local families who had been invited came in and took their places, and those included Sarah and Joe, who had married a fortnight earlier in a quiet ceremony. He and Marianne had agreed to keep Sarah on as a maid, despite her being married. She would instead train for the position of house-keeper and return to her own home at nights.

The Vernons were not there, of course, not after Perry had learned of Robert's selfish maneuver to frighten Marianne. The Belfords had been invited and were sitting in their places, and after Miss Belford's kindness to Marianne, he was more than eager to further that acquaintance.

Perry squinted at the open door and lifted his eyebrows in surprise as he saw Neck stride in. He had, after some reflection, invited his three friends from London, fearing it would be an affront not to do so. He had hardly expected them to come. Neck lifted his hand and grinned, then turned back to wait for Raife, who followed him in. Perry wasn't entirely thrilled with the idea of Lorry being anywhere near his betrothed and was relieved when the two took their seats without giving signs of expecting another.

Then all other thoughts fled as the church grew quiet. Accompanied by his mother, Marianne stepped into the church, and his vision blurred when he focused his eyes on her.

Upon returning to Brindale, he had been surprised by how well she looked with her hair in the new style that sent sprigs of curls around her face and the modish gowns which fit her petite figure so well. But now... The sight of her now rendered him speechless, left him without breath.

Holding a small bouquet of her mother's roses, she stepped toward him in a gown of the palest pink, with silver trim that somehow caught the reflection of light and color in the church. Her brown locks had small pink blossoms pinned in each curl, and her rosy cheeks resembled two more. As she drew near, she lifted her eyes shyly to his, a smile trembling on her lips, and he was done for. Today, he would vow to love and protect this woman, and that was precisely what he meant to do for the rest of his days.

"Dearly beloved, we are gathered together today in the sight of man and of God to witness the holy union of this man and this woman..."

In Perry's brief visit with the rector to plan the wedding ceremony, he discovered that the man of the cloth scarcely knew Marianne, though she had grown up in his parish. This did not cause him to look upon the rector with favor, because he felt he had not done his duty by the orphan under his care.

But now, the sound of the familiar words from the few ceremonies he had attended—words that pertained to him— he was ready to forgive the rector. After all, it was through his offices that Perry might wed Marianne.

Every word of his vow, Perry uttered with quiet fervor. Marianne would see that she was not alone and that she never would be again. Her voice spoke the same vows with her own quiet conviction. Then came the moment when he slipped his ring on her finger, the moment when they were pronounced man and wife—when he was given leave to kiss his bride.

Hardly had the rector spoken the words than Perry leaned down and whispered, "Our first kiss as man and wife." Then he pressed his lips to hers.

Her hands were on his arms, and she kissed him back. A cloud that had passed over the sun at some point in the ceremony released its rays once again, filling the back of Perry's eyelids with pricks of light. Or perhaps those were simply from the electric sensation that came from kissing her.

And then there was applause, and even a hoot or two that could only be Neck. It was certainly not Raife.

The ride back to the castle was too short for many stolen kisses, but Perry did his best with what he had been given. After their wedding breakfast, they would travel to Essex so he could show her his childhood home, and they would continue on to the Peak District for their honeymoon.

His uncle would not stay much longer, but his mother was contemplating making her home at Brindale, a thought which suited everyone. He did not like the thought of his mother alone, and his betrothed had delighted him by declaring that it had been long enough that she had not had the joy of a mother's presence and hoped she would stay.

The wedding breakfast at Brindale was perfect, as Mrs. Malford produced something worthy of the occasion with the help of hired servants. The dining room was filled with laughter and talk, and—unexpectedly—with Raife and Miss Belford seated side by side in conversation that seemed equally engrossing for both. Even Marianne was able to participate and laugh when teased, showing no hints of her earlier shyness.

After the breakfast, as Marianne bade him wait while she freshened up in a private room, his uncle stepped apart from the mingling guests and approached him. "Well, Peregrine." Perry waited, grateful his uncle had refrained from calling him "boy."

"I still can't say you have chosen as well for yourself as you might have, had you allowed yourself to be guided by me—"

"Now, Uncle..." He may have been patient with the baron's prejudice before, but he was a married man now. His loyalty was to his wife.

"Hear me out, boy." Lord Steere frowned and cleared his throat. "Peregrine, that is to say. You are a married man now. What I was about to say is that Mrs. Osborne has turned herself out well, and it does her credit."

It was Perry's turn to frown. Why was his uncle talking about his mother at this juncture?

Oh. His brow cleared. The "Mrs. Osborne" referred to his wife. "Thank you, sir."

"Her disposition tends toward sweetness, so you will have to see that you don't pamper your sons and watch them grow up to be milksops."

Perry just managed to restrain his laughter. "No, Uncle."

"And if you have girls, you will need to have a governess brought in to educate them in all the accomplishments of a lady."

Perry was done with the lecture. "I'll have you know that Marianne will be perfectly capable of educating her own daughters in the art of...."

His voice trailed away as Marianne came into his vision, pausing in the main hall near the front entrance. The pale gown on her slender frame was lit by the sun streaming in through the open door, and her dark brown curls set, as they were, near her smiling face made her teeth and eyes gleam white. Her smile caused the rest of his surroundings to become a blur.

In time, he remembered he was about to commit the offense of abandoning his uncle without taking leave, and he caught himself. He held out his hand. "Thank you."

Lord Steere bestowed one of his rare smiles and shook Perry's hand in return, even going so far as to clasp him on the arm at the same time. Then Perry went over to the crowd that was beginning to congregate around his wife, holding his arm out to her.

"Shall we?"

Slipping her hand through the crook of his elbow, she said, "We shall."

The wedding night would be spent at the cottage, where they would be free from the company of servants and guests. As they exited into the outdoors, the sun hid behind a cloud once again, in the temperamental way of springtime. There, a small group of guests waited for them.

They were to go to the cottage on foot, accompanied by their well-wishers for a portion of the distance. Marianne had a spring in her step at his side, and she sent a playful, happy grin his way that warmed his heart. She was every inch the lady, though his uncle couldn't see it. And even if she were not, Perry simply did not care any longer. Any society that wouldn't accept her into it was not a society he wanted to be part of.

They had rounded the northern tower and were walking east around Brindale's pond when Marianne stopped suddenly.

"Oh! Dearest!" The nickname was new, and he loved it. "I have forgotten to throw my bouquet. Let me do so now."

He caught on to her enthusiasm, and faced the crowd, some of whom had already thought it time to turn back to the castle.

"Your attention, if you will. Mrs. Osborne would like to toss her bouquet for anyone who might be interested in catching it."

There was a pause and a noticeable lack of movement. Then his mother put her arm around Miss Belford and led her forward to the front. When it soon became clear that she was the only one, she put her hand on one hip, appearing to make the best of it.

"If you must, Mrs. Osborne. Aim well. There is only one of us."

Marianne turned and lifted the bouquet in the air, before facing forward again. She adjusted her position on the path, coming close to the edge of it which led to the muddy slope down into the pond. Perry was about to call out for her to take care, all in good fun, for surely she had seen the danger and would not allow herself to be dunked on her wedding day of all things.

He did not have time to utter a word, because she whirled around again to set her sights on Miss Belford, and in doing so, one foot slid down the slope. As though everything happened in a sluggish dream impossible to wake from, she gave a shriek as she tripped and rolled into the pond, falling on her hands and knees, and dousing her bodice and face before she came up sputtering.

Lord Steere's nostrils thinned, as people came rushing toward the edge to help. Perry lifted his hand to stop them, his eyes challenging his uncle against saying a word of disparagement.

"She is my wife. Allow me."

His wife was a forlorn, pitiful object, much like a small, sodden bird, with her carefully styled hair now plastered to her face and the blossoms flattened against her head. Her dress clung to her in a way that hastened Perry's steps as he simultaneously removed his jacket. Then, *he* slipped on the mud—he could not avoid it—but as he was more prepared, merely got drenched up to his thighs. He splashed over to her and threw his coat over her shoulders and pulled it around her front.

He reached up and gently brushed a wet lock of hair from Marianne's cheek, his heart full of his great affection for her. Perhaps he had not chosen a wife fit for society in every way, but he'd chosen a wife fit for him.

"Oh, Perry," she said in a mournful tone, at odds with the twinkle in her eye, "What a sad day it was when you exchanged your bachelorhood for my hand."

"I exchanged my bachelorhood for your love," he replied promptly, matching her twinkle with one of his own. He would warm her up as soon as they reached the cottage.

"Then what a sad day that was," she insisted, her hopeful gaze resting on him as she waited for his playful contradiction.

But he did not tease in return. He killed the contemptible notion before it could take flight. "You have it all wrong, my dear. It was the *best* day. Do not ever doubt me when I say that your love is better than life."

And without regard for whether his uncle had stayed to watch—or anyone else, really, for were they not newly wed and could do as they liked?—Perry leaned down and seized a kiss from his wife's lips. Her cold lips. It might be late spring, but the water was not warm. He would have to make haste and carry her out of this pond, knowing that any further steps she tried to take on her own would likely result in her slipping back into the water again, bringing him down with her. Yes, he would carry her.

But first he would make sure her lips were warm enough to continue the journey.

NOTES FROM THE AUTHOR

Susan Ferrier wrote the book *Marriage*, which was published in 1818. I bent time and used it in my story set in 1810. Kindly overlook that discrepancy.

I give all credit to *The Complete Servant* by Samuel & Sarah Adams, published in 1825 for the perfume and cosmetics recipes Marianne found in her mother's handwriting. She would likely have had such recipes handed down, but the Adamses formalized the recipes for public use.

The servants' dialect was inspired by *A dictionary of the Kentish dialect and provincialisms in use in the County of Kent.* Although I likely got some of it wrong, I did my best.

The quote, "rashers of sindg'd bacon on the coals' by morning" is from the original poems by John Dryden, Esq. *The Cock and the Fox*, 1773

OTHER BOOKS IN CASTLES & COURTSHIP

ABOUT THE AUTHOR

Jennie Goutet is an American-born Anglophile who lives with her French husband and their three children in a small town outside of Paris. Her imagination resides in Regency England, where her best-selling proper Regency romances are set. She is also author of the award-winning memoir *Stars Upside Down,* two contemporary romances, and a smattering of other published works. A Christian, a cook, and an inveterate klutz, Jennie writes (with increasing infrequency) about faith, food, and life—even the clumsy moments—on her blog, aladyin-france.com. If you really want to learn more about Jennie and her books, sign up for her newsletter on her author website: jenniegoutet.com.

* Photo Credit : Caroline Aoustin

Printed in Great Britain
by Amazon